Touch

LOVE, HURT, TOUCH, HEAL

Casey Costra

Forward Press

© 2016
Forward Press
Lewes, Delaware

Forward Press is dedicated to works of fiction
which call attention to social problems or their solutions.

ISBN 978-0-9982853-0-6

The characters in this book are fictitious.
Any resemblance to real persons, living or dead,
is coincidental and not intended by the author.

The author may be contacted at:
CaseyCostra@gmail.com
Or through the website at CaseyCostra.com
Book cover design by www.jdandj.com

Table of Contents

Chapter 1	5
Chapter 2	17
Chapter 3	21
Chapter 4	26
Chapter 5	31
Chapter 6	37
Chapter 7	40
Chapter 8	47
Chapter 9	51
Chapter 10	58
Chapter 11	65
Chapter 12	72
Chapter 13	77
Chapter 14	85
Chapter 15	89
Chapter 16	93
Chapter 17	104
Chapter 18	106
Chapter 19	111
Chapter 20	117
Chapter 21	120
Chapter 22	125
Chapter 23	131
Chapter 24	134
Chapter 25	141
Chapter 26	144
Chapter 27	147
Chapter 28	152
Chapter 29	156
Chapter 30	162
Chapter 31	168
Chapter 32	173
Chapter 33	178
Chapter 34	184
Chapter 35	190
Chapter 36	197
Chapter 37	200

Chapter 38...209
Chapter 39...219
Chapter 40...224
Chapter 41...231
Chapter 42...236
Chapter 43...242
Chapter 44...247
Chapter 45...252
Chapter 46...258
Acknowledgments...263

Chapter 1
October, 1995

Face it. Only eight days left. Some big blow-up, even some little glitch—not going to happen. Time to let go of his five-year hope. Rosa was eighteen now and she'd marry the little prick next week.

The traffic through Bayonne was backed up bad. Tony drove from Staten Island to the dealership in Jersey every day since Mr. Forte got him the job, and he knew how long the trip oughtta take. He passed the poor bastard who caused all the traffic—standing by his broken down Plymouth Breeze. Figures. Glad he worked on Toyotas. He patted the steering wheel of his 4Runner.

All those years while he dreamed and waited for Rosa, other girls nosed around. Mechanics have muscles, especially if they'd been high school jocks. When he was young, maybe twelve, he'd combed his hair like Elvis, slicked back on the sides. Little curl on the forehead. His father made fun of him, so he had to keep the look. By ninth grade, half the kids in high school called him Elvis Prezzi. Girls liked it—Italian girls anyway, the only kind in the neighborhood.

He had been uninterested in the girls that hung around. Unavailable. Waiting for Rosa to figure out what a dick Joey was. But she never did. Somehow, being unavailable attracted girls. As of today, dammit, he was available. Which one?

At work, he couldn't think about which girl, because he had a couple mystery motors to work on. They gave him most of those jobs because he liked the challenge, unlike the lazy stunadi who only wanted the easy-money work. But now, sitting in the traffic, he thought about the girls he ran into most everywhere he went. He didn't want to be alone when Rosa and Joey stood at the altar in St. Anthony's and Rosa gave herself to that strunz' forever.

Almost home. He turned left into the alley and right into his parking spot. Crossing the little patio between his car and the kitchen door, he said how ya doin' to old Mr. Jacome next door, fussing with his tomato plants like always.

Mama and he ate dinner—pasta, a couple sausages, salad. Simple. Mama worked, and there were only the two of them anyway. She knew enough not to talk about what everybody else in the neighborhood yakked about, the big wedding. Or ask was Tony okay. Unlike his father or probably his sister, he could handle his hurt, and Mama respected that.

Upstairs in his room, he decided on Lucia. She was the most persistent, she was a cop so she must have guts like Rosa did starring on the b'ball court, and she even sorta looked like Rosa. Most guys he knew wouldn't date a woman cop, but she'd be interesting to figure out, like when a car came through with a weird engine somebody swapped from another model. Besides, he was looking for some consolation sex, and she once said that if he ever needed anything, just ask.

He left for the tavern, the overgrown bar whose sign said "Bellastero's" but nobody in the neighborhood called it that. It had been "the tavern" all his life. He didn't know why. Probably nobody did. He was inside for less than a minute, hadn't even gotten his beer, when he noticed Lucia.

Heading to the bar, he walked by her, gave his usual polite nod and collected her usual happy greeting. He saw her beer glass was empty, so he bought two beers. He turned around and there she was. He gave her one.

They talked for a couple minutes, or rather she talked—nervously. How could she be a cop?

He waited for a pause so he could drop the bomb, feeling the smile building inside. This was gonna be fun, hitting her with his little surprise. "Do you want to get together next Saturday? The pizza place. Get a pizz' and a beer. Lunchtime, maybe?" While Rosa got attached to her damn disgraziat'.

She stood up on her toes and pecked him on the lips. "Yesss. This is so great." Back down on her heels, she chatted for a while, not nervous anymore. As she left, she put on a cop face he'd never seen before. Two different women. "Thanks. I'll see you next week."

The next week when he walked into the pizza place, she was already there, at the table where he usually sat.

She leaped up and kissed him again. "I ordered the one you like. Sausage and onions, right?"

They went through the pizza and a couple beers, talking about her job. "I was already working 911 dispatch, sending help. I figured why not be the one who did the help. So I applied to the Academy."

After maybe 45 minutes of that, Lucia left for the ladies' room. When she got back, she didn't sit down, just stood there cop-faced. "Do you want to hang around here, or do you want to come over to my place?"

Would it be weird if he screwed Lucia at the exact time as Joey screwed Rosa on her wedding night? Yes, it would. But otherwise he'd go home and beat off. Better Lucia.

She led him to a studio apartment in an older building. A gun safe beside the door, an eating table with two wood chairs, a couple upholstered chairs that faced a TV teetering on a waist-high shelf, and on the other side of the shelf, her bed. Nothing hanging on the walls. She had no sofa where they could sit next to each other, so they sat on the edge of her bed.

When Tony woke up Sunday morning, it took him a moment to realize where he was. He lay on his side looking at Lucia as she lay purring in the early dawn light. Who was this person? Wild sex on the surface, but all for him. Watching, feeling, even asking—was this good, what did he want to do next? Wild. But did she get anything out of it? Did she even try to? Not that he could feel.

He rose quietly and slipped into her bathroom. While he was in there, he used her toothpaste to rub a finger across his teeth, her big woman's brush to slick his hair back in place, and his thumb to form the little curl hanging over his forehead. His stubble was pretty bad, same as every morning. While he eyed her razor on the edge of her tub, the door flew open.

She hopped around him and took a seat. "Whew. What were you doing in here so long?" She glanced up at his sculpted Elvis hair. "Oh." Back on her feet, she kissed him lightly on the cheek. "Um, not good." She grabbed the razor and tossed it at him. "Here." She handed him a bottle of hand soap to lather with, and nudged him sideways with her hip, claiming half the mirror.

Her hair had bunched and tangled. While shaving, he watched her in the mirror. With long energetic brushstrokes, she straightened the strands back into place, tucked behind her ears and hanging down her back. Like Rosa.

He glanced lower in the mirror, to her breasts. He loved her bikini lines—three light patches. Like dashboard lights, they showed at a glance where the most important instruments were. He gave the nearest one a little twist. His own instrument peeked above the rim of the sink.

She returned the little twist, at the same time nudging him toward the door. "Out. I'll join you in a minute."

By mid-morning, his suspicion turned into certainty. "You're not even trying to cross the finish line. Have you ever gotten there? Not just with me. Ever?"

"I don't know. Maybe. But you do, and that makes me happy."

"Well, you don't. And that makes me unhappy." He French-kissed her again, his tongue probing her mouth, same as when they'd first started the night before. "Do you like that?"

She took a few seconds to recover, running her tongue across her lips. "Yes. I do."

"Good." He gently pushed her shoulders. "Lie back." Starting with her forehead, he kissed his way down.

When he got to her navel, she held his head. "Wait. What are you doing?"

He lifted his lips off her skin, just enough to speak. "You know what I'm doing."

"I don't know. Nobody's ev—"

"You had your turn. Now it's mine." He moved in and probed. For quite a while. Maybe this wasn't going to work. Maybe she really couldn't.

Finally, a low moan. Several moans, not so low. She grabbed his hair and kicked her legs on his back. The finish line.

He lifted his chin, rested it on her hair, and looked up between her breasts.

She raised her head, a crooked smile on her face he'd not seen the night before. "Give me a minute and I'll help you—"

"No. You finished, and that made me happy. Hang on. I want to be happy again." He dove back down. This time, she moaned louder, pulled his hair harder, and kicked his back longer.

As she lay limp on the mattress, he scrambled up to lie beside her. She rolled sideways, kissed his neck, and rested her head on his right shoulder, her arm on his chest. He felt her knees touch his hip. Her body relaxed even more and she purred in his ear. He closed his eyes and joined her.

Five months later, on a sunny cool day in March, he woke her by waving a mug of coffee in front of her nose.

She lay there, eyes blinking.

He touched the hot mug to a breast.

"Alright, alright. I'm awake." She sat up.

He gave her the mug and sat beside her. "Do you want to go shopping for a ring at the Staten Island Mall?"

"What?" Her palm on his cheek, she turned his head toward her so she could look into his eyes. She didn't blink, so he couldn't either. She didn't say anything.

What the hell? She wasn't going to say yes? How could she not say yes? Isn't this why she was chasing him all that time? What would he do if she said no?

"Yes, I do. Are you sure you do?"

"I asked, didn't I?"

"Yeah, but you skipped a couple steps."

He pondered. He asked her. She said yes. What steps? Oh.

He slipped off the bed onto his knees. Her crotch was straight ahead, filling his vision.

Still holding her mug in one hand, she used the other to curl a knuckle under his chin and raise his eyes, past her breasts and up to her face. "I'm ready."

"Lucia, will you marry me? We could go ring shopping at the mall."

"Yes." She dropped her mug. It bounced off the bed and splattered them both with hot coffee. With both hands behind his neck, she pulled him up for a long kiss.

Done, she pushed his head back enough to look him in the eyes again. "That was wonderful, Tony. I've dreamed about this moment for so long. You have no idea. So long." She wiped her eyes with the sheet. "But that was step two. I still want step one. I think I deserve it."

"You did deserve it. You've been coming for months now, and I love it every time you do."

"You're right, Tony. All because of you. Because of how I feel about you. But technically I think that was supposed to be step five or six. You know, after the rings and all. You almost got step one there—only one word off."

Deserve? No. Coming? No. He had to say it? He hadn't been showing her for months now? "Lucia, I love you. Will you marry me? And go pick out a ring?"

She held his wrists and put both his hands near her crotch. Uh, in her lap. "Tony, I have loved you so much. This is the happiest day in my life," She lay back on the bed. "Where do you want to show me how much you love me first? Here or in the jewelry store?"

They made it to the mall in the afternoon.

For such a no-nonsense woman, Lucia and the women in her family took a ridiculously long time to plan a wedding, but she finally made an honest man out of him. Their relationship changed— more official, more committed. In their church and in his mind, marriage was an unbreakable thing. Babies someday, though her job would make it complicated to be a mother.

The neighborhood saw him differently, too. A job, a wife, a place in the community. A man of respect.

They'd been married more than three years. They still lived in Lucia's studio because the rent was cheap and they were saving the down payment on a house. The studio would be way too small for a family. They'd decided they were ready for kids, talked about it all the time. A couple weeks before, Lucia's pill prescription ran out. She didn't renew it.

They had a new personal computer, and a phone connection to the World Wide Web. When Lucia worked second shift, sometimes Tony used to beat off to the computer porn. Unbelievable porn progress, the computer. You didn't have to sneak into some sleazy store in Jersey, far away from the neighborhood. And the porn on the web changed all the time, always something new. But now they were trying to have a baby, Tony quit that. It had gotten boring anyway, and he had to save all his joy-juice to make the baby.

Lucia had her secrets, too. He knew, because sometimes he'd come home and open the boxes from her catalog orders. Between the deliveries of no-iron sheets or nonstick frying pans, there'd arrive little boxes of weight-loss supplements, or hair-straightening stuff or bronzing sun-tan oil. She was in her mid-twenties now, and she hadn't gained a pound of weight. The only places she could lose pounds from, he'd miss them if they were gone. Her hair had always been straight. Why did she need straightening stuff? He did like her tan though. Anyway, he never said anything about her beauty boosters, and neither did she.

They spent holidays with his in-laws. His Mama too, because she was alone now that he was gone. His sister was a flight attendant with Alaska Airline, a job she took the minute she graduated high school, and didn't even come home for holidays.

He liked Lucia's family, and he enjoyed spending time with her parents, with her brothers and sisters. None of them were much to look at, though. Pudgy, nondescript. Amazing such a frumpy bunch had produced Lucia.

That year, bloated by the Thanksgiving lasagna, they both slept late the following Friday. Lucia had never been into Black Friday shopping—any shopping, really. Probably why she bought from catalogues. He awoke with a big morning-stiff boner. She lay there, eyelids half open, as he got up and headed for the bathroom.

When he stumbled back to bed, she said, "Lie there and think good thoughts. I'll be back in a minute." She made her own bathroom dash.

She had him stretch out on his back. She kneeled astride him, rolling her hips slowly back and forth. This was one of her favorites.

When his bent neck cramped, he stopped watching the motion of her breasts and lay his head back on the bed. He closed his eyes to concentrate on the feeling of her movement.

The movement stopped. "Goddam it! You're still imagining I'm Rosa DeAngelo, aren't you?" She climbed off him. His shriveling dick flopped into his pubic hair.

Shocked, he was silent for a few seconds—a few seconds too long. How could she tell?

She stood over him, piercing his heart with the hurt on her face. "Early on, I could understand, but four years you've been with me. Four years. We're trying to have a baby."

Then she was gone from his sight and he lay there alone. He closed his eyes, willing the whole thing away. Something hit him in the ribs a couple times. He opened his eyes halfway. Lucia stepped back. She'd dressed, sort of. Sweatpants and a stretched-out, faded red pullover she'd owned since before he met her. He'd loved it when it was newer, because it was tighter back then, and because of its particular shade of red.

Rex-Aid red. Where Rosa worked. Where she wore their red shirt. Boy, was he in trouble.

Lucia seemed calm, all recovered and almost cheery. Her smile made him more nervous than if she still looked mad.

"Boy, it's teeny. Can you pull it back inside when it's scared, like a turtle?" She bent over further and whispered toward his waist. "Don't worry little dickie, mommy won't hurt you." Straightening up and switching faces, she gave a cop-voiced order. "Get dressed and get out of here."

"Leave?"

"No. Not like that. You know how much you love it when I say, 'We have to talk?' Well, we have to talk."

"I know we do, Lucia. I can see that."

"Good. You go walk around a couple of hours and think of what you want to say. I have some visual aids I need to get together, and I have to think what I want to say, too. I don't want you here while I'm thinking. So beat it."

He threw on some clothes and got ready to go.

"Don't just mope around," she said, "and stay away from the tavern. Think about what you want to say, because I'll be listening close."

He was half way into the hall when she called out. "Bring some subs back with you. The cook is taking the day off."

He walked around as instructed, then sat on the bleachers of the Little League field. No game today. Some people walked their dogs. He watched the dogs sniff around until they found a good spot. How did they decide?

He stood up and walked some more. In a store window, he didn't look like a man deep in thought. He looked like a man deep in worry, even fear.

Confess, obviously. Then what? He walked way up the Avenue

to her favorite sub place and took special care not to screw up her usual order—no cappicol', no onions, no hot peppers, extra oregano.

She liked Raspberry Vitamin Water, but the only place that sold it was Rex-Aid. She'd have to settle for regular water.

Maybe he should have stayed away longer to pretend he had thought more, but the olive oil leaked from the subs and greased up the paper bag, so he headed home.

Lucia sat them down in the two upholstered chairs they never used, the ones she called the guest chairs. The chairs faced the back of the TV on the room divider, because they'd turned the TV to watch it from their bed. She scooted her chair around to look straight toward him, so he did the same. She had a paper bag on the floor next to her chair. He had nothing. Should he have something, too? She never told him the rules.

"Let's start at the beginning," she said.

Tony made a serious face. "Okay. You were good looking, and you seemed interested in me, so I—"

"That's not the beginning. That's probably past the middle."

"What's the beginning, then?"

"I don't know about you," she said. "For me it was eleventh grade. You were a senior. You were a jock. You were popular. You had your beautiful Elvis hair. And when you passed me in the hall, you gave me a smile and a little pistol-finger wave—waist level, cool. Even when you were with your buddies. No other popular guy ever smiled and waved at me, not even when they were alone. When was the beginning for you?"

"Like I said, I noticed you when—"

"When did you start up your obsession with Rosa DeAngelo? That's your beginning."

"I wouldn't call it an obsession."

"I think I would. When did it start?" She was demanding, with the cop face. Once he'd asked her about her cop face, how she switched over. She didn't even know she had a cop face.

"I was still in high school and she was in middle school."

"When you were a senior, you fell for a seventh grader instead of me. Is that what you mean?"

"Sounds bad, doesn't it? That's why I never did anything. I mean, about the way I felt. I'm not a child molester. I was waiting for her to grow up."

"Wow, way back then. The first I knew about it was when you

started going to all Rosa's games. She was in ninth grade, right?"

"Yeah, ninth grade. That's when Joey DiFalco grabbed her. He's two years younger than me, so he was still in school, twelfth grade."

"I was there, too. All the games. Did you notice?"

"You were?"

"That's what I thought."

"You were into hoops?"

"No. I was into you. I know about obsessions."

"How come I didn't notice? You're a beautiful woman."

"Thank you. You must not have thought so back then. Three years you never looked. I was desperate to make you see me."

He stared at her. The body, the long black hair against her tan. How could he not have noticed?

She bent over to reach into her bag. "Do you want to see my yearbook picture?"

"If you want me to."

She brought out the 1991 *Metropolitan*. It flopped open to one of the pages with the senior portraits, and she handed him the open book.

He looked, but her picture wasn't on either of the open pages. He looked at the pages before and after it. Not there either. The Seniors' pictures were in alphabetical order. He turned back to the original open page and looked for her name.

The picture over her name showed a chubby girl with hair puffed out on the sides of her head. Wispy longer hair curled down to her shoulders. The hair was highlighted, bleach on black. The wide hairdo made her round face wider.

He remembered this girl. She was always around. But this girl wasn't Lucia, no matter what the name under the picture said. Probably a screw-up when they printed it. "This isn't you."

"Sure it is. I look just like my sister and my mother. See the resemblance?"

He peered at the picture. "Maybe."

"Here's one from a year later." She opened a photo album and handed it to him. On one side was a photo of her whole schlumpy family standing in front of a Christmas tree. On the other was a full-length portrait of the girl Lucia claimed was her. She had a short haircut layered in short waves. Better than the puffy cut, but the full-length portrait showed a wide face set on top of a body that was wide from her neck to her ankles. Not really fat, but wider than average.

"Right after that one, I went to the basketball games and watched you drool over Rosa DeAngelo. Joey had snapped Rosa away from you, thank God."

She reached down into a different bag. "Here's some pictures from the next year."

She handed him two pictures, front and profile like full-length mug shots, of the woman he married, the woman he loved. Well padded, but thinner everywhere than the last two pictures. Her face looked even thinner because her hair was tucked behind her ears and ran straight down her back. The splotchy white skin had turned to gold.

"This is the real you," he said. "We used to run into each other at the tavern. And the bowling alley, right?"

"Yes, we did. As if I gave a damn about bowling. The real me? Not then. Maybe now."

"You used to flirt. I remember one day I said to myself, 'That Lucia—I think she likes me.'"

"Well, good for you. I had to flirt my ass off. There were other women."

"Yeah. But you were my favorite."

"Sure I was. The week Rosa got married was the week you first asked me out. Just a coincidence. Right?"

"No." Hey, wait a minute. "This 'we have to talk' was supposed to be about me imagining you were Rosa. Instead, it's about you tricking me into dating you."

"About me tricking you into marrying me, actually. That's why we have to talk."

"No matter how you changed your looks, you're not Rosa. I don't even know what Rosa's really like. I married you. I loved you."

"Loved?"

"I was talking about when we got married. Of course, it's still "love."

"After what I just told you?"

"Yes."

"Don't say it so quick. Now's the time to decide. I'm not Rosa. Do you love the non-Rosa me?

He didn't have to think, but he paused a second so she'd feel better when he said it. "Yes."

She stood up, pulled him from his chair, and led him around the room divider to the bed. Joy and relief—the shadow member of their love triangle was gone.

Chapter 2

The calendar that ruled their lives hung on the bathroom wall. Next to the toilet. Rosa had hung it low enough to enter her daily info, high enough for Joey to look it over. She wrote down all the observations she used: basal body temperature, cervical mucus, cervical position, piss-strip reading. For eighteen months she sat there each morning, went through her observation ritual, and wrote down her results, with different color pencils hanging from strings tacked to the wall.

Joey worried, and it didn't help he couldn't understand the calendar. One thing he understood well enough—the first red day. Most months, he'd punch another dent in the drywall.

Then they'd repeat it again. From her position on the toilet, she'd yell through the bathroom doorway their prospects for the day. "Take a rest," or "worth a try," or "this is it—all day long."

Rosa's cycles varied, which didn't help, but the doctor said Joey's little fishies were the main problem. He didn't make many, and the ones he made couldn't swim very well.

Every time, she had to be on the bottom. Afterwards, she lay on her back with her pelvis tilted toward the ceiling, to give the fishies a head start. Sex was work—stressful work.

One month, Rosa said from her seat on the toilet. "Blood again." She fought to keep from sobbing. Shoulders hunched, staring unfocused at a chipped tile over the tub, she braced herself for Joey's violent punch through the wall.

"Goddam it." Instead of hitting the wall, he hammered his fist down on the top of her head. Her jaw slammed shut and chipped a tooth.

He fell to his knees immediately, wedged between the sink and the tub. "Please.... I didn't mean.... I love you. Never again. Never. Please."

Not looking at him, Rosa dug at the chipped tooth with her tongue. She knew the stress they were under and she almost pitied him. Her headache pounding, she said, "This is the last time, Joey. I mean it, never."

But nothing would ever again be the way it was.

All the DeAngelos had babies but her. Dino and Pete had two kids each, even though Pete and Paola had been separated for a year. Pete hit her once too often, Paola said. Should Rosa be separated, too?

Aggie, who couldn't carry the dirty sheets to the washing machine without getting pregnant, had four with another on the way.

Rosa and Joey still lived in the apartment over his motorcycle shop. It wasn't big enough for a family, and they'd always planned to move. But there they were. She still worked at Rex-Aid. She'd always planned to quit when the baby came. But there she was.

Sometimes she took care of her nieces and nephews. They loved their Zia Rosa. When one cried, its mother would hand the kid over to Rosa and the crying stopped. Mama said she had a magic touch with little kids.

Rosa's and Joey's mothers were not religious women, but they both began to walk up the hill to St. Anthony's Church, to light candles at the altar of St. Anne, the patron saint of fertility.

Aggie gave birth to her fifth, a girl. While she was still nursing the little one, she got pregnant again. Mama and the DeAngelo aunts thought such a thing impossible.

Soon after Aggie's news, Mama called. "Don't you have tomorrow off?"

"Yes."

"Come over for coffee with me and Aggie. I'm making your baby sister take care of Aggie's older ones."

Her baby sister was now in eleventh grade, not inclined to be made to do anything, but Mama had the Eye, and if she threatened to use it, her kids obeyed.

"Okay. What's up?"

"Let it be a surprise, but I think you'll like it."

Next day, the three of them met at Mama's big kitchen table. Aggie brought her baby girl, who fussed until she was handed to Rosa.

Mama served coffee and almond biscotti. Rosa's curiosity grew. Mama swept her hand toward Aggie. "You want to start?"

"Okay. Did you know, Rosa, that Al planned a vasectomy?

"No."

"Yes, but the new one snuck through before he closed the door. No way we ever thought we'd have six kids. We can't afford five. So Mama thought—"

"Why don't you and Joey adopt the new one?"

Rosa thought a few seconds "I like it. I like it a lot. It would take so much pressure off Joey and me. These last couple of years have been hell." The baby startled herself awake and cried again. Rosa rubbed her back. She put her head back on Rosa's shoulder and fell quiet.

"How will Joey take it?" Aggie asked.

"I don't know. He's so damn stubborn. He might—"

"C'mon, Rosa." Mama tapped one finger to her temple. "Women know how to handle their men. It's his idea. He just hasn't thought of it yet."

Papa was a lot more laid back than Joey. But Rosa didn't say anything.

Back home, she tried to figure a strategy, but nothing came. Joey would never give up living through this hell until they'd "won." He wouldn't want someone else's baby. He'd want his own baby.

She decided to wait and see if she bled again. One last chance.

The first day of the blood, after he'd punched through the wall, she said in a rush, "Mama thinks we ought to help out Aggie by adopting the baby she's carrying. Can we do that, Joey? It doesn't mean we'll stop trying to have a baby of our own."

"You want to give up? I don't give up. And you won't either."

"I just said we wouldn't give up."

"You know you will. You can't do all this"—he slapped the chart—"and take care of a baby too."

"You're right, I can't." She ripped the mangled chart off the wall, scrunched it up, and threw it in the little bathroom trashcan. "I can't keep—"

He punched her on the jaw, knocking her head against the cast-iron tub. She lost consciousness, awakening to terrible pain. Her upper teeth had cut through her cheek. Her lower teeth flopped around, jawbone maybe broken. Her shirt turned red with blood. Her head pounded. Her soul squeezed her love until it turned to liquid and leaked away, like the blood running down her shirt.

Joey was down on his knees again, begging. She stumbled past him and made it home to Mama, who called 911. The surgery lasted three hours. With two plastic surgeries after that. Then laser treatments that almost erased the scars.

She never returned to the garage, not even to get her things. She'd hadn't been a single woman since she was fifteen. Now she was twenty-two and her life had to be her own. No husband to be with. No babies to love. Everything she ever wanted was gone. Some days the weight of sadness bent down her back. She looked at the ground. Other days the lift of possibility stood her up straight. She saw the horizon. She willed herself to have more horizon days.

Chapter 3

Lonely. Sad.

Rosa passed people on the streets. They'd ask, "How ya doin'?" She'd say, "Fine." Because nobody wanted to hear, "Sad."

Everybody knew her, the girl whose husband smashed her face. For the first year and a half, until the second plastic surgery healed and the laser treatments ended, she wore her scars like a label on her cheek—"victim."

The worst part, the part that disgusted her, was she missed him. She tried to convince herself she just missed love, but she missed his love. She missed her eighteenth birthday, with the ring, the family party, and the first time she took him inside her. Her eighteenth birthday was going to be the high point of her life?

Since she was fifteen, she wanted to marry Joey and take care of their babies. Now that was gone. There was no other guy she wanted instead. No babies. She'd have to do something else, until she found another love, another husband, a real father. But what? Work a register at Rex-Aid.—that would be her life?

Sure, she had Mama and Papa. And her family. And Aggie's six kids – the first five plus the baby boy that might have been hers. But Mama and Papa lived four houses away from Joey, and Pete had moved back in with them after his divorce. Dino's house and Aggie's house were only a block or two away. She couldn't live near her family, because of Joey.

So she lived with Sandra, one of the girls from work. Fifteen blocks from Mama and Papa, six blocks from Rex-Aid. A one-bedroom apartment on the third floor. Too small for two girls, but affordable. No matter what shift Rosa worked, whether she got home in the afternoon or the evening, Sandra was out partying with her boyfriend, Louie. Either she came home after Rosa had gone to sleep, or she didn't come home at all. Rosa wished Sandra stayed home more, so she'd have someone to talk to. She was tired of feeling alone.

Once, when they both had the same day off, they shared a six-pack. Sandra said, "I think Louie is the real thing. Finally." She teared up for a second, then broke her mood by chugging down the rest of her beer.

Sandra went into the other room, rustled around for a few minutes, and came out carrying a gift bag with purple tissue paper sticking out the top. Standing over Rosa, who sat in their one good chair, she put the bag down in her lap. "Here. Take these. I have a real boyfriend now, and you could use some help."

Rosa peeked inside. Two plastic penises, a shiny blue one and a bigger dark one. She stared up at Sandra. She'd heard about these things, but never seen one. Her fingertips had done the job perfectly well since she was thirteen.

The things wouldn't cure lonely, but Rosa might have been curious—if they hadn't been Sandra's hand-me-downs. Ugh. "Have you...used...?"

"They're washable." She reached into the bag with two hands and pulled them out, wiggling her ass and shaking the things at Rosa like a pair of maracas. "Do you have any beer left?"

Rosa shook her ahead.

"We should have bought more." She salsa-danced to the kitchen sink. Squirting dishwasher soap the length of each one, like mustard on a hot dog, she lathered them one at a time, slowly rubbing them up and down.

She nodded with her chin at the squeeze bottle of dishwasher soap, "Antibacterial." Once rinsed and patted dry with a paper towel, she handed them to Rosa with a ceremonial bow. "You'll have a good time with these. I miss them already."

Because she had nothing else going on in her life except sadness and hurt, Rosa for the first time took an interest in the goings-on at Rex-Aid.

The store had a new Manager, Mrs. Frenio. Like most of the Store Managers, she had worked her way up from a cashier's job. Short and stocky, she was older and more experienced than their last Manager, but also more tired of the Rex-Aid rah-rah bullshit that was supposed to motivate her low-paid employees. She had veteran Assistant Managers and employees like Rosa, and she preferred to stay out of the way and let them do their jobs.

That took some re-training, because the last Manager wanted to know every detail.

Sandra said, "Mrs. Frenio, we're running out of the super-strength Kotex."

"What are you telling me for? I haven't needed them for years. Ha-ha. Just tell your Assistant Manager and she'll check the inventory to see when they'll come in. The registers should have told the computer to reorder them." She walked away stage-muttering, so everyone could hear. "Kotex. Next thing, somebody will tell me we're running out of rubbers. Don't need them either. Damn."

The computer ran the inventory unsupervised until it screwed up, then an Assistant Manager took care of the problem. Same with payroll. And the hourly tally of receipts. And the monthly inventories to calculate how much stuff was stolen since last time. Mrs. Frenio supervised the changeover of seasonal merchandise, hired and fired, evaluated employees, and doled out the few ten-cent raises that her budget allowed.

One day she invited Rosa to the back room. "How come you're still a cashier after all these years?"

"Well, I used to be married. Now, I guess I have more—"

"Don't tell me. I know that story. I got dumped, too. Why do you think I gave enough of a damn about work to become a Manager? Anyway, what I wanted to tell you—the Regional Office finally authorized us to go back up to three Assistant Managers like the store used to have. You're it."

"I'm what?"

"The third Assistant Manager. Jeez, Rosa. If you want to be a manager, you have to at least pretend you're paying attention."

"Oh, wow. That's great. Thank you, thank you."

"Don't get too excited. It's ninety cents more an hour and you'll have to work the late shift to close the store. You're the low Assistant on the totem pole."

In her new job, she was one of Sandra's bosses. Their friendship frosted a little. No more shared six-packs. Her roommate had spent most of her time at Louie's place anyway. Now she almost never came home.

Rosa worked the same shift every day now, from one in the afternoon to ten at night, with an hour lunch break when the rest of the world ate dinner. One night she came home to find Sandra sitting in the apartment's chair.

"Louie and I are getting a place together. I'm sorry, but I'm moving out." She waved her hand at a small pile of boxes and shopping bags. "The rent's paid until the end of the month. I hope you can find another roommate before then."

The next day, when Rosa got home from her shift, the little pile was gone. Sandra drank too much, and wasn't really a friend, but still.... She dreaded the process of interviewing strangers to find another roommate. The apartment was so small. Any annoying little habit could make the place unlivable.

A few days later, Aggie called. "Can you have a dog in that apartment?"

"Well, management allows them, but I'm not sure I could fit one in. It'd be harder to get a roommate. Why do you want to know?"

"To dump a puppy on you, of course."

"You have puppies? Didn't you spay Dillie? Or are these IUD puppies?"

"Not really."

"Not really which?"

"Well, we intended to get her spayed, but when you have six kids, there are a lot of things you don't get around to."

"Anyway, come look at them. They're cute. Dillie is mostly cocker spaniel and they look like her. Whatever the father was, he had weak genes."

"I can't believe this. Any living thing that hangs around your house ends up giving birth."

"No. We finally got the vasectomy. A little swelling and Al complained for days. You'd think he had a baby. Anyway, the point isn't we have too many kids and animals to love. The point is you don't have even one."

Touch

One of the puppies picked Rosa, repeatedly bumping his nose against her ankle. Aggie's kids had already named him Charlie. She took him home.

She reviewed her new ninety-cents-an-hour higher budget. If she didn't go out and spend money on restaurant food, which she didn't much anyway, she could afford the apartment alone. Charlie had annoying habits—mostly chewing the wrong things—but he was a safer bet than squeezing in a new roommate.

Because of Charlie, she had to exit and enter the store one more time every day. She couldn't leave him alone from one until ten and come home to anything pleasant, so Charlie used up her lunch break.

One day she noticed two things she'd never paid attention to before. On the way out to walk Charlie, she needed only a glance to see the displays along the check-out line looked like crap. Messy and full of stuff nobody would ever buy on impulse, like 12-packs of Dr. Pepper. They weighed too much to carry home without a car, and whoever heard of a New York Italian drinking the stuff, anyway?

On the way back, she noticed a new store about to open in the vacated K-Mart section of the shopping center. *Le Salon de l'Amour*. A love room? What the hell was that?

Chapter 4

The procession assembled at Fresh Kills Park, south of St. Anthony's. Group by group, they left for the church. First, the squadron of motorcycles turned on their flashing lights and slowly rode away. The Emerald Society bagpipers stepped out, keening music so sad his heart would have dissolved if it hadn't done so already. The honor guard of eight officers, four on each side, accompanied the flower-covered hearse at a slow march. Then twenty or more police cars followed. He and the Family Liaison Officer sat in the back seat of the first car, Mama and Papa in the second. The rest of the family members followed, along with New York City's mayor, police chief, other politicians and police brass.

Police officers lined the route, sometimes four or five deep—about 10,000, the liaison officer told him. They had come from New York City and upstate, from cities as far away as Boston, Philly, and Washington, and from small cities and towns everywhere in between. As the hearse approached, the officers slowly raised their hands to their foreheads, and one-by-one they snapped off a sharp salute as the hearse rolled past.

Once at the church, the honor guard carried in the coffin, draped with the NYPD funeral banner. He didn't know why, but the police used an American flag with green stripes instead of white. They set the coffin down at the end of the aisle, parallel to the altar rail. Two officers took their places as guards at the casket's head and foot. Inside the small church, fellow officers from the 52nd Precinct in Brooklyn lined the walls, standing at attention with their badges blackened. Officers led the family to their pews, then a few neighborhood guests.

The city's important people filled the rest of the seats.

He heard impersonal eulogies from the mayor and other bigwigs who had come to honor the fallen. The Liaison Officer, who had not left him since he'd brought the Police Chief and the Chaplain to knock on their door three days ago, whispered who each person was and what would happen next. He nodded each time, but none of it mattered.

The Chief was to describe the events which had earned these honors, how the officer had died heroically in what the police called an LODD, a line-of-duty death. That part he wanted to hear again. The Chief spoke in police jargon, so the Liaison occasionally whispered an explanation.

The dispatcher had radioed an address for a shots-fired domestic. Lucia and her partner were closest and arrived on the scene first. Following protocol for a shots-fired, they waited down the street until back-up arrived, until a Lieutenant could determine if the situation called for a hostage-rescue team.

While they waited, crouched behind their unit's open doors with guns drawn, a shooter from a second-story window fired a dozen rounds. Two hit her partner. Yelling "Officer down, officer down," into her collar radio, Lucia crawled around the unit and dragged her much larger partner to a safer place behind the rear wheels.

As Lucia moved to help him, everybody else took cover to see what would happen next. Inactivity and silence. Twenty minutes later, the domestic victim, already shot and bloodied, staggered out from the apartment-house door with a baby in her arms. The shooter hit her three more times. She lay prone on the sidewalk, while her baby cried an infant's scream, loud sobs punctuated by breath-gasping whimpers.

Lucia was the nearest officer. She crawled from her place of safety to pick up the baby under one arm. Shuffling backwards on her knees, she used her other hand to drag the woman to safety behind a parked van. Lucia, Tony's beloved Lucia, was hit once, but she brought the lady and the baby back safe.

Too long later, after a hostage-team sniper killed the shooter in his window, waiting EMTs raced onto the street. Lucia's partner, hit twice, was seriously but not critically injured. The victim, shot five times, somehow survived and was hospitalized in stable condition. Lucia, hit only once, had already bled out and died on the street, huddled against the tire of the Chevy van. The baby was unharmed.

Lucia was a hero, the Police Chief said, and he posthumously awarded her some medal, and then an Honor Medal, which he called the NYPD's highest. They were given to her family, meaning Tony. He didn't want these reminders of her death. There were officers everywhere now. Where were they when she had died a slow death, curled up on the street all on by herself? He gave the damned medals to her parents.

The service was long, but it didn't matter because he was too numbed to move or to listen. The Church said its regular Requiem Mass. The last time he'd taken communion was when he married Lucia. This time, his throat went dry, and he had trouble forcing the wafer down.

After mass, the police ritual resumed. While everybody stood, the honor guard took her casket away. He broke down. His nose ran and his knees wobbled. He was afraid he'd fall. The Liaison Officer wrapped his arm around Tony's back and held him upright. Lucia's sister cried into her husband's chest. The Emerald Society's pipes played "An Inspector's Funeral," an unbearable sob of a song, designed to make hardened officers cry. He tried to pull himself together and walk tall, like a man worthy of Lucia, but he couldn't do it.

The procession re-formed, and the cars followed the hearse between the files of saluting officers, who had reassembled along the new route. They rode south to Resurrection Cemetery, where the priest read some more words and Lucia was put into the ground. A bugler played "Amazing Grace."

Officers and friends pulled the family away. Lucia's Mama collapsed. His father-in-law and he stood her up, put their arms around her waist, and escorted her limp-legged body back to her seat in the police car reserved for the parents. The police dropped the family off at Lucia's aunt's house, its kitchen overflowing with piles of donated food and drink. The Liaison Officer said goodbye and everything official ended.

Women set out the food. Men sat around on folding chairs.

Her Nona's brother, a short man with white hair bristling in a horseshoe around the back of his head and more white hair on his upper lip, lowered himself down into the chair next to him. "You lost a good woman. I don't think we ever did right by her. We didn't know the courage she must have had. But you did."

His eyes watered and his mustache quivered. "I need a drink." He levered himself up from the chair and walked away.

Lucia's aunts in the kitchen didn't talk about Lucia. Still too hard, maybe. Instead, they wondered at the funeral service.

"Such an honor. The mayor even."

"And to think. For Lucia. Right here in our family."

"She left the kids something to live up to, that's for sure."

"Ten thousand police. From out of state. From all over."

He couldn't listen anymore. He went into the bathroom to be alone for a minute. Her fellow officers let her die on the street. So they had to stage their show to make themselves feel better. To make her family feel better. Well, bullshit. They should have heroically protected her at the scene. Like she'd protected her partner. They could have skipped the whole circus.

Sitting in the living room with a plate of untouched food balanced on his knees, he could hear Lucia's Mama and her Nona. You couldn't talk quietly to Nona anymore.

"Did you see how close she is to Dorothy Day?" Mama said.

"Doris Day?" Nona's face took on the look of frustrated concentration. She brightened. "From all those Rock Hudson movies? They say he was a fairy. Can you imagine?"

"No. Dorothy Day. You know, that woman from the Bowery. They're making her a saint."

"Oh, yeah. Her." Nona's face again showed her struggle to remember.

"It's a comfort to me they'll be so close. Forever." Sniffling when she said, "forever," Mama didn't sound comforted.

"Yes. A comfort." Nona's face settled back into repose.

He wished he had something like a supposed saint to comfort him.

His own Mama's fork fell out of her hand. She set her plate on the floor and sat still in her chair.

She was exhausted. Tony took the opportunity to tell everyone good-bye.

The aunts forced Tony to take home shopping bags full of food. "To get you through the next couple days," they said, though it was enough for weeks.

He had decided to stay with Mama for the first few nights, because he couldn't face his and Lucia's apartment. So he drove them both, and all that food, back to her house.

The next Monday he had to go to work. It was a relief to worry about cars. If a car was broken, he didn't have any emotions about it, and neither did the car.

He never moved back to the apartment. He let it go and stayed with his mother, in the room where he grew up.

Chapter 5

Mrs. Frenio fixed up an office area for Rosa in the Rex-Aid back room. A shelf hung at desk height with a keyboard terminal on it, hard-wired to the Regional Office's inventory control system. Pinned to the wall around the shelf were notes Rosa had written to herself.

"The bigger the display, the bigger the sales."
"Fewer choices, easier impulses."
"Catholic seasons sell."
"Smaller, lighter, cheaper."
"High margins good, high turnover better."

The last one was a tweak at Mrs. Frenio, who used to buy whatever Regional had on the biggest sale and stick the stuff out there, no matter how long it took to sell. The Dr. Pepper 12-packs were a result of that philosophy. Rosa remembered when Mrs. Frenio explained her system.

"Do they sell?" Rosa asked. "Hasn't some of this stuff been sitting here forever?"

"It's hit or miss. It all sells sooner or later, and we get the big discounts, no matter when it sells."

"Wouldn't we make more money if everything turned over quick? I mean, because we displayed things people in this neighborhood would see and grab."

"And how would we know that? Ouija Board?"

"No offense, Mrs. Frenio, but you're Italian-American. Don't you know what we like?"

"No offense, Miss DeAngelo, but this is a working class Italian neighborhood. I have a house in a nice suburb on the South Shore. No, I don't know what your 'we' likes."

"Wow. Do Italians on the South Shore drink Dr. Pepper?"

"No. But on sale at half the price of Coke, I figured people would try it out."

"But they're too heavy to carry home, no matter how cheap they are."

"Okay. One point for you. I never thought of that. Most Rex-Aids, the customers drive to the store."

"Here, most people walk."

"Yes, I know. Don't rub it in."

After their talk, Rosa was allowed to experiment for a month with a few items, and the check-out area's sales went up. Next step—she got three months to manage the inventory and displays. If the sales increased by 10% or more, year over year, she'd stay in charge.

There was no mention of any more money in her paycheck, but even if she didn't earn any more money right now, she figured her new skill should be worth something, someday. Besides, Rosa liked this work more than she liked standing behind a cash register. Cashiers had to smile at every customer, no matter how nasty. By the end of the day her jaw hurt, especially where Joey had smashed the bone.

Part way through the three months' probation, a local police officer was killed—Lucia, the wife of her brother Pete's friend, Tony what's-his-name. She was shot while saving a baby. Other people too, so she was a hero.

Thousands of cops came to line the road to and from St. Anthony's. Before they took their places, they swarmed the Rex-Aid, hundreds of them, buying out everything there was to eat or drink in the store. The store had the highest one-day numbers in its history, and so did the check-out area, So Mrs. Frenio made Rosa start her probation all over again. The higher sales had nothing to do with Rosa's choices, she said. Rosa couldn't argue with that.

The French love salon's sign went up on the façade over the window. Curious because love was what she longed for, Rosa checked it out on her way to work. Through the darkened window, she could see raw drywall with wires sticking out the holes where switches and plugs would be. "Not anytime soon," she muttered to herself, and headed across the mostly-empty parking lot to Rex-Aid.

Touch

For the next six weeks, every Monday on her way to work, she'd stop by the love salon. Depending on how friendly they looked, she'd sometimes chat with the construction men. One week, she talked to a couple of guys laying tile. One of them went to high school with her baby brother. She felt like an old maid.

"How much longer till this place is done?" Rosa asked.

"We'll be finished by tomorrow."

"No, I mean all done, everybody finished."

"See, we're tile. The only trade after us is paint. We can't walk on the tiles for 24 hours before we grout. After that, the job could be done in two days, if the owner's in a hurry."

"What's it like in there?"

"Nice. The two baths are really something. We had to work almost a week on those. Everywhere else, we're laying regular commercial tile, but good quality. Porcelain—and on the diagonal. That always costs more. More interesting, too, because it takes more skill." He handed her a triangle of tile he'd just sawed to fit in a gap against a wall. "See."

She examined it, pretending she could see how much higher quality it was from any other tile she'd ever seen, or how much more skill he needed to cut a corner off a tile. She could tell, though, the tile probably cost more than the scuzzy red-brown commercial carpet they had at Rex-Aid.

Fridays were Rosa's big day at work. At the start of her shift, she'd sit in the back room with Mrs. Frenio, who'd eat her lunch with one hand while the other hand's fingers flicked around a keyboard, pulling up sales and inventory charts.

When the first chart came up, Mrs. Frenio was so startled she talked even though she had a mouth full of tuna sub. "You're up five per cent over last week. That's big for one week. What'd you do?"

"Well, this weekend is the Sunday for first communion and confirmation. Most churches, anyway. We had big bins of cheap plastic photo frames saying, 'First Communion,' or, 'Confirmation,' or some other Catholic thing, I don't remember what."

Mrs. Frenio swallowed her mouthful of tuna salad. "You sold that many picture frames? Because they had 'First Communion' on them? Come on."

"There were other plastic Catholic knick-knacks, too. Christ-on-a-cross nightlights for $1.59. They sold big. Cost us 35 cents. Brightly colored packets of saints' cards, too, down on the kiddie shelves. A kid wants one of those for a buck fifty, what parent is going to say, 'No saints for you?'"

Because she'd taken another bite, Mrs. Frenio just nodded for Rosa to continue.

"Memorial Day is coming up in three weeks and St. Anthony's Day two weeks after that. So we've put out big bins full of 50-foot strings of little plastic American and Italian flags. Plastic Statue of Liberty torches with little light bulbs. We've got the same thing coming in next week, but they're shaped like St. Anthony candles. Stuff like that."

"But I have stocked the store full of Memorial Day paraphernalia already."

"Sure, but your things are better quality. Real flags, not my printed plastic ones the size of a postcard. I've got the Memorial Day impulse stuff. Small, light, cheap. Like the soldier-shaped chocolate bars wrapped in a tinfoil flag."

"What?"

"You heard me. Chocolate soldiers. Maybe you eat them to remember our country's fallen. They were on the Rex-Aid inventory list. Is it too embarrassing? I can take down the display."

"No. Go ahead."

It was Monday again. The *Salon de l'Amour* finally looked open. She peered through the window. Nothing looked scary, so she decided to go in and find out what the place really was, what it had to do with finding love. As soon as she got through the entry, a guy stuck his head through a door on the other side of the tiny waiting room. He looked at her and yelled over his shoulder. "Birgit, we have a client."

From somewhere in back, somebody answered. "What do you mean, we have a client? We aren't even open. Quit screwing around, Karl. We have to finish setting up the therapy rooms."

Karl, an older man with close-cropped white hair and a build like a piano mover, asked, "You are a client, aren't you?"

"How would I know? I don't even know what you do. I don't know what a 'love lounge' is."

"Love lounge?"

"If it was Italian, that's what *Le Salon de l'Amour* would probably mean, a cocktail lounge for love. Or maybe a love room, a love parlor."

"I guess it means most of those things in French, too, though I don't speak French that well. English, German, Danish, a little Dutch – those I can speak."

"So why the French name?"

"Marketing. Do you think *Elskovsalon* would attract many people? Seriously, though, the 'love' part has nothing to do with the treatment here. Afterwards, depending on how you personally want to take advantage of the treatment's effects, that's when the 'love' might come in."

"'Love' would be welcome. First, though, I want to get rid of lonely."

"That's easier. I'm pretty sure you will do that. Do you mind if I touch you? The wrist, the forehead--nothing embarrassing." He touched the underside of her wrist with two fingers, like he was taking her pulse. He touched her forehead with three fingers, said "ouch" and stepped around behind her to touch the forehead with the fingers of both hands.

"No wonder you're lonely. You were mistreated, weren't you?" Before Rosa could answer, he stepped in front of her with two hands up. "Would you touch the tips of my fingers and thumbs? Like 'patty cake.' That's how you say the children's game in English, no?"

She touched him as he asked. She felt the slightest tingling in her fingertips, like static electricity. He jerked his fingers away from hers, like they'd been burnt.

"Birgit. No kidding. This is important. You have to touch." He held Rosa's wrist and led her out of the little waiting room. Rosa let herself be pulled along. She was curious who was behind the door, and what was so important.

Birgit was a tall Scandinavian woman with stereotypical long blond hair. Middle aged, maybe in her late forties. She touched Rosa in the same places, played the same patty cake. "Holy…. You're right, Karl."

"I told you."

Turning to Rosa, she asked, "Are you available for a treatment now?"

"No. I'm due at work any moment."

"Call in sick?"

"I wouldn't feel right. It's too late for that. What's the big hurry, anyway?"

"If you are just starting work now, how late do you get out?"

"Ten."

Birgit looked at Karl. He nodded. "Okay, we'll stay here that late, setting up the place. Come knock on the door as soon as you can."

"Wait a minute. What is the treatment? How much does it cost?"

"If you have to go to work, we'll explain the treatment when you get back. Cost? Three hundred dollars. But for you?" Birgit looked at Karl again. He nodded again. "Nothing. Just pass it on."

"Pass what on?"

"Tonight. We'll explain it tonight."

Rosa left for work. On her lunch break, she walked Charlie over to get himself dog-sat at Aggie's house. Rosa wouldn't be available to walk him that evening. She didn't know what she would be doing instead. Something more exciting, she was sure, than waiting until Charlie finally decided on the right time and place for her to pick up dog poop.

Chapter 6

Tony always wished Lucia had stayed a 911 dispatcher. He'd worried every shift. He knew he'd fall apart if he lost her, and he had fallen apart. But he did not know, never guessed, that losing Lucia would make him less a man. In his heart—and in the neighborhood—he was barely a man at all.

His wife died heroically in a gun battle, while he was home watching TV. He was washing dishes when the Chaplain and the Police Chief came to tell him. She had a hero's funeral, and he cried, and they gave him her hero's medals to make him feel better. He'd felt chest-empty awful through it all. He should have been shot, not her. He should have protected her, but he let her protect him.

She took a tough job as a cop. He stood under cars up on their lifts. Sometimes oil dribbled on him. He went to work the day he graduated from high school. It was a great job back then. It was still a great job. But it was the same job. At least it was a man's job, though now the shop had a few women. At least it was a job he was good at. At least it was a job where he got respect.

He went to work for eight hours, and at work he was a man. Back in the neighborhood, he felt like a boy. He lived at home in his boy-child's room and his Mama washed his clothes and cooked his suppers. He helped with the chores.

When he wasn't a man at work or a child at home, he was some wounded kid for people to pity. At the tavern, he hated the looks and the whispers, the pity—especially from women. Women his own age approached him, comforted him like he was a forlorn boy, and then flirted like they wanted to take him home.

You're a little boy who needs cheering up. I'm the motherly type and I can help. Let's fuck. Ick.

When the first woman approached him and he realized what she wanted, he thought of Lucia and how far he'd fallen. He almost puked. A spittle of beer escaped his lips and landed on the woman's shoe. She left for the ladies' room. The beer burp worked so well he filed the idea away in case he needed it again.

Even Pete pitied him, for chrissake. Pete, who lost his wife and kids to divorce. Pete, who lived at his parents' home just like him. Pete, who couldn't hold onto a job because he couldn't control his temper.

Because Pete pitied him, his buddy had formed a new bowling team and asked him to join. "The men's league," he said. "One night a week, we'll get you out with the men."

He wanted to tell Pete that beating his wife didn't make him a man. Who else was he adding to the team, Joey DiFalco? Joey was running his motorcycle shop as if nothing happened.

But he didn't say any of that because Pete was right. He had to try things that might help. Bowling with guys who couldn't just sit and drink and pity him, because they had to bowl every once in a while—maybe that would help.

He joined the team.

He needed to buy a ball and shoes, and a team shirt. Pete had signed them up as the "Italian Stallions." Original. Amazing the name was still available.

On opening night, two beers into the first game, the men sprawled out among the banquettes, feet hanging over the seats in front and bellowing back and forth like walruses on their rocks.

The guy with the belly so big it hid his belt called out, "Hey, Pete, what happened to Rosa? I don't see her at the registers no more."

"She's a manager now."

"Manager? She needs a man to manage her. What she needs, you ask me." He pretended to cradle his balls. As if he could find them under there.

"Keep it in your pants. I'm her brother here." Pete looked around. "I didn't hear anybody ask him. Did you guys?"

Tony answered with a loud, "No." He was going to spend his bowling nights talking about Rosa?

His turn to bowl came around. He pulled himself to his feet and walked by Pete. Under his breath, he said, "This what you meant, spend an evening with the men?"

"Sure. Why not?"

Asshole.

His first ball started well enough, then curved into the gutter.

Walrus derision all around.

Better than pity.

Chapter 7

The love salon's waiting room only had space for four chairs, the stacking kind with stainless steel frames, little pieces of wood on the arms, seats and backs covered with black vinyl. Expensive tiles on the floor and the cheapest chairs? Temporary, maybe. They made the place seem a bit less legit. Why had she agreed to this? Love. Lonely. She turned her attention back to the couple in the chairs across from her.

Karl started. "We touch. We—"

"No shortcuts, even though it's late." Birgit got up and gave Rosa a shopping bag, full of pamphlets and brochures. "You can look at these later. We'll tell you everything that's in them before we start."

She motioned to Karl. "Go ahead."

He looked at Rosa and held his hands to his temples. "If your eyesight dims, what can you do?"

"Get glasses?"

"Yes, or contacts, or laser surgery, or take out the cataracts. The point is most people can fix the problem and see as well as ever." He moved his hands to his ears. "If your hearing fades?"

"Hearing aids?"

"Or cochlear implants or whatever. Again, you do something, and most people can hear again. Smell and taste though, we aren't so lucky. Not much we can do, at least so far. Now our fifth sense, what about that one?"

Rosa ran down the list. Oh, yeah—what he started with, touch. "People lose their sense of touch?"

Birgit took over. A tag team. "Sure. Some have a serious problem. Diabetes, maybe. Or surgery. But everyone loses sensitivity, it just happens so gradually we don't notice."

Probably true. Rosa had come to rely on Sandra's blue buzzer. Without the buzz, it was hard to reach her goal. She never had the problem before.

Birgit extended her leg toward Rosa. Rosa pulled back. Birgit shook her head. "Come here. Feel the hem of my pant leg." Rosa did. "What's the thread count? How many threads per inch?"

"I have no idea."

"Me neither. If we worked with fabrics all day, like in the fashion industry, we'd know. Design staffers develop a better touch-sense for cloth than you and me. We don't need it, but we could work up to their level if we wanted to."

"Fashion?" Karl snorted. "Let's get back on track. Rosa, what do we feel with?"

"Our hands, I guess."

"You knew love." He talked with a softer, gentler voice. "I mean, before you were traumatized. Right?"

"Ye… yes." Was this really his business? Where was this going?

"Okay, when you were with him…. Was your lover a him?"

Next, he'd ask if she liked three-ways. Him and Birgit. She answered anyway. "Yes"

"I didn't want to presume. Okay. With him, were your hands the only part of your body you used to feel with?"

She remembered the feel of Joey's body—so smooth, so strong. "Of course not."

"Right. We sense with every inch of our skin. There are nerve endings everywhere, some places more densely packed than others. They touch something and send signals to the brain about what the touch—"

Birgit leaned forward. "When we experience trauma—any kind of trauma, accidents, falls, but most especially unexpected blows from people we trusted—our skin shuts down. We call those most terrible experiences love trauma—child abuse, spousal abuse, abuse of the elderly. A lover beat you, didn't he?"

Karl frowned at Birgit. "You don't have to answer that."

"He means," Birgit said, "we already could tell what happened when we touched your wrist and forehead. Trauma closes down your sensitivity, your ability to touch. Starting at the trauma site, but spreading through your skin's nerve cells everywhere. You are more or less shut down. Except for—"

"Your fingertips." Karl's turn to hunch forward in his chair. "They're more sensitive than ninety-nine per cent of the clients we've ever worked with. Imagine your ability to touch if your whole skin wasn't so hurt."

Birgit stood up and put her hand on Karl's shoulder. "Because of our work, our fingers are so sensitive we can't hold hands. Our fingers would hurt, like a burn. When we touched your fingertips, we hurt too. Not bad, but definitely a little scorch."

She massaged the gray stubble on the top of his head. "Now you know why we're here in the middle of the night about to give away a complimentary therapy. If we remove the effects of your trauma…. Well, with your fingertips and a few days training, you could be a touch therapist yourself."

Karl and Birgit took Rosa on a tour of the back rooms. Two therapy rooms, each with their own bath and changing room, and a little office. The tile guy was right about the bathrooms. Identical, each had a large shower with both a regular showerhead and a hand-held shower spray. A modern sink stood above a long counter, connected to a changing area with a full-length mirror. Soft towels and thick cloth robes lay stacked in piles. Bright light filled the space—too bright, maybe. Would anybody want to see herself naked under lights like those?

After the tour, all three sat in one of the therapy rooms, the two of them on the therapy table, Rosa on a rolling stool. "The therapy," Birgit said, "consists of us touching almost every spot on your body with our sensitized fingers." She touched the side of Karl's neck with one finger, bouncing a few times, then did the same to his arm.

"There are lovely places with lots of nerve endings, you know which places I mean. The general vitalization of the rest of your skin will make them more alive. If we touched those areas themselves, they could get so sensitive a lover's touch might even hurt. Nobody wants that. We stay away from those areas."

Karl sat there placidly. This was woman-to-woman talk.

Birgit continued, "In Europe, the clients are always nude, and the therapist has the skill to know where she needs to stop touching. Here in America, where so many women are not comfortable naked, we can do the therapy on women wearing their own underwear. With this option, we stop where the underwear begins. Depending on the underwear, unfortunately we may miss some areas that should have had the therapy."

Karl looked at his watch. "One other thing. Normally, one therapist touches one client, but since it's already eleven o'clock, we'll both share the therapy, to finish in half the time."

Birgit stopped rubbing Karl's head and faced Rosa directly, "Are you ready? Is this something you want to do?"

Was it? She didn't know these people. They were obviously weird. On the other hand, if she ever found someone to caress her again…. "Yes. Let's do it."

Birgit sent her off. "Take a thorough shower and dry yourself completely. Come out in a robe." Wear your underwear or not. Your option."

Showered and dried, she stood in the bathroom deciding. No matter what Birgit said about Europeans, Southern Italians were not blasé, probably less blasé than Americans. She looked at herself in the mirror. She was almost thirty, but she still looked pretty good. The nude therapy was supposed to be better. If she was going to do this, she might as well do it all the way. Think of them as doctors. Yeah, right.

She hustled out of the shower room before she changed her mind.

"Leave your robe on for now," said Birgit, "until we've taken care of your head, hands, and feet. We start with the edges and work toward your core."

They still didn't know if anything was under the robe. The big, embarrassing reveal was postponed. She wished she'd gotten it over with.

The couple helped her onto their therapy table, set in the middle of the room. Lying on her back, Rosa watched Birgit on her right, and rolled her head to see Karl on her left. She brought her head back to center, waiting.

They attacked her hair. Long, normally hanging down her back, on the table it splayed out in all directions. With one hand, they pulled strands of it out of the way, with the other, they pressed their fingers down on the skin of her scalp.

She could tell which touch came from Birgit, which from Karl. Her finger pushed down harder and didn't stay as long. His bigger finger made a softer touch that lingered longer.

Right away, he noticed. "On the top of the head? Somebody hit you on the top of your head?" He didn't wait for an answer. "Slow down, Birgit. Long touches, or we might have to do her scalp again. This hair is too much of a pain to do her head twice." They both pushed down longer, rotating their fingers. She'd never get the tangles out.

When they had done her forehead and moved down her face, Karl felt her injury and her surgeries. "I have a big trauma over here. Anything on your side?'

"Not so far."

"You might get to her feet before I get through her face. You do her neck and her hand. The hand won't take any time at all. Keep going, both feet if you get that far, while I work on her cheek and jaw."

He softened his touch, took longer with each one, and slowly rotated his finger each time. After he'd covered her cheek, he went back over the same area a second time, softer yet, and a third. Though he kept getting softer, with each repeat her cheeks hurt more. By the third time, she could feel her pulse in front of her ear, where she'd never felt it before. He ran his fingers over her cheek, like she felt her legs when she shaved to find the places that needed another swipe. When he found something, he rubbed around, searching out the exact spot that needed one more touch. He held his finger on just that spot and did his long, rotating touch one last time.

Finally, he moved on to her jaw, which had been shattered and put back together with metal pins. He whistled, softened his touch another notch, and went over the area again and again. By the time he was done, her pulse banged a fast rhythm under her chin and her whole jaw throbbed. The old plastic surgery sites hurt even worse. He touched so gently, but by the end she hurt so much. Touch therapy sounded so gentle, but it wasn't for sissies. Not as bad as waxing, but bad enough.

"I'm sorry I hurt you, but when skin goes from completely numb to fully alive, it will feel like it's hurt. Soon you'll adjust to its new vitality."

By the time he finished her hand and forearm, even though he spent almost no time on her hand, Birgit had touched her feet and both lower legs.

"Time to get up," Birgit said. "We need to do your back. I'll help you take off your robe. Then, we'll get you back up on the table to lie on your stomach."

She swung her legs off the table. She didn't need any help to take off a robe. And if she was going to strip, she wanted to do it herself. When her feet hit the tiles, she hopped from one foot to the other. Her soles hurt and she tried to lift them off the floor.

"No, no. Stand in one place. Spread your weight on the whole bottom of each foot." She did what Karl said, but it made her waver forward and back. Karl ran around the table to hold one shoulder. Birgit held the other. When she was standing steady, they removed her robe and lifted her back on the table. Being naked was a big deal to Rosa, but neither appeared to notice.

The therapy table was firm, not to say hard. Even with the hole for her face so she could breathe, squashing her breasts on its surface wasn't pleasant.

First they touched the back of her neck, her upper arms, her thighs. Only then did they touch her back, working down from her shoulder blades to the top of her butt.

She felt fingers bouncing on both butt cheeks.

From Birgit's side, "She has a sit-down job?"

Karl's voice. "No, it's just part of the overall numbness of her whole body. Except the fingers."

They both continued working on her ass. The fleshiest part they'd touched so far, their fingers dimpled down further into her muscle. Or maybe her fat. She grimaced. Face down, nobody noticed.

"This is why it's so much better not to wear underwear," Birgit said. "We would have missed this whole area."

Whoopie. She winced at another finger-stab.

They finished her butt without touching anything but her cheeks. She'd been bracing herself.

Time to roll over. They helped her get comfortable on her back. Rosa thought her front looked pretty good. Joey certainly thought so. But Karl didn't pay any attention. She was a job to do, not a woman to notice.

The underside of her upper arms came next, then across her collar bone and upper ribs. Things got fleshy right below that, and they didn't touch any of it, moving to her armpits instead, and tapping their way down her ribs. Leap-frogging down to her knees, they touched her upper thighs, veered around each side to her hips, then finger-pushed her stomach, finishing with a flourish around her navel.

Rosa was exhausted. No, her skin was exhausted. Her head hurt—top, cheek, jaw. They were right. Her skin was more sensitive, and right now it wasn't happy.

Birgit covered her with a sheet. "You'll have to rest and recover. You saw how hard it is to walk at first." She gave Rosa a water bottle with a top she could suck out of. Birgit followed Karl into their little office and shut the door.

She awoke to the smell of red wine. Birgit and Karl blew on her face and gently shook her shoulders. They stood her upright and put on her robe. Birgit held her arm and walked her to the changing area, where she had to help Rosa get dressed. Rosa's skin tingled all over, like she'd been spanked, not touched. Her fingers fumbled with the button at the neck of her knit Rex-Aid shirt.

Rosa and Birgit waited while Karl locked up, "Because you're a special case," he said, "be careful how you touch people from now on. You can brush against someone, you can even hug, but don't touch anyone with your fingertips extended, like we did for you. At least, not for the next month or two. Okay?"

"Why?"

"Because it won't be just a casual touch. Understand?"

Not really. But she could guess the general idea.

Karl apologized for not walking her to her apartment, but they had to catch their bus. Midnight had come and gone. The bus only ran once an hour.

Rosa walked home teetering on her sandals, feeling light-headed, lifted up. Like returning from the tavern after she'd drunk the perfect amount and not a half drink more—which never happened that long after midnight.

Chapter 8

The service department VP, Mr. Checci, called Tony into the office. He'd only been there a couple of times before. Plaques and awards covered the fake wood paneling. Old issues of *Underhood* and *Professional Car Service* lay on file cabinets and tables.

Invited with a gesture, he sat on one of the hard chairs facing Mr. Checci and waited for the boss to get off the phone.

Mr. Checci leaned back all the way, feet on his desk. He held the receiver away from his ear, listening. When the murmur from the phone paused for a breath, he jumped in. "Yes, well, I've got somebody here. Interesting idea. I'll get back to you." He put down the phone and smiled a cheerless grin. "Everybody wants something."

Not Tony. He didn't even want to be there, wondering why his biggest boss wanted to talk.

"Listen, I need your help. We're getting more and more recalls from Toyota—stupid stuff like the driver's mat comes loose and jams under the accelerator. That one includes just about every Toyota we ever sold."

"I know. What's the problem? The cars come in, they're simple jobs, and some junior guy does the work."

Mr. Checci took his feet off the desk and sat up straight. "Right. That's our system. But it can't keep up with the volume we've got. We want to set aside a couple of service bays just for the recalls. Use our two apprentice kids, hire a couple more, and get the jobs moving like an assembly line. Bring the car in, do the fix, get it out, and bring in the next. Every car's the same work. There's no thinking involved. Get 'em in, get 'em out."

"What do you want from me? The no-thinking repairs? No thanks."

By this time, Mr. Checci was leaning forward, set in his professional sales posture, focused totally on Tony's face. "No. Well, sorta. We want you to be in charge of the junior guys. Show them the job, then check they're doing it right."

"I should give up working on cars with real problems for that?"

"Yes, you should. The pay's higher. You'll be a working foreman—a first-line manager. You'll get a good salary instead of piecework, trying to beat the book-rate all day."

"For what? Teaching the kids, checking up every once in a while, and sitting on my ass? No offense to managers."

"It's a little more involved than that. You'd spend time out in the service sales department, scheduling the cars coming in, making appointments."

"Oh, Christ." Service sales people were the worst. They sold work the car didn't really need, then told some lie about why it wasn't done yet. Just being around those guys—the slime would rub off on him.

"You won't be selling anything, just coordinating customers to keep the recall bays filled. Most of the time, if it makes you happy, you can go out and get your hands dirty helping the young guys move the cars."

"I'm going to do recall work?"

"Maybe. Just to help out."

Shit. He could say no and piss off his big boss, or he could say yes and make more money. They'd set him up. No way out.

"Why me?"

"Frankly, you're in a rut here, and your daily gross is down since you lost your.... I mean, it's understandable, but we thought you could use a change."

"How much more money?"

"About twenty percent, give-or-take, plus another week's vacation and a little more company help with your retirement plan."

The deal sounded better than he thought it'd be, and he had no choice anyway. "Okay."

Mr. Checci leaped from the chair, stepped around the desk, and gave him a professional two-handed, close-the-deal handshake. Thirty seconds more of small talk, and the man was leading him toward the door.

Touch

He walked back to the Service Department to see Sal, the Shop Foreman. A cross-breeze blew through the service entrance, past the mechanic's work stations to the exit in back. Sal's office hid all the way toward the rear, across the aisle from the Parts Department.

He had to pass by all the guys, each with a comment to contribute.

"Hey, you still with us, pal?"

"Checci, huh? He needed help pulling his head out of his ass?"

"Which is it, man? Up or out?"

Man-talk to ask if he was alright. He answered with a little head-tilted nod. Not good, not bad.

Sal's office was surrounded by glass, so he could watch his mechanics, and they could watch him. Sal saw him and opened the door. "How'd it go?" he asked.

"Did you know about this?"

"They told me this morning. Did you say yes?"

"Did I have a choice?"

"Welcome to management. You thought getting cars to go was hard? Wait till you're jump-starting mechanics."

"Do you know the plan? Where we're going to work?"

"You get the four bays up front."

"But two of them are already oil change."

"Oh, he didn't mention it? You're in charge of that, too."

"What? I'll go tell him I changed my mind."

"Want to know why they're doing this?"

"Not particularly."

"Toyota keeps giving away free oil changes when someone buys a car. They pay us for the service, but not much. This fuck-up with the floor mats, they pay us by the job to fix that. We're losing money on both of them. To make money, we got to do eight, ten oil changes an hour, four or five a bay. The floor mats – five, maybe six. That's after we pay you and the two new kids you're going to hire.

Sal sat down in his chair. Maybe he wasn't used to standing that long. "Right now we don't do three an hour of either one."

"I'm going to fix this?"

"Yeah. You're going to have twice as many bays and four apprentices with quotas. And you're going to stand behind them kicking ass."

Sal talked some more, but Tony had heard enough. He'd gone from a guy solving cars' problems to a guy kicking kids' butts.

49

The service department already had two apprentices. They liked the new assignment—better than their current work as gofers for the mechanics, running back and forth to the Parts Department. Good thing they were happy, because they had no more choice than he did.

The next day, he went down to the high school auto shop where Mr. Forte had helped him graduate sixteen years ago. He had been like a father to him, after he'd lost his own—not that he missed the drunken bastard—but Mr. Forte had retired years ago. The new Shop Teacher, Mr. Mello, had long hair and a beard whose smell of pot would keep him high until his next joint. The place was a shithole compared to when he was in school. Tools lay scattered on the floor, nothing stored where it belonged.

Still, the guy gave him the names of his two best graduates. Mello sent them over to the dealership and Tony checked them out. Their attitudes were okay, for mechanics. They'd already gotten themselves tats. They didn't seem any worse than the jack-offs working there now, so he hired them both.

All set to push cars out the door.

Chapter 9

Rosa showed up for work the day after her touch treatment. The girls went nuts.

"Wow. Look at you."

"Had a big date, huh?"

"On a weekday?"

"Does he have any brothers?"

Even Mrs. Frenio winked and threw Rosa a knuckle kiss.

Rosa tried to explain about touch therapy. A couple of girls giggled. The others' faces went blank, as if she were talking about trigonometry. She pointed out the door. "Right over there. Go see for yourself."

"*Amour* for women. Like some kind of gigolo palace?" Four girls took a peek out the Rex-Aid doorway, as if they expected to see naked men dancing out *Le Salon de l'Amour's* door.

If someone had told Rosa about touch therapy yesterday morning, she wouldn't have understood, either. One more try. After that it was up to them. "If you like the way I look, go over there and talk to them yourself. Or don't. It's up to you."

None of the Rex-Aid girls went across the parking lot. In less than the length of her work shift, they'd reverted to the movie-dream explanation. She had found a special guy, a dreamboat who could light up a girl's face in one night of love.

Twice, Rosa went into the employees' restroom to look in the mirror. What were they talking about? She saw a happy Rosa, nothing more. She did feel like a different person, but she couldn't see a different person in the mirror. Twisting her head this way and that, all she saw was Rosa with a smile. They'd never seen her smile before?

Rosa had the day off. Way too early in the morning, Mama called to invite her to lunch at Aggie's. "Just us three girls." Rosa called Aggie to make sure she knew about Mama's plan. She didn't, but she liked the idea anyway. All six kids were in school now, and she had more free time during the day.

"I've got sausage and peppers, and Anisette for the coffee," Aggie said. "Stop by the bakery and pick up the bread."

Rosa brought Charlie to play with his friends and relatives in Aggie's back yard. She dropped him off and crossed the well-worn back porch into the kitchen. Outside, clothes drying on the lines gave off their familiar wet-laundry scent. Inside the kitchen, the much stronger odor of sausage and peppers made Rosa salivate as soon as she stepped through the door. Aggie worked facing the stove and Mama talked to the back of her head. Three places were set around Aggie's end of the long table. As Aggie kept cooking, Rosa gave her a squeeze and kissed Mama's cheek. She set the bread on the table and sat down facing her mother.

"Oh, Rosa." Mama broke into happy tears. Aggie whirled around, but Rosa's chair faced away from her. "I'm so happy for you." Mama sniffled. "Finally. Nobody deserves it more."

Aggie slipped into her seat at the end of the table. She handed Mama a paper napkin while she peered at Rosa's face. "Not a makeover. Mama's right—a guy did this for you, didn't he?" She reached out to give Rosa a hug, squeezed her hard, and kissed her on the cheek as she let go. Rosa puzzled. That was more than a sister-sister kiss. Oh, yeah. Her sensitized skin.

"I'm sorry to let you two down. Whatever you're talking about, there's no guy involved. I wish there was."

Aggie looked at Rosa and gave a little laugh. "Right."

Mama stared. She lowered her eyes and shook her head. "Oh, Rosa, Rosa. Such misery. My heart goes out to you. Can you stop yourself, or is it too late?"

Rosa raised her eyebrows, her eyes darting from one side to the other. "What, what?"

Aggie looked at Mama, then back at Rosa. "Oh, shit. Mama's right. He's married, isn't he?"

Touch

Aggie stood and headed back to the stove, then turned her head to speak over her shoulder. "Some think a shared man is better than no man, but you're going to end up hurt. Wife or mistress, the women always end up hurt."

While they ate, Rosa explained how she'd gone for touch therapy at *Il salone dell'amore*—translated into Italian for Mama. "It's new. In our shopping center. Stand facing Rex-Aid and it's down on the left. It's only five blocks away from here. If you like my look, just walk down there and sign up."

Aggie wasn't buying it. "Massage, mud bath, hot rocks, you name it—nothing changes your looks this much."

"I can't even see any new look, except I smile more. It took away the hidden hurts that were still there from Joey. I feel lifted up, but I don't look that different."

Mama and Aggie together. "Yes, you do."

Mama hugged her. "I'm glad you finally got over what he did, that"—she looked both ways, but whatever she worried about wasn't around so she finished her sentence—"testa di cazzo."

Rosa and Aggie both stared. Neither remembered ever hearing Mama say something like dickhead. Both Rosa and Aggie had called Joey a testa di cazzo many times. Other phrases too. Aggie encouraged Mama. "Yeah, a real pezzo di merda."

Aggie's ploy worked. Mama added, "Right. From a porca stronzo." Rosa and Aggie applauded. Rosa couldn't believe Mama said "pig asshole." Mama grinned, then clapped her hands once. "No more. From this family, he's gone."

After eating, on their third cup of Anisette-spiked coffee, Rosa had finally convinced her family she wasn't screwing a married man, although they were still dubious about the love salon and touch therapy.

Mama came up with a three-drink idea. She gave Aggie the Italian version of the American "OK" sign, thumb and forefinger in a ring, hand moving in and out. Mama's new vulgarity was on a roll.

"Holy crap! Do you really think so?"

Mama nodded her head to the right and wrinkled her forehead. "She said, 'There's no guy involved.'"

They both stared at Rosa.

"What?"

Mama asked, "Do we know her?"

"Do we know who?"

"Your new honey. The one who did this for you. We're family, Rosa. You can talk to us."

Rosa took a minute to absorb this. She poured herself another cup of coffee and Anisette. "Anyone want another cup?"

"No. My kids will be home from school soon, and I don't want them to see their mother plastered."

"I shouldn't drink so much coffee. It keeps me awake at night." Mama put a splash in her cup, then filled it up with Annisette.

Rosa took a deep breath. "No, there's no new honey. No old honey. There's never been any honey. I'm not a lesbian."

"Rosa, dear. Nobody thinks you're a lesbian. You and Joey. I mean, before… I thought maybe you were a bisexy."

"Bisexual? Mama, what do you know about bisexual?"

"Maybe more than you think."

Rosa and Aggie looked at each other.

"An old story. Before I met your Papa. Not worth talking about."

Mama grasped Rosa's shoulder. "But you, we're talking about this week. That's worth talking about."

It took a while, but Rosa erased their bisexual fantasies about her. At least, she thought she did.

Mama finished her coffee-flavored Anisette. "Are you in the club? If you're keeping that a secret, I think you should. I don't think the other members want you blabbing about it."

"The club?"

"Sure. The zingers club. There's one right in the neighborhood, you know. Well, I guess you probably do know. One of Nina's daughters and her husband—they belong. Nina told me. She said we ought to form one for seniors. She was joking, I think. I told Papa. He didn't think it was funny—I mean he really didn't think it was funny." Mama laughed. Apparently she still thought it was funny.

"Mama, you mean a swingers club?"

"Yes. Didn't I say so? Well, as I was saying, you should keep it to yourself."

"Good idea, Mama. I will. Don't you go talking about it, either."

Mama held her finger to her mouth. "Shhh."

Aggie put the plates and cups in the dishwasher. "My kids will be home soon."

Touch

Rosa walked Mama home and got her settled in her chair. She hung Mama's coat in the closet and turned to say good-bye.

Nearing the chair, she heard the gentle sound she remembered so well—the regular breathing of Mama's soft snore.

"Sweet swinging dreams, Mama." She grabbed Charlie's leash and left.

On the way home, she realized something. She didn't have a guy, she didn't have a honey, she didn't have a club. According to Karl and Birgit, though, she had very special fingers.

Closing the bedroom door to keep Charlie out, she approached her experiment carefully. She had to put the blue buzzer right on the spot and buzz, thinking good thoughts the whole time.

With her special finger and her new skin, all she had to do was touch-rotate her finger anywhere in the general vicinity. No dreamy fantasies, no too-slow build up. A couple of touches gave her a jolt, a jolt that took quite a while to stop quivering and settle down. Another touch, another jolt. She hadn't had so much fun alone since sixth grade, when she first learned about the special thing that only grown-up girls could do.

Wiped out by her session, she staggered to the kitchen to drink a glass of water. She returned to her bed, thinking to take a nap.

Charlie jumped up to join her, as usual. Absent-mindedly, she scratched behind his ears, one of his favorites. He whined, leaped off the bed, and ran out of the room. Creeping back into the doorway on his stomach, he lay his jaw on the floor, his big eyes looking up at her. She made soothing noises, but he wouldn't come any closer.

The next morning, Charlie was perfectly happy to wear his leash and walk with her, but shied away from her touch. She stopped by the love salon on her way to work, to ask them what happened.

Birgit shrugged. "I can guess, but first tell me what you did with him?"

Karl looked like he was about to scold her. "You petted him with the sides of your fingers, right?"

"No, I scratched him."

"We told you not to do that with your fingertips, just two days ago. The dog will get over it, but learn your lesson."

"Okay. I promise. My lesson, though—that was my other question. Do you two earn more than a couple dollars over the minimum wage?"

Birgit laughed. "I certainly hope so. But we're not open yet, so right now we're earning less than the minimum wage—like zero cents an hour. All the grand opening publicity and advertising is on hold, because construction on the other franchise in Brooklyn was delayed a week."

"You said I could be trained in a few days. Can I really?"

Karl's turn to laugh. "Who knows? We never found anybody like you before. It took us months to build our fingertips up to the level you already had when you walked in."

"Can you train me? I have...." She did a quick calculation. Her savings, plus her next paycheck, minus the rent, minus the minimum payment on her credit card. "Five hundred and forty dollars."

"Yes, I'd like to. It'll be interesting. Whoops. Let me check with the boss." He turned to Birgit, the question silent on his face. She circled her finger in front of her chest—get on with it. "Yes. We can talk about money later. We don't want to leave you penniless."

Great. Maybe she wouldn't be a Rex-Aid cashier her whole life. "Tomorrow morning? Nine o'clock?"

"Fine. The sooner the better. We won't have time once we're finally allowed to open." Karl grinned. "I hope we won't."

Birgit shook her head. "Earth to Karl. Yoo-hoo. Who are we going to train her on? We're both fully charged and ready to go. God knows she is."

Aggie. She'd give up on that married lesbian swinger theory. Maybe she'd convince Mama. "I have someone. Does childbirth leave trauma we can fix?"

"Not as much as you'd think. Must be some evolutionary thing. Women are the tougher sex, anyway. Right?" Birgit answered her own question with a nod of her head. "But touch therapy can help anybody. A person doesn't have to be traumatized like you were."

"Ok. See you tomorrow. I'm bringing my sister."

She walked across the parking lot to work.

Still outside in the parking lot, she could hear the commotion in the store. Once inside the door, pandemonium. Girls ran around with plastic tubs full of shelf stock. Mrs. Frenio balanced on a step stool dusting the expensive items behind the registers, stopping to call out orders to her clerks below.

Touch

She spun toward Rosa, duster extended, and took a second to regain her balance. "Rosa. Thank God you finally showed up."

Rosa glanced at the clock. She was five minutes early.

"You have to clean the check-out area. I wouldn't let anyone else touch it. Not just ordinary clean. The cleanest it's ever been. And make sure the display is arranged the best you possibly can."

Chapter 10

They were in their oil-change bay, the two kids sitting on boxes of oil filters, Tony leaning against a wall. Sonny and Leo, to Tony's disbelief, couldn't do an oil change any better than the average guy in Tony's neighborhood. He had to train them as if they'd never been through Auto Shop.

"If you didn't even learn how to change oil right, what the hell did you do over there?"

"Every year," Leo said, "Mr. Mello found a classic car and we restored it. This year we did a '57 Chevy Nomad. Really cool. The school holds an auction to benefit the shop. This year, the Nomad sold for $66,000."

"How many kids worked on the car?"

Sonny raised his hand, like he was still in school. "Two classes. Thirty-five of us. A lot of work goes into restoring a car."

"Of course. Lot of work. How many graduates got jobs in restoration shops this year?"

They looked at each other and shrugged. "Nobody. I don't even know a restoration place around here."

"A couple places for cars. Another asshole who restores motorcycles. All one-man, two-man operations. They don't hire anybody."

Tony raised his voice a notch, less like a buddy and more like a boss. "Let's compare a '57 Chevy to the modern cars your friends would repair if they ever got a job."

"Of course they're different, but Mr. Mello says the principles are the same."

The poor kids. No wonder they couldn't do a decent oil change. Mr. Forte had been replaced by a bullshit artist. "He says that? What principles? Same engine block and head configuration? No. Same cam and valve set-up? No. Fuel intake systems? No. Exhaust systems? No. Electronics? No. Belt drive and accessories? No. Drive shaft and rear-wheel drive? No. Suspension? No. Brakes? No. Frame, body shell, paint? No, no, no. Even the tires are different."

Leo tried one more time. "But we learned the basics. Now we can apply them to the newer cars."

"Basics? You couldn't have worked on more than one thirty-fifth of an old Chevy. If I'd known you had learned so little, I wouldn't have hired you. But now you're here, you'll learn to change oil at production speed. Hardly a job even for an apprentice, but..."

The shop was open six days a week and the mechanics each worked five. Guys picked their day off, in order of seniority. Once in a while, a senior mechanic had a dentist appointment or something and took a weekday off, but usually they picked Saturday.

Tony told friends, "Don't get your car fixed on a Saturday."

He took Tuesday off to go look at the school's auto shop and talk to Mr. Mello.

Working amid the same mess he saw last time, three kids in the shop struggled to start the engine on a ten-year-old hatchback. All high school kids looked young to Tony these days, but these three were still two years short of borrowing daddy's razor.

He watched them for a few minutes. "Do you want to figure this out for yourselves, or do you want a hint?"

"Who are you?"

"Tony Prezzi. I graduated from here more-or-less the year you were born. I just hired Sonny and Leo."

"Whoa. Okay, a hint."

"The car's not getting gas. Hope the fuel filter's shot—cheap and easy. If it's the fuel pump, it's a hassle to get at but a few hours of minimum-wage work could buy you a reconditioned replacement. The fuel injectors—that would be something electronic. They wouldn't get plugged up all at once. If it's electronics, good luck with that. It's more like repairing a computer than fixing a car."

They looked for the fuel filter. One kid flopped onto his back and ran his hand along the fuel line. Tony watched, smiling. They were almost cute. Any mechanic would have seen the filter, because on this model it sat in plain sight attached to the firewall.

Taking pity on them, Tony tapped it with his finger. "Is Mr. Mello around?"

"He's out on break." The tallest kid pinched his thumb and index finger to his lips.

"He's toking somewhere? On the job?"

"Yeah. Pretty cool, huh?"

"No. Better weed than booze, probably. My old man didn't die from dope. But on the job? Has he got a habit? Is that why this place is a shithouse?"

"I guess."

"Good guess. Where is he?"

"In his truck. The tricked-out Toyota." They pointed out the garage door.

Smoke fogged the truck's windows. A hazy outline of a head showed through the smoke. He decided he'd wait until the guy finished his break.

Tony left the kids working. Curious to see the new equipment bought from auctioning off the classic cars, he wandered through the shop. He couldn't find any.

"Sir! Sir!" A tall woman in a pantsuit stood in the shop's doorway, waving him toward her. He headed her way. Crisp, thin, good looking. About his age—no, probably older. The frosted dye job made her look younger than the age on her face.

When he got close enough, she gave him an elbow-locked handshake, the kind women use to keep strange men from getting too close. "I'm Ms. Gennaro. Can I help you?"

"Tony Prezzi. Hello." Her tone of voice implied he was supposed to know who Ms. Gennaro was, but he had no idea.

"Are you a prospective parent? I'm sorry, but you need a visitor's pass. We can't let people wander through the school unaccompanied—for the safety of our students. I'm sure you understand."

"No. Not a parent. I graduated from this program," he pointed his thumb over his shoulder, "sixteen years ago. I just hired two kids who graduated this year and, frankly, they don't know anything, so I came by to see what the story was."

"I gather you saw. I don't know anything about cars, but I can look through the doorway and see what the problem is. Did you meet Mr. Mello?"

"No. He wasn't there."

"Out in his truck, heh?"

She strode into the shop, stepping her short heels over the tools on the floor and waving at the three kids, "Hi, boys," They stood at attention until she lowered her hand and gave them a subtle "as-you-were" move.

Once at the garage door, she stared at Mr. Mello's truck. "Sir, would you do me a big favor? You could help me and our auto shop program, which you seem to care about."

"What?"

"Come with me to his truck and let me introduce you to Mr. Mello. When I write up our encounter, and I've written up a lot of them already, I'll have more impact if I can mention one of our graduates' employers saw him, too."

"Okay." She sounded like Mr. Mello might get himself fired. He'd seen enough in the shop and he'd heard enough from Leo and Sonny. He was happy to help.

As they approached the truck, the door opened and pot smoke billowed out. Ms. Gennaro stepped back. Tony, too.

"Miss Jenny! Nice of you to visit. You too, mister. Beautiful day to be outside. I love this time of year." Happy to see her, happy to see him, happy about the weather, just a happy guy.

Looking at her again, his grin collapsed into a pout. "You're going to fill out one of those forms again, aren't you? Well, I'm not going to let a little form ruin my day." He shut the door.

"Would you mind accompanying me to my office? Not to fill out his form. I can do that later. I need to talk about our auto shop problems, with somebody who knows about auto shops." Ms. Gennaro walked across the grass towards the school's main entrance, long legs moving right along, apparently taking for granted he'd follow her.

Her office said "Principal" on the door. Not a surprise. Backed by bookshelves at the rear of the room, her desk faced the office door. A round conference table stood nearby. She pulled out a chair for him at the table. He sat. She walked around the table, hung her suit jacket on the back of a chair, and slipped into the seat across from him.

"If you graduated sixteen years ago, you must have been here during Mr. Forte's time."

"Yes, I was."

"He's a legend."

"He should be. He used car manuals and car electronics to teach me reading and math. He cared." Tony hadn't stayed in touch since Mr. Forte retired. He should have. "Without Mr. Forte, I wouldn't have graduated. He got me a job, a great job. I'm a high school graduate and a good mechanic because of him."

"I'm sorry I never met him. He lives with his daughter now, upstate somewhere. Syracuse, I think. Too bad we've never been able to replace him with anybody half as good."

"Why not?"

She tapped the edge of her table. "I'm so glad you asked." She fixed her eyes on his.

He held her gaze just long enough to feel okay about himself.

"A person can get licensed as a Voc-Ed teacher only two ways."

She wrapped a fist around her first finger. "One, get a college degree with an education major and then get at least two years full-time experience in the field you will teach, like auto mechanics. How many of those people do you suppose we find running around?"

"None."

"Correct."

She wrapped the fist around her middle finger. "Two, have a high school degree and five years full time work experience in the field. In auto shop, things get complicated because the teacher also needs ASE certifications—whatever they are—in the important auto-repair areas. I think the minimum is two. Maybe three." She'd unwrapped her fist, leaving her middle finger up. They both looked at it. Her face reddened and she bent it into her palm.

"ASE. Automotive Service Excellence. I have five certs, I think. You retake the tests every five years or you lose them."

"Well, good. You would qualify. But we can't hire people like you because the starting pay is so much less than a mechanic earns. Hang around for twenty years of annual pay-step increases, you might earn more than a mechanic, and teachers have a decent pension, if the City doesn't go broke before we all retire. But that's all we have to offer."

"If that's true, how could you hire Mello?"

"I said we pay much less than a mechanic earns. A dysfunctional mechanic, an out-of-work mechanic—we can pay people like that more than they used to earn."

"You already have Mr. Doobie. I thought teachers were almost impossible to fire."

"True. Almost impossible, but not totally. I've worked on him ever since I got transferred here. He's at the stage he's supposed to be out of the classroom, doing busywork somewhere until the tribunal tells him good-bye. I keep writing him up, to help the tribunal reach the right decision."

"Good job. I see he's no longer in the classroom. He's in his truck."

"I can't leave the auto shop with nobody. We'd be forced to close the program down. I can't kick him out until I find a replacement. I had a long-term sub lined up, but at the last minute he got a permanent job." She leaned over the table.

He automatically leaned back in his chair. "Sorry to hear. Those kids are learning nothing. The whole point of the shop program is so a student can get a job when he gets out. None of these kids are qualified."

"Would you take the job? You more than meet the requirements. I can kick him out today and you can start fixing the mess tomorrow."

"Ma'am. What you were saying about how much more a mechanic already earns? I've been promoted to manager. I earn a lot more than a mechanic."

"You're a manager? In an auto shop?"

As of last week, but she didn't need to know that. "Yes."

To lean himself back, he had put his palms on the edge of the table, like he was ready to leap up and run.

She half rose from her chair, leaned too far forward for the top she was wearing, and reached across the table with both hands. She covered the fingers of his left hand, squashing them flat on the table. "If you're a manager, we can start you three pay steps higher, about five thousand dollars more a year. Will you take the job?"

63

Tony raised his eyes. *Look at her face, look at her face.* He gave a tentative try to pull his fingers out from under her hand, but she didn't let up. "I'll earn only about seven thousand dollars less than I earned as a mechanic, and much less than I earn as a manager. Do I understand the deal?"

"Yes. That's all I can offer, but the kids need you. Will you take the job?"

"How about if I get back to you?"

"Promise?" She relaxed her hold.

He stood up, shook hands—she bent her elbow this time—and fled from her office.

Chapter 11

The next morning, Rosa dragged Aggie the five blocks to Le Salon de l'Amour. Aggie would not have come for herself, she said several times, but she came to help her sister out.

"What will you do to me?"

"I told you, touch your skin from head to toe."

"Think, Rosa. You're my little sister. I used to carry you around. Now we hug. You've had your grubby little fingers all over me by now, and I don't feel the magic."

"I don't know that much about it. I think you have to touch in a special way, and the sensitivity wears off after a while. You need the therapy again. I don't know how often. Besides, we had clothes on."

"I'm not going to have clothes on?"

"I didn't. But you can wear your underwear if you want."

"You were nude?"

"Yep."

"Will I look like you? Because if I do, Al will send the kids out to do chores as soon as he gets home from work. We'll do the bedroom bounce every day, instead of once a week on Saturday night."

"I hope you get bounced twice a day, but the point isn't looks. The point is how alive you feel, in touch with everything."

She absent-mindedly brushed the back of her hand down her cheek, caressing the spot where her bruise used to be. "The treatment makes you aware of all the world's wonderful textures. I feel breezes I never felt before. If Rex-Aid would let me, I'd wear long silk skirts and forget about the underwear. For the sensuality of it all."

By then they'd reached the Salon. Rosa opened the door, but Aggie grabbed it too, and held it half shut. She mumbled, "Too late now," and finally let Rosa open the door.

Birgit had watched the indecision in the doorway. "If that's how we have to drag a customer in here to give away the therapy for free, we're going to be in trouble."

Rosa stopped herself from agreeing. This neighborhood was a weird choice for a Salon location. Look at the reaction of her co-workers.

Birgit told them Karl was in Brooklyn, trying to speed things up at the other franchise. She gave Aggie the spiel about the eyeglasses and the hearing aids and the possibility to renew the sense of touch.

Aggie walked back from the shower room, hair wet and wearing a robe. Rosa guessed her sister wore underwear under the robe, but Aggie opened the robe enough to show her bra-less cleavage. She and Rosa exchanged winks like two teens being naughty.

After rubbing her hands around Aggie's head, face and neck, Birgit let Rosa touch the scalp and watched every touch. When Rosa had finished, Birgit touched a spot just behind Aggie's hairline on the left.

She took Rosa's hand and made her rub the same spot. "Feel that?"

"Sure. Same as everywhere else. I already touched there."

"No, not the same. I hoped you would feel the difference. Aggie, how did you get hit?

"Basketball. Slammed down to the court. The bitch got a penalty and I had to shoot two free throws even though the basket was too blurry to see. I had a devil-horn bump for weeks."

"Rosa, you couldn't feel the difference between the trauma spot and the rest of the scalp?"

"No." She rubbed the area again, but still nothing.

Birgit went over the spot once, with those slow, finger-rotating touches. "These touches are more effective, but we only use them when necessary. I'll let you find out why for yourself. Aggie, do you have any other traumatized places?"

Aggie opened her robe and revealed her Ceasarean scar. Rosa tried not to stare at her sister's bare body, so much like her own. Aggie had two C-section babies, though there was only one scar. "The doctor deliberately made the second cut exactly where the first one was – not to sever more nerve endings."

"Did you hear that, Rosa? 'Sever nerve endings?' Surgery scars are the toughest places we have to touch. In Europe, specialists work only on surgery patients. Here, we're too few for that."

"Are you going to do her scar?"

"I want you to try." Birgit held out her own arm. "Practice on me."

Rosa touched her arm.

"With a rotating touch."

Rosa did.

Birgit took hold of Rosa's wrist and rotated her finger further.

Rosa practiced the rotation several times, on different parts of Birgit's arm.

"Softer, Rosa."

Rosa tried.

"Still softer. We will touch her many times. Very softly. Remember how you hurt, even though Karl's touch was so soft?"

"Yes." She would hurt her sister. Touch therapy became an anxious business.

She touch-rotated, softly, slowly. As she circled her wrist, the wrist rolled her finger slightly from the thumb side of the fingertip to the middle-finger side. Birgit said the subtle roll helped.

Twenty minutes later, Rosa's wrist was killing her. She shook her hand every few touches.

Birgit took over the work on the scar. "Your wrist? You just learned why we rotate only where necessary. You'll build up your little wrist muscles and learn to touch with both hands. Still, some of us have to wear braces when we're not working."

Rosa stood, shaking her wrist, while Birgit worked on the scar.

"No, no. This isn't my session. You are doing this for your sister. I'm not. Touch her feet and legs, hands and arms. We'll see if you can feel where to stop touching in the areas around her breasts and vagina, then we'll turn her over."

Rosa didn't bother to feel where to stop. Looking at her sister's vagina was embarrassing enough. She wouldn't touch anywhere near it.

The session finally ended. By then her fingers hurt as much as her wrist. Aggie purred in her sleep under the sheet.

Birgit and Rosa washed their hands again, thoroughly, like doctors. Birgit poured some soothing cream into two finger bowls and gave Rosa one. "We did the best we could on the Caesarean scar. We couldn't help as much as we would with a regular surgical scar because she was cut twice."

Awake and dressed, Aggie asked, "Did you guys give me something while I was knocked out? I feel a little drunk."

"Bad drunk or good drunk?" Birgit asked.

"Good. Definitely good."

"The short-term effect of the therapy."

Aggie took Rosa back to the big mirror in the dressing area.

Aggie peered at her reflection. "I can't see any difference. Can you?"

Aggie's skin was filled out, her frown lines and half her wrinkles gone. Despite her dark tan skin color, the same as Rosa's, a reddish undertone chased away any trace of pallor. Aggie's grin had grown wider. Transformed.

In the mirror, they still looked like sisters, their skin and grins identical. Standing next to Aggie, Rosa saw for the first time the change everyone else had seen.

They hugged and Aggie left for home.

"Let's finish the lesson," Birgit said. "What did you learn?"

"Touching's hard."

"Sure. You have to build up the endurance in your wrists and fingers, work on the left hand, and—"

"Learn to feel. I couldn't feel anything. All her skin felt the same to me. Even where her bump had been, and I knew about the bump."

Birgit squeezed her arm. "Good. First lesson learned. Feeling is harder than touching for everybody. For you, how to feel is the only part you have to learn."

She gathered up the therapy table's cover, the towels, the robe, and led Rosa to the washing machine. "I thought your magic fingers would make you able to feel easily, too. But in that aspect, you'll start out just like the rest of us did."

"Thank you so much, Birgit." Rosa wanted to stay and talk, but she checked her watch. "I have to leave for work. All hell is breaking loose over there, and I can't be late."

At Rex-Aid, they expected a visit from some important headquarters people—to inspect the store, Mrs. Frenio thought. "But, I don't know for sure. They're from national headquarters in Connecticut, not from the regional office. Nobody from national has ever come to the store before."

Mrs. Frenio leaned over and arranged the school notebooks into a neater pile. "They'll come this afternoon or tomorrow."

Some office assistant had told Mrs. Frenio she'd call the morning of their visit, with a more exact time of arrival. She hadn't called yet, which should mean the execs wouldn't come until the next day. Mrs. Frenio kept everybody ready, in case they showed up by surprise.

Every time a customer bought anything, some clerk slipped to its shelf to pull the remaining products forward. Products stood in even ranks along the front of their shelves, like soldiers lined up for inspection.

Mrs. Frenio fussed with her seasonal displays, back-to-school season now, which had started on July fifth, the first day after the Independence Day season. In the back office. Mrs. Frenio made Rosa take down all her reminder slogans off the wall. Too messy, she said. To remember them, Rosa typed a list and printed it out: Catholic seasons sell; red, white and green always; fewer choices, more impulses—twenty-one altogether.

Rosa's check-out section needed little work. She moved her displays, vacuumed the rug, and put them back. She raised the false bottoms on a couple of cardboard tubs, to make the products seem like they mounded higher. "The bigger the displays, the bigger the sales." One hour and done.

Mrs. Frenio called Rosa the next morning at half past nine.

"Headquarters called. Two executives are coming this morning at eleven—Mr. Miller and Mr. Bates. I never heard of either, but I don't know the national people. I guess they want all the Assistant Managers here, because the woman told me to make sure you're here. You're the only one wouldn't be working then. You have to come in early."

"How early? I have to shower and dress. Then it's a ten-minute walk to the store."

"Ten o-clock. You three Assistants and I need a last-minute meeting, to make sure we know what to say. You know—to get on the same page."

"I can't make it by ten. You start your meeting and I'll get there as soon as I can."

She ran around getting ready. Luckily, she had no clothes decision. Black pants, the red Rex-Aid shirt, and her name badge. Her laundry had piled up, because she felt so great and laundry was not a feel-great activity. She still had almost-clean pants and a clean shirt. Her regular underwear was all in the laundry, so she threw on a set from the big-date drawer.

Luckily, Charlie was in a hurry, too. Otherwise, she would have needed to follow him around, with her plastic bag at the ready, until the mood struck. She hustled him back into the apartment.

Rosa got to the meeting about twenty after ten. It didn't matter that she was late, because the agenda had only one item, listen to Mrs. Frenio fret.

At eleven, a short stocky man slipped in the door. Wool pants and a wrinkled blue dress shirt—nobody from the neighborhood. Everybody looked at him expectantly, but he paid no attention to the staff. Not fifteen feet from the door, he got hooked by Rosa's impulse displays and pawed through a basket of dinosaur-shaped pencil sharpeners in a bin marked ninety-nine-cents.

He did not have much to look at, though, because of her rule about "no choices, more impulses." All the dinosaurs were identical green Tyrannosauruses. He went on to pick up a transformer pen out of the next cardboard bin. Cheap plastic things, they unfolded from a robot-toy to an awkward ballpoint pen. A dollar ninety-nine, and so popular she'd already re-ordered them twice. Like the dinosaur pencil sharpeners, they were manufactured in different types and colors, but her display carried only one type.

Another man came through the door, a total contrast to the first. Tall, with black hair shaved around his ears and curly on top, he wore fashionable black-framed glasses. His dark silk suit set off a red tie, perfectly knotted in the collar of his white shirt. Shirt cuffs emerged from his suit sleeves, showing red cufflinks which matched his tie. He kept his left hand in a fist and the fingers on his right hand were shortened and without fingernails, as if he'd been in some kind of accident. He wore freshly shined Italian loafers peeking out from the perfect break of his creased pants. "Headquarters" radiated from his outfit.

Mrs. Frenio hustled over to shake his hand. The short, wrinkled man joined them and shook Mrs. Frenio's hand, too. Standing next to her, he could have been her brother, the same height and stocky build. But she died her hair and he was halfway bald.

Pretending to be busy, the employees peeked at the two men as they talked to Mrs. Frenio. The short one asked a question, his voice rising at the end, "...DeAngelo?"

Mrs. Frenio's eyebrows arched. After a brief hesitation, she led the men toward Rosa.

Chapter 12

The weekend after she'd made the job offer, Ms. Gennaro—Meg, her name was—called to ask if Tony was free for dinner. No woman had ever asked him out before.

They ate Greek at a fancy diner farther south on the Island, talking about their lives. She'd never married. He told her of Lucia.

Over the baklava, he said, "I've decided. I'll take the job."

"Hold that thought until later."

What? Wasn't getting his "yes" the whole point of the invitation?

"You want to stop by for coffee or a drink?" She did her thing again, where she leaned too far over the table and the neck of her blouse flopped open. He didn't bother trying to look at her face.

He didn't want to insult her, so he said, "Sure," even though she was older than him, and the skinniest woman he'd ever dated.

She lived near the diner, in a regular suburban house with a driveway leading to an attached garage. Grass grew on all four sides.

They lived in two different worlds. In the neighborhood where Tony lived, the houses were attached, with their front doors a few feet from the sidewalk. If there was any grass at all, it was a little patch between the back of the house and the alley.

Inside the door, in a living room with a few pieces of modern furniture, like a picture in a magazine, she gave his shoulder a little squeeze. "I'm having whiskey, what will it be for you? I have beer, wine, hard drinks, whatever you want."

He would normally have said beer, but he said whiskey.

She came back from the kitchen, not with a couple of shot glasses on a tray, but with two short cocktail glasses full of booze, triple shots at least.

Touch

After the booze, she rubbed his shoulder. "Do you mind?"

He wasn't sure if he did or didn't.

She slid around in front of him and rubbed both his shoulders, moving down to his biceps. "Nice." She rubbed his chest, slipping one hand between his shirt buttons.

He wished he wore his work pants. They were sturdier and it wouldn't be so obvious what was happening below his belt.

He felt her fingers furrowing through his chest hair. "You don't have to do this. I already said yes."

Her fingers went still. "That's insulting, Tony. You think I'd seduce you just so you'd take a job? You think I use my body to hire faculty?"

It was only insulting if it wasn't true. "I thought—"

"You thought wrong. You've been on my fuckworthy list since that first day we met. Pardon my French. Your looks, the way you cared about the shop, about how the shop shortchanged its graduates…. Not many men meet my fuckworthy criteria. When I find one, I try not to let him wriggle off the hook." She resumed with her fingers in his chest hair. "Enough talk. I don't have to justify myself. Let's go into the bedroom and continue this conversation on a lower plane."

Meg had a supply of different styles and sizes of rubbers in a nightstand drawer. She looked at Tony, then wrapped her fingers around him and insured she was sizing him up at his full height and girth.

She pawed through the drawer and pulled out a packet. "This one's perfect." She put the rubber on him. She put the rubber and himself in her.

By three in the morning, lying on his back and trying to keep his fingers rigid in the position she wanted, he fell asleep. She'd used every part of him that could serve her purpose. She'd put him on top, bottom, front, back, sitting, standing, lying. After the first two times, she'd stopped selecting his rubbers, reaching into her drawer and throwing him a handful.

She woke him at six, as the sun began to light the room. She went easy on him this time—just an hour or so, just one rubber.

It seemed unlikely, but he had to ask. "Did you keep going while I slept?"

"No. A sleeping woman needn't stop the fun. But a sleeping man is basically useless."

He lay flat on his back, talking to the ceiling. "I assume it's been a while, or is that presumptuous?"

She lay right beside him, her hand on top of his. "It's been long enough. Fuckworthy men are hard to come by."

"Depends on your standards, I guess."

"Mine are high. But even if they look and sound good, I sometimes hook a fuckworthless guy, a fish not worth the work of catching him. Not your problem, though. You're fuckworthy in every sense of the word."

"It's a word?"

"It is to me, and you fit the definition."

"Thank you." He rolled on his side to look at her face. "But this is a one-nighter, right? I say yes, and we're finished."

"I've made an executive decision. I won't be your boss until all the paperwork goes through and you've signed the contract. It's a chancy legal position. You're not going to sue, are you?"

"No. So when's our next date?"

"It's Sunday. Do you go to mass?"

"No."

"Then, after breakfast."

The paperwork took four weeks. Four two-day dates.

She kissed him as she gave him a pen to sign the contract. "Sorry, Tony. I dragged it out as long as I could."

"It was good while it lasted, wasn't it?"

"You know what they say. All good things come to an end." She put his signed contract in a file fat with previous paperwork. She shook his hand. "Welcome to the faculty, Tony. I'm sure we'll work well together. By the way, you're the only one. Your average faculty guy is decidedly not fuckworthy."

By the start of school, every tool and machine in the shop was cleaned and stored the way it should be.

The three kids with the hatchback had done a lot of the work. He'd made a deal with them. Mornings, he helped with their car, and he paid for the reconditioned parts. After lunch, they helped him with the shop. The kids' car was done, except for paint because the shop didn't have a paint booth. The shop was ready, tools in place, machines working, and even some new equipment.

The classic car auction bonanza was nonsense, as Tony should have known. By the time Mello bought a car for fifteen thousand and put thirty thousand dollars' worth of restored parts in it, the sales price wasn't so impressive. Fortunately, Mello had never gotten around to requisitioning any equipment for the shop in the three years he sold his classic cars, so Tony had something to work with.

As the school year got underway, Tony demonstrated the make-up of modern brakes on his 4Runner, with four groups shifting from the disc brakes on his front wheels to the drums on the rear. After that, he had students bring in cars, from their families or wherever, that could use a free brake job.

By late October, he had the year's plan set. One car system every two weeks. He still didn't know about requisitions or report cards or any school stuff, but Meg and her assistant helped with that.

In late October, Bob Beretto cornered Tony while he was microwaving a pizza-slice in the tiny teachers' lounge. Bob taught Gym, or Exercise Science, or whatever the latest name was.

"Tony, I have a problem you could help me with."

An opening line like that, he didn't want to hear the rest. "What?"

"Rita Esposito—you probably never met her—she's been on maternity leave. She told me she won't be doing anything extra when she comes back."

"Of course not. She has a baby."

"Well, some women want to work the same as before they.... Never mind. My problem is, she was our women's basketball coach. I have to find another one. You know who'd make a perfect candidate?"

"Uh, no."

"Someone who played varsity here for three years. Someone who once took quite an interest in our women's team, back when they were league champs. Someone who knows basketball and also knows the women's game—the smaller ball, the shorter shot clock, the closer 3-point line. All that, and women's height, make for a different style of play. Most men don't know squat about any of that, but my perfect candidate might."

Tony shifted his feet. His one-slice lunch was getting cold. "What about the Assistant Coach. Why not give her the job?"

"I would, but she transferred out of the City system at the end of last year. Took a job in the 'burbs. Her husband got a better position out there."

"Just for kicks, how much does it pay?"

"Thirty-five hundred."

"Wha? Doesn't it take as much time as teaching?"

"No one does it for the money."

"That's for sure."

"Our coaches do it for love of their game, and because they know how sports can teach a kid values like nothing else. Values that can change kids' lives."

Plenty of other things must teach values at least as well as sports. With his emphasis on quality work, Tony was already teaching values.

Phil pointed at Tony's soggy piece of microwaved pizza. "It's getting cold."

Smart man. Observant.

"I'll let you eat. Take a couple of days to think it over. But let me know quick. If you say no, I'll have to improvise and I'm out of time."

Tony half knew his answer, but he needed time to be sure. He did know the women's game. He would rather work with girls than the asshole jocks like he'd been at sixteen. Hell, he liked women more than men in general—which was why he might have to say no. If he fixated on some teenager like he'd fixated on Rosa, his whole life would blow up, a crater would open under his feet, and he'd slide down to hell.

He was older now. He'd loved Lucia and there'd never been another teenage Rosa. He could handle himself.

He zapped his pizza slice again. Thinking about what to do, he swallowed the limp piece of soggy mess without tasting it—one plus for the offer already.

He slowly walked back to his auto shop, remembering basketball plays, and players in ponytails.

Chapter 13

With a not quite convincing grace, Mrs. Frenio gathered the four of them together. "Mr. Miller and Mr. Bates, please meet Miss DeAngelo. Mr. Miller is VP of Marketing and Mr. Bates is VP of In-store Management." Rosa decided to remember them as MM and BIG, the G meaning the Good-looking one.

Rosa reached out and shook their hands. "Please, call me Rosa."

Mr. Bates said, "Lou." She could feel the trauma in Mr. Bates' skin. Probably anybody could.

"Phil." Mr. Miller.

Mrs. Frenio said, "Ella."

Rosa stifled her amazement. Ella. She never knew Mrs. Frenio's first name. How stupid—like a little kid surprised to learn teachers had first names.

With no small talk, no "nice to meet you," Phil asked Rosa, "Why only one kind of dinosaur, one kind of robot?"

"My displays are alongside a moving line of people waiting for a cashier. People grab something or they don't. If they have to stop and decide, they'll probably look but not take time to choose. I have a rule, 'Less choices, more impulses.' I bet we'd sell five times the candy and gum, if the contract distributors didn't pile one hundred choices in their little space."

Mr. Miller—, Phil—grinned. "I've been in marketing all my life, but that's a new one on me. Your overflowing displays, those are standard—"

"One of my rules, "Bigger displays, bigger sales.""

"Yes, well, your rule is standard retail practice. Look in any supermarket. What's this with the rules? You have a list?"

"Do you want me to show it to you?"

Mrs. Frenio prevented any answer. "I spotted Rosa's natural ability and put her in charge of the check-out area."

"Good thing you did." Mr. Bates led them farther down the check-out lane. "The checkout-area sales in this store started to rise. Some seasonal bump, the guys from regional thought, but the sales graph kept moving higher and higher. They sent a man over here to check out the situation, and he described the displays and told us about Miss DeAngelo—Rosa."

"I thought he came here to talk to me."

"Of course, Ella. That, too."

Phil noticed the red, white, and green containers full of items with the same three colors. "What's this about? The Rex-Aid colors are red and white—no green."

"Another rule: 'Red, white, and green sells.' Plus some of these items are to decorate for the Feast of the Assumption. That one is, "Catholic seasons sell.'"

"O...kay. But why the green?"

Lou rolled his eyes. "C'mon, Phil. Italian neighborhood, Italian national colors."

"Oh. All right, I get that, but Catholic seasons? You mean like Christmas and Easter? Doesn't every store do that?"

Rosa grinned. "Nobody does those holidays Catholic, like I do. And how about the Feast of the Assumption. Is that big in your other stores?

Lou smiled. Phil looked puzzled. "'Do it Catholic? What does that even mean in a retail sense?"

"Okay. Christmas, little nativities. Easter, plaster Christs-on-a-cross for your bedroom wall. St. Anthony's day, plastic statues and candles. All Souls Day—that's Halloween—plastic flowers to decorate gravestones for the winter. Virgin Mary's Day in early December, religious calendars for the next year. February, we've got Carnival, Lent, even St. Agata's Day."

St. Agata. She smiled. What a great saint. "She's Sicilian and the patron saint of breasts—long story—so women with lumps and 11-year-old girls buy her statue. My older sister had a bunch of them. They worked for her, but her name was Agata, so they would. She gave them to me when I was eleven." Another man might have lowered his eyes to check how well they worked, but unfortunately Lou's gaze never left her face.

She spread her hands. "None of the Catholic stuff costs more than a couple bucks apiece."

"How about St. Louis? He's not big in this neighborhood?" Lou asked.

"Was he Italian?" Luigi. Maybe he was.

"Maybe."

"I'm not sure. I don't think he'd sell."

Lou was Catholic, she guessed. But he'd know where his name saint lived. Not that he had to be very Catholic to know the seasons. She knew them, for chrissake, and she only went to mass for family baptisms or confirmations, weddings or funerals. She had crowds of aunts and uncles and cousins, though, whose occasions forced her into the church too often.

"That's only a couple of your rules, right?" Phil asked. "Go get your list. I want to see them all."

Mrs. Frenio told them the list was in the back room. Why didn't they go talk back there?

"No. I want to see the rules and the displays both at once," Phil said. "Ella, why don't you go bring us the list."

Mrs. Frenio stood there. "It's not my li—"

Walking backwards a few steps toward her office, with a fake smile, "Sure, I'll get our store's list. One copy for each of us?"

Once Phil and Lou had their lists, they walked through the check-out aisles, talking to each other about the rules and the displays. Rosa's new friend Ella and she stood behind the checkout counter, not saying anything unless one of the men asked Rosa a question.

The two more senior Assistant Managers, who Mrs. Frenio had psyched up in her meeting but who hadn't even been introduced, stood and fumed together in the store's middle aisle. The older one had a good Eye. Rosa took a few steps back so Ella would serve as her shield.

Eventually, Lou said, "Hey, it's way past lunch time. Why don't we all go get a good Italian meal, since we're in a real Italian neighborhood?"

Except for pizza and subs, nobody in the neighborhood went to Italian restaurants. Why pay more for the food you eat every day, especially since it wasn't as good as what you ate at home? 'Medicans came from their American neighborhoods to eat Italian.

Mrs. Frenio wasn't local. Rosa had to pretend she knew which Italian restaurant was the best. They all got in Phil's Cadillac and drove six blocks to the most expensive Italian restaurant. The atmosphere was good. Maybe the food would be, too.

The food was so-so. Lou ordered a bottle of Barolo wine, which was like Papa's Italian Table Red except it burned your throat less and cost twenty times as much. The bottle ran out before they'd finished the secondi, the main course, so he ordered another. When everybody had finished eating, there was still half of the second bottle left, a lot of money's worth, so Phil poured everybody another half glass.

Rosa flashed back to a pre-prom dinner when Joey and the guys tried to get the girls liquored up. She hoped this was a rerun. Lou wasn't going to choose Mrs. Frenio over her. She didn't think so, anyway.

After the meal, they got down to business.

Phil pulled a crumpled copy of Rosa's list from his pants pocket. "Rosa, much as I admire your list, half the items, like your rule about bigger displays, are well known marketing maxims. I'm impressed you figured them out for yourself, but you shouldn't have had to."

He gave Mrs. Frenio a look and then gave Lou a minor league version of the Eye. He probably eyed the best he could, but he wasn't Italian. He didn't have the knack. "If we had good enough training, the managers would know these things. What do you think, Mr. In-store Management?"

"I agree. Our department caused the problem, and we will fix it. Of course, we'll need a big boost in our training budget. Marketing might have to take a hit."

"I see. Let's hash it out back at Headquarters."

Finished with Lou, he turned back to Rosa. "The other half of your list brings two innovations to Rex-Aid. First, your "fewer choices, more impulses" rule. I wouldn't have thought it probable, but your sales figures are a convincing proof of concept. Congratulations." He reached across the table to pat her shoulder. Rosa refrained from saying thank you and reaching across the table to pat his shoulder, too.

Touch

"All your remaining rules boil down to, "know your local market and carry the items they want to buy." Shame on us for not encouraging our managers to do that. I'm Rex-Aid Marketing, and I spend all my time negotiating the best deals with our national suppliers and contractors. It never occurred to me that a big chain like us could have our stores go local. Well, we can. You've shown that." He patted her shoulder again.

"Yeah, well. Great overview, Phil. You know your marketing." Lou looked around the table. "Time for cannoli, don't you think?"

"Just a second." Mrs. Frenio held her hand palm out. "Before we finish with the business, I need to say something. Since I arrived, we've been a management team in our store. We all marketed all our products. Rosa was a long-time employee when I arrived. I promoted her. I recognized her talent. I put her in charge of check-out. We're a team."

Lou nodded his head, "Of course, Ella." He raised his hand to call the waiter.

"Your right, Ella, we've been unfair," Phil said. He raised his patting hand, started for her shoulder, but decided on the back of her hand. "You are the store leadership, and we need to give you credit for how your store's gross has grown. Not many managers of an older store could have accomplished what you did. When we get a chance, you and I need to talk about your marketing in the rest of the store."

Mrs. Frenio's broad smile, as new to Rosa as her first name, made her almost pretty.

Lou ordered Sicilian cannoli, the best kind, the only kind her family ever bought from the bakery. He ordered another bottle of wine. "You can't eat dolce without a good Moscatel." Rosa had been eating dessert all her life, and she'd never tasted Moscatel, so he was wrong about that, but if he wanted everybody drunk enough to drop their pants, that was fine with her.

"Rosa, let's go freshen up," her new teammate Ella said. "If we're going to have more wine, I'll need to freshen up first."

Once in the ladies room, Ella gave Rosa her orders. "I'm going to 'discuss the rest of the store's marketing' with Phil tonight. We're both too drunk to drive too far, so I'll probably take him to the little Hilton here. So forget about him, even if he patted your shoulder." She peered in the mirror to add another layer of concealer under her eyes, painting it on with her pinkie.

Yes! But just to make sure. "Phil's your boss. Isn't that against some rule?"

Ella held her two hands out, palms up. "On the one hand, I respect the rules." She lowered one hand a little. "On the other hand, I haven't gotten laid in at least five years." She lowered the other hand a lot. She bounced both hands in their relative positions. "Getting laid wins."

"It hasn't been five years, but it's been long enough. Does the same deal about the rules apply to me and Lou?"

"By all means. Be my guest. He seems interested, don't you think?"

"I hope so."

Back in the dining room, the cannoli and wine had arrived. Lou poured them all a small glass. The cannoli were okay, just like all the other food.

Before Lou could make his move with the wine, Rosa took charge. "No more wine for me. We can't hold our liquor like those two. Right, Ella?"

Ella nodded.

"So why don't you guys finish the wine for us." Rosa emptied the bottle in the men's glasses, filling each to the brim, like a girl trying to get her guy liquored up for the prom.

Fifteen minutes later, Phil and Ella were about to get in her car.

Phil tossed Lou some keys. "Here. Take the Caddy and drive Rosa to where she wants to go."

Was Lou too drunk to drive? Maybe. But some things were worth a risk.

Lou held the door for Rosa, then went around to get in and take the wheel. He backed out of their parking space, driving mostly with his left hand, the wheel held between his thumb and his closed fist. He turned to her. "Where to?"

Where did Rosa want to go? Take him back to her little apartment with the pile of laundry hiding behind the bed? No. If Ella got the Hilton, why not her? She'd never stayed in a nice hotel since her one-night honeymoon in Manhattan.

"Lou, my place is a mess. How about we get a room in the Hilton?"

Lou put the car in Park and turned to her. "Sorry if I gave you the wrong impression, Rosa. I don't spend the night with anyone."

"I thought you liked me. I like you, and I want to know you better."

Not with anyone? "Religion?" She put her hand on his. The back of his hand had a silky smooth texture, no little hairs, unlike any skin she'd ever touched. She stroked it with her fingers, enjoying the sensation.

He slipped his hand out from under hers. "Religion?" He laughed. "No, God's kicked me in the ass too much for that."

Silent for so long he made her worry, he looked straight ahead at the stores, closed in the dusk but still with a few bits of neon, and the street lights, with glowing rings lent them by the windshield's glass.

He shook himself and turned back to her. "You 'want to know me better.' Why? What for?"

"I…well, you know."

"That's not going to happen, Rosa. I'm sorry. So do you still want to know me better?"

"Yes. I mean, if you want to."

"Okay. This is new for me, but maybe…. Which way to the Hilton?"

They checked into the hotel, no luggage. She didn't think the Hilton was that kind of place, but the clerk pretended not to notice.

In the room, he hung his suit coat over the one chair. He left on his tie, didn't even loosen his collar. He sat in the chair and she sat on the bed across from him. She caressed a cufflink. Stunning. Silver and red.

From his sleeve, she was irresistibly drawn to the skin on his hand, the one with the fingers. In the cross light, she could see the patchwork. Some skin patches lower, white and glossy, other patches raised, red and scaly. Some patches were moist, with a faint odor of sun tan lotion, others dry. Scars stitched the patches together, like a quilt of textures. Whether red or white, raised or sunken, glossy or scaly, none of the patches had the furry covering of little hairs, like the back of other men's hands. She closed her hands around his finger stumps, smooth and rounded at the tips, like little peni…. She touched the ends.

He inhaled, a sharp breath.

"I'm sorry. Does that hurt? On the tips?"

"A little. Are you one of those kinky broads who gets off on amputees? The men in the clinic talk about finding a woman like you, but I didn't think they really existed."

"No, but I do have super sense of touch. The patchwork of textures on your skin fascinates me."

"There are a lot more textures where that skin came from, but I'm not sure I want to be your super-touch research subject."

He leaned back in his chair, taking his hands out of her reach. "Since we're not going to spend the night banging away, let's start with some civilized talk. I see you don't wear a ring?"

"No. I was married once. My husband hit me, so we're divorced. Your left fist doesn't have separate fingers, so you can't wear a ring. Are you married? I mean, as long as we're asking."

"I was, and I'd wear the ring if I could. She died." He ducked his head for a second, then looked back at her. The bleakness of his face brought her close to tears, but his own eyes were dry.

"I'm sorry." They sat silent awhile. "Did…do you have any children?

"A boy and a girl." He reached behind him to his jacket pocket and pulled out a billfold. He showed Rosa a studio photo of two dressed-up kids. A girl about five and a boy about two. Dark hair like his. "Nicole and Tom. Nicky. We used to call him Too. Whatever Nicky did, he wanted to do. He'd say, "Too.""

"I bet he's moved beyond that by now. Do you still call him Too?"

"Yes, he is. Beyond that. And yes, he's still Too."

He jammed the photo back into his billfold.

He stood up, looking somewhere beyond her. "Oh, bullshit. He's dead. They're all dead."

He picked up his suit jacket, mumbled, "Sorry, bad idea," and walked out the door.

Chapter 14

Lou had paid for the room. Rosa might as well sleep on the deluxe mattress. But she couldn't sleep. Her fingers yearned to imagine Lou and touch herself. But what kind of disgusting woman would do that after looking into his bleak face? She'd stay at least until six in the morning, when the free breakfast started. But, lying awake in that sorrowful room, how could she stay another minute?

She walked the hour back to her apartment, the streets around her changing from street-lamp night to the first flush of dawn. Back home, she called work and told one of the ticked-off Assistant Managers she was too sick to come in. Rosa's buddy, Ella, had called in sick an hour before.

After a nap, she headed to the Salon. She wanted to ask about Lou's hands. Had Karl and Birgit had ever seen anything like them? Could the therapy help him?

Why did she care? She hardly knew him. Some women fell for wounded men and tried to fix them. Rosa didn't think she was one of those women. But Lou wasn't just hurt. He was literally tall, dark, and handsome. Attractive, confident despite his injuries—he'd be a leader somewhere even if he wasn't a Rex-Aid VP. Rosa liked him. His rejection hurt, but she understood why he was unable to say yes. He was the first man since Joey that she wanted to have as both a bedmate and a friend. The first step was to learn what happened to him, and Birgit might know.

She had the whole day free. Maybe she could also get another lesson. Since the Salon was so close to Rex-Aid, she sidled along the store fronts, keeping her eye out for red-shirted women on a smoke break.

Karl was in a therapy session, even though the salon wasn't officially open. He was so famous in Europe, Birgit said, that word-of-mouth had begun bringing him clients.

Rosa asked Birgit about Lou's hands.

"Burns. Almost certainly burns. The patches are pieces of skin harvested from places where he wasn't burnt."

She grabbed a piece of paper and drew three lines dividing skin into two layers. "Outer and inner. They use a precision potato peeler to cut through the center of the inner layer."

She drew a dotted line between two of the lines. "All the nerves, blood vessels, sweat glands, and hair follicles are in the inner layer. Where the burns destroyed all the existing skin, that's where they put the outer patches, the ones they just peeled off."

"What keeps it in place?"

"Under the bandages, new blood vessels grow into the layers of fat and muscle." She drew arrows from the inner skin to the muscles below. "Skin grows new veins and arteries easily. Every time you get a little cut, for instance, tiny blood vessels grow across it and help the skin heal."

"What about where they potato-peeled the skin?"

She drew more arrows going from the inner level to the outer layer. "The outer layer of your skin is just dying skin cells. The inner layer left in place grows out naturally and eventually forms a new outer layer. It will have hair, nerves, sweat glands, everything."

"The back of Lou's hands had no little fuzzy hair."

"Right. No nerves either. No sense of touch, heat, cold. Or sweat glands. The potato peeler chopped through all of those. The roots are still back in the original place. They can regrow. But the outer half, stuck down where the burn was, got cut off from the roots, so none of the nerves or hairs can stay alive."

"When I stroked the back of his hand, he couldn't feel me?"

"No. If you pushed hard, his muscles would feel the pressure, but his skin? Nothing."

No wonder he wanted her to stop. "Can't touch therapy help at all?"

"We've tried, many times, but no. There's nothing left to sensitize. Sad, because burn victims need touch therapy more than anyone."

Poor Lou. His wife, his kids, and burns, too. God kicked him in the ass, all right. "Thanks, Birgit. You know a lot about skin."

"When we finish your training, you will, too. A touch therapist who doesn't know about skin would be like a hairdresser who doesn't know about hair."

Karl finished his session and joined them in the waiting room.

Rosa asked Birgit, "Can I get another lesson? I called in sick from work."

"Sure. But you didn't bring a client. How are we going to train you?"

Karl motioned toward the door. "Just troll the sidewalk and haul one in."

"I can't. I called in sick, and they'd spot me from Rex-Aid."

Birgit sighed. She went out the door and came back with Mama's friend, Mrs. Testa.

When the lady heard she would lie nude while one of the DeAngelo kids worked on her body, Mrs. Testa headed for the exit. Pausing at the door, she asked Rosa, "Does your mother know you're doing this?"

Of course she did. Rosa had given the therapy to Aggie. There wouldn't be a cousin left who hadn't heard.

Birgit headed out again. This time, she returned with an Italian girl bundled up in a coat and scarf, though it was August. Karl mumbled, "Eighteen-nineteen years old? How much sensitization could she need?"

Birgit explained the whole process.

The girl's lip quivered. "I don't know if this will help me or hurt me."

Karl pointed at Rosa. "Part of the training."

"I'm sure it will help," she said. "It certainly won't hurt. Don't worry."

The girl's quivering lip moved to the next stage, tears running down her cheeks. She did not move or answer. Were Karl and Birgit sure this was a good idea, working on a young, emotionally unstable girl? But the girl was standing right there, so how could Rosa ask? If she should stop, they would say something. Rosa introduced herself and asked the girl her name.

"Carmella. Carmella Lessera."

"A beautiful name."

87

She sniffed her runny nose. "Thank you."

Hesitantly, she removed her scarf. Her neck had two black-and-blue spots in front, other marks on the back.

Karl took over. This girl did need the therapy.

After he'd finished his explanation, she agreed—to the therapy and to the three of them working on her.

She went in to take her shower. Rosa and Birgit prepared the therapy room. When Carmella came out she got up on the table wearing her robe. When she opened it, she had on her underwear. In addition to her neck, more bruises showed on her stomach, her left shoulder, both thighs. Yellow-black spots on her thighs were half covered by her panties, as were marks that started on her upper chest and disappeared under her bra.

Birgit took her hand. "We can't help heal your sense of touch if we can't work on all your trauma areas." She helped the girl off the table and led her back into the shower room. The girl held Birgit's hand and followed like a person with no will of her own.

After a few minutes, still holding her hand, Birgit led Carmella back to the therapy table. Usually a calm and centered person, Birgit had a look on her face that made Rosa want to run and hide. All three helped the girl onto the table.

"Would you please open your robe," Birgit asked.

The girl held it closed.

"Please."

She let it fall open.

Her breasts were horribly discolored, and her privates looked like someone had kicked her.

Carmella had a Joey. Ten times worse than a Joey. While Karl and Birgit professionally planned how to help her, Rosa held her hand and cried. First Lou, and now Carmella. Was she some kind of pain magnet?

How to help Carmella? Who to call? The cops, obviously. But they couldn't make her safe. Her family, probably. But they hadn't kept her safe so far.

There must be someplace where women like Carmella could be safe. Maybe Paola, Pete's ex, knew. Rosa would find a safe place, even if she had to bring Carmella home herself.

Chapter 15

Her dark hair pulled back into a game-day ponytail, she wore a slight grin of confidence. The high school girl's exaggerated please-like-me smile? Not on her face. Still, a luscious lower lip caught the light, and he liked that lip way too much.

The ball rested on her right hip, held in place by her dangling arm. Her weight on her left foot swung her hips to the left, balanced with a slight slant of her shoulders. Her stance created a sinuous curve from head to feet. On her left side, her uniform shirt hung straight down from her breast to mid-thigh. On the right, the shirt had no room to fall, the ball bunching it up just below her breast. Oh, God.

Seventeen and so beautiful he ached with longing every time he saw her again, she paid no attention to him, just stood there with her ball, not noticing she made his knees go wobbly when he walked by.

Surrounded by the trophies her teams had won, Rosa's poster-sized photo highlighted the school's trophy case. Sports pictures and sports-page clippings from the *Staten Island Advance* and even the *New York Times* flanked the poster in the school's display.

If he looked at her, she was too much. If he looked away, he felt self-conscious. He walked briskly by, with long steps and eyes drilled straight ahead, as if in a hurry to get to the coaches' office. He had some urgent coaching need, some brilliant basketball thought, which required him to pass the poster and reach the office as quickly as possible.

When he became a coach, he thought of game strategies and practice routines. He didn't think about what came before that. After one week of try-outs, he had to choose his team. Twelve girls. Another thirteen young ones, he had to reject. He delayed posting the final roster from Friday to Monday, because he couldn't bring himself to do it. A terrible mistake, because he spent the whole weekend unable to sleep. On Sunday, he thought up a three-girl practice squad, to be ready in case of injuries. Only ten girls left to hurt.

He snuck into school early on Monday, posted the final roster, and hurried to work in the shop. He couldn't be there to watch the faces of the girls he'd rejected, the ones he'd taught a new life lesson—no matter how hard they tried, they were not good enough.

Of the twelve girls who'd made the team, three were DeAngelos—one of Angie's girls, Dino's daughter, and Pete's daughter. Tessa had a different last name because she'd been adopted by her stepfather, but she'd inherited Pete's toughness, and some of his temper.

He had worried about favoritism. He'd anguished at the start of the try-outs, but no DeAngelo girl was on the cusp. They belonged on the team. Wasted anguish.

Tony divided the team into five starters, three regular subs who would get a lot of minutes, and four more he was grooming for next year when the seniors left. Tessa was his starting center, and each of the other groups had its DeAngelo.

He had managed to find one full-time and one part-time assistant. Rosa would have been ideal in theory, if he could have handled his feelings. Fortunately, Jojo, the center from Rosa's championship team, was available every day after school. She worked 5:30am to 2:30pm managing the breakfast and lunch shifts at McDonalds.

Tony didn't know the inside game, the blocking out and the constant battle for position, so he needed Jojo. Her partner, Lee, had played for another school. She worked rotating shifts at the Hilton front desk, and she came to help when she could.

They lost their first game, badly. He held his first post-game meeting in the locker room. He had ten minutes to convince his girls they weren't permanent losers, then he'd have to leave so they could shower and change.

"Did you ever take a test and get a disappointing grade? Disappointing because you knew you could do better?"

Silence. Girls sat on benches and stared down at their knees.

He picked Tessa, the captain, the one with the temper. Leaning over so his mouth was a foot from the top of her bowed head, he asked quietly—not gently, no gentle in his voice at all—but quietly, "Well, did you?"

She looked up at him. "What a bullshit question. Sure, we're better than your stupid 'test.' Next time we'll only lose by twelve points. That's supposed to make us feel better?"

The rest of the girls looked at him now, not at their knees.

He spoke to them all. "No. You're supposed to feel bad. You flunked the test. You had the knowledge and the skills to do better, but you didn't use them. You failed."

He looked back at Tessa. "You. You're the captain. They elected you their leader. You didn't lead well enough, did you? You failed." She lowered her head and resumed her study of her knees.

He raised his voice. "I'm the coach. I watched my team play worse than they ever played in practice. I tried everything I knew, and my team did not get back on its feet and fight. I failed. I failed the test."

The girls stared at him. He let the silence build, went around the circle engaging eyes. "You know how that makes me feel? The same way your play ought to make you feel." He held the pause. One, two, three, four beats. "Angry. Damn angry."

He paced inside the circle of girls, too energized to stay still. "Who am I angry at? Not the other team. They did their job. Not you out on the court, because you did what you thought you could. I'm angry at me. I'm not going to let my team go through this again."

He pointed one-by-one at each of the twelve girls. "And you know who else I'm angry at? You. Not you back there on the court. You right now in this room. Because I don't see angry. I see sad. Sad does not get better. Sad does not win. I want to see angry girls. Angry at yourself. Angry at your performance. Angry because you gave the team less than you could. Angry at me, because I let you down."

He pulled a flimsy gray metal can, full of dirty towels, into the middle of the space. "Stand up. If you're angry, kick this thing." A girl tapped it with her toes. He pulled back and soccer-kicked it full force, sending it flying against a locker. "I have to leave now. When I come here tomorrow, this thing better be flattened like a beer can in the gutter. And my players better be ready to practice like they've been angry, like they will not let anyone do this to them again." He let the door slam behind him.

He heard the can bang around on the other side of the door. Girls shouted. Jojo slipped out the door and gave him a high five.

After the girls had flattened the dirty-towel can—which he had to pay for—he and Jojo could feel the new intensity in the team's practice sessions. They won their second game.

Next, they played a league powerhouse and got wiped out. After the defeat, he gave them no big locker-room dramatics. "They were better than us. All we can do is work to narrow the gap. Don't worry about it. We've got the next game coming up. That's the one we have to work on. See you tomorrow for practice."

The girls won their fourth game, giving them an even record at the semester's end. Their next games were at the New Year's Tournament. They'd play one game if they got knocked out in the first round, three games if they made it to the finals. Before then, wedged around Christmas, he could schedule only three more practices.

At the last practice, Dino's kid told everybody her Aunt Rosa, the team's hero and inspiration, had spent Christmas with the family and would come to the tournament. The girls jumped around and pumped their fists, until one asked, "What if we stink up the court?" Everybody paused, then reassured each other, but no more pumping fists.

Tony's stress level soared. The tournament would be his best chance ever to impress Rosa. His hands would not stop shaking.

To hide the shakes, he clapped one of the cheerleaders' rhythms. "Let's go, let's go. Let's…really go." Jojo and the girls picked up the rhythm. He sent them to the locker room still clapping. Jojo gave him the thumbs up.

Stop shaking, start clapping. Make the anxiety work for him. He laughed. Sports self-psych nonsense. But if he really could….

Chapter 16

Carmella lay on the table, Karl and Birgit working on each trauma spot as best they could. Soft, twisting touches, until they'd done so many she whimpered in pain, and they had to move on to another trauma. Rosa could have touched her non-traumatized skin, but she thought it more important to find out what happened and call for help.

"My fiancé... I do things that make him angry. It's my fault, really. Lenny can't help himself. I try to do like he wants, but I mess up sometimes. He doesn't mean to hurt me. It just happens."

Rosa fought to keep her mouth shut. She wasn't a therapist. "Do you live with him, or with your family?"

"With him. I don't have a family. Not really. My Mama and cousins and those live in the Bronx. That's where I grew up. Lenny, too. He thought we'd be better off coming here, because the rents are cheaper. Besides, I've got almost nobody left. My brother's in the service, and Papa died when I was little. He went off the road."

"Could you go home and live with your mother? At least until your bruises heal?"

"She doesn't have a house any more. She lived with my aunt, but we don't know where she is right now. Besides, she always said that's just how men are, and I should get used to it. She drinks medicine for the pain, and Papa's been dead eight years. That's what she calls it, medicine."

"Where do you want to go to after this?"

"To Lenny's apartment, of course. Where else would I go? Ow. You're hurting me."

Karl and Birgit each moved on to a new black and yellow patch of skin.

"Do you think I should call somebody to help?" Rosa asked her.

"Why? Help what?"

"I think it's required." Rosa called 911. The dispatcher said Carmella wasn't an emergency, since she wasn't under assault at that moment. He gave Rosa three numbers to call: the police nonemergency number, a help line for victims of physical or sexual abuse, and a screening center which could connect to shelters for abused women.

Karl and Birgit appeared totally immersed in their difficult work. But their therapy only revived her sense of touch, which was the last thing Carmella needed, unless somebody could get her away from Lenny.

After hearing fifty times how important her call was to them, Rosa finally got to talk to some nonemergency police person. He said he couldn't talk to anybody but the victim, so Rosa gave Carmella the phone while she still lay on the table being touched.

"Carmella Lessera."

She gave him her address and phone number. He must have been entering her information in their computer. Rosa could only hear Carmella's side of the conversation.

"Lenny Renzi"

"Yes. He's my fiancé. We have an apartment."

"No."

"No, he didn't do anything he shouldn't have."

"Ow, ow, ouch."

Birgit switched to another discolored place.

"No. Not Lenny. Just these doctors or therapists or whatever they are. They're helping me feel better."

"No. Why would I press charges? I told you he didn't do anything he didn't have to."

"Okay. Here she is."

Rosa took back the phone. The cop explained how they couldn't do anything without the abuse victim's cooperation, and how common it was for victims not to cooperate. He told her to use whatever influence she had to get Carmella away from this Lenny person. A shelter for abused women, where they had group therapy, would be best.

He gave Rosa a number to call, which turned out to be the screening center number she already had. She called the number. A volunteer answered, took the information, and said someone would call back.

Touch

When she hung up, Karl told her to touch Carmella's non-trauma areas, basically all of her back and lower legs. The only traumatized areas left were on her breasts and genitals.

"For this client," he said, "I don't think a man should be present when Birgit works on those traumas. You do what you know how to do, the clear-skin places, and I'll leave." He went into the little office and shut the door.

Rosa had to stop because a shelter called. The woman said she was, "Mary from St. Rita's."

"Is this Carmella?"

"No, this is—"

"Is she there? Put her on."

Rosa did. This Mary person talked so loud Rosa could hear. Everybody could hear.

"Now, Carmella. I understand you got banged up. Is that right?"

"Yes. But it wasn't Lenny's—"

"Are you banged up or aren't you?"

"Yes. I guess…"

"I'm sorry to hear that. What you need to do is take a little time off to get better. Doesn't she girls? Wait a minute. Helen—come here and put this dang thing on speaker. I can never remem…. Okay, girls. Her name's Carmella."

A raggedy choir of women sang,

"Hey, Carmella, come on down.

"You'll feel better.

"You'll heal better.

"With us around."

Mary came back, but her phone was still on speaker, so her words were hard to make out. In the background, women talked and little kids played. "Carmella, you got any kids? No? That's all right. We got plenty. You stay there and one of our volunteer ladies will come pick you up. That okay with you?"

"Well, I don't—"

"Good. You promise? No backing out at the last minute. Let me hear you say 'yes.'"

"Okay."

"Not okay. Yes."

"Okay. Yes."

"Good enough. Put that other woman on the phone, will you?"

Rosa took the phone.

"What's your name again?"

"Rosa. You would have known if you hadn't cut—"

"You got another room to talk in?"

She went into the other therapy room. "I'm in ano—"

"Good. Good. Just give me your address. One of our volunteers will go get Carmella as soon as she can. Your job is to keep her busy, talking, or whatever you're doing there, until our volunteer shows up. If Carmella tries to run, talk to her best you can, but don't tackle her or anything. She's got to come here on her own, but we don't want her to have time to change her mind. So keep her busy. Got that?"

"Yeah. I get it."

"Good. Bye. I've got to call our volunteer and get her going."

Rosa took a moment to recover, and returned to touching Carmella's legs.

Rosa had just got out of the shower. Charlie tucked his nose around to sniff her like he always did, while she tried to towel off. She looked to see if she still had any clean underwear. It was November and the apartment was cold. She needed to dress before she froze. Could she get to both the supermarket and the laundromat before she had to go to work? She was putting Charlie's leash on when Phil called. Mrs. Frenio's one-nighter Phil. The Rex-Aid marketing VP Phil. That Phil.

"Rosa, Lou and I have a joint project we're working on. Training store managers about effective store displays. He's dealing with screening managers, and also the program evaluation—all that side of things. I'm in charge of the marketing content."

"Good. Our store needs that. Probably others, too."

"Believe me, we've got stores in worse shape than yours. Listen, the reason I called is we'll kick the project off at a two-day planning session, December 2nd and 3rd, Thursday and Friday. Lou discovered this free-wheeling design process, called a charrette, to pull all the stakeholders together and come up with a rough plan."

"A charrette? I never heard of it."

"Basically a bust-your-butt free-for-all. We start with the goals, then brainstorm how to accomplish them, break out into groups to work on the pieces, then put it all together into a package we can present to Jim by Friday at 4:00pm. Then we party. Or sleep. Some folks will probably work all Thursday night to get it done. That's the whole idea, compress a two-month design process down to two days."

"Who's Jim?"

"Jim Townsend, our CEO. He's not going to say no. He's already approved a budget. He's going to approve the plan, or tell us to tickle it here or there so it works for him. After that, we go to a small implementation committee."

Jim. Now she had three HQ first-name buddies—Lou, Phil, and Jim. Two VPs and the CEO. Rosa wondered what this had to do with her. She guessed Phil would get around to telling her, so she held the question.

"On the implementation committee, we'll have my top assistant and Lou's, a training type and a marketing pro, a couple of people from the regional offices, a good manager we haven't picked yet, and you."

"Bigshots and then me. Why?"

"You're our expert on market localization. You'll be working out of Headquarters here in Connecticut. We'll need you for the charrette, so get here on December first to give yourself a day to settle in. We'll put you up at the Residence Inn until you find yourself something more permanent."

"What about my job now?"

"Forget about it. I already called Ella and told her to find your replacement. You're promoted. I don't remember the exact salary, eighty something, a lot more than you're getting now. Any more questions?

"Eighty something what?"

"Eighty thousand a year. I'll see you December second. My office assistant will get you all the info about where and when. Bye." Click.

Three weeks until she had to move. Eighty thousand! She had sick days left, so she told Mrs. Frenio what days she'd be sick. Eighty thousand!

She found somebody to take over the apartment lease, her biggest worry. She still had to clear out her stuff. Dump it in Mama's basement—maybe her nephews would help. Eighty thousand!

And what about Charlie? He couldn't stay at a Residence Inn if Rosa was going to work on that two-day comesegiam' thing. Rosa reluctantly gave him back to Aggie, where at least he'd be with his relatives. Maybe she could come get him later, when she had a permanent place to live. Eighty thousand!

After she trained three more times at the salon, to the point when she could feel where skin had been traumatized—some of the time—Karl and Birgit declared her an Apprentice Touch Therapist.

She visited Carmella at St. Rita's again, and Sister Mary made her promise she would come back to visit when she was home for Christmas. Carmella had become one of the women who sang over the phone. Sister Mary, who was in charge of admissions and discharges, and everything else, said Carmella would probably be ready to graduate sometime in January, if they could find her a job.

When she arrived at the comosegiam', the charrette, Rosa's name tag said "Deangelo," which sounded like "Dean jello" to her, and she told the woman that. It also said "Senior Marketing Consultant," her eighty-thousand. That part was fine.

The woman at the reception desk smiled. "We'll take care of that right away, Miss DeAngelo. Why don't you help yourself to coffee, and we'll have a new name tag for you by the time you come back."

The coffee table had three kinds of coffee. She poured a cup of "Dark Roast," which turned out to be half way between Italian and American. Another table had napkins and platters of mini donuts and mini versions of those gooey Danish pastries that 'Medigans eat.

She was putting on her new name tag when Lou came up to her. He wore a different suit, a different red tie, and different red cufflinks—all of them more impressive than what he wore to Staten Island.

"Hi, Rosa. Excited about the charrette? I am. We never had one of these before."

"Yes. It's exciting just to be here. The Residence Inn is wonderful."

"Good. It's important you're comfortable. We have so much to do here, it'll get intense. I have to move on and greet the other participants. See you again soon."

Apparently they were pretending the scene in the Hilton never happened.

Phil shook her hand. "So glad you're here. I don't think you know how important you are to this process. Remember, you're my Senior Marketing Consultant now. Everybody knows you were a store

Assistant Manager, but that's not what you are now. Don't be shy. Speak up, because we'll rely on your input."

The group could intimidate all right, full of name tags with fancy titles, but Rosa wasn't shy. Nobody in her family was shy, or they wouldn't have survived Mama. Rosa didn't know many shy Italians, unless they didn't have a mama, like Carmella.

The room for the charrette had a movie screen up front, round tables with six comfortable chairs each, and other small tables against the wall with computers, printers, and copiers. The chairs were on wheels, and people were already using them to glide from one table to another. There were thirty people in the group, only a few of them women. The stores hired almost all women. She'd never worked with so many men like this.

Lou stood in front of the movie screen. "Welcome to our first Rex-Aid charrette."

After his welcoming remarks, he pushed a button to put words on the movie screen, mostly the same words he was saying. "Remember, our goals for the charrette are: first, to re-think effective store displays; second, to figure out how to teach that to our managers; third, to come up with a company-wide system for managers to train their assistants; and fourth, to revamp our displays along new principles: to maximize impulse purchases, and to customize each store's inventory for its demographic profile."

People looked at each other and whispered. People at Rosa's table thought there was no way they would get all that done by Friday afternoon.

Lou quieted the whispers with a wave of his hand. He spoke quietly, for such a tall impressive guy, so people concentrated to hear what he said. "Let's start by introducing ourselves to each other. Stand up and tell us your first name and your job. We're on a first name basis here. Fifteen seconds each, please. We can't take all morning with this. I'm Lou, VP for In-store Management."

When they got to Rosa's table, she stood and called herself the Senior Marketing Consultant.

While she was sitting down and as the next person stood, Lou said, "Rosa's the inspiration for this charrette. Most of our goals come from her ideas and accomplishments. Next."

Rosa started out at the inventory-localization table, but Lou had made her famous so she was in demand everywhere. The whole process was to move people around, to get input from all the "stakeholders." She imagined kids sword-fighting with stakes from a picket fence.

Her image fit. Stakeholders each had their own turf to defend during the planning. She discovered Phil's marketing people disliked her. She was an outsider with disruptive ideas their boss said they had to follow. They needed to listen to her, because Phil said so, but they didn't like it.

Lou's people, who had to come up with the training parts, all wanted her to stay with them, so they could "pick your brain." She was more comfortable with the store-management execs, because they liked her, but she worked under Phil in marketing.

By afternoon, she'd come up with a personal strategy. Stop hanging out with Lou's people, and fight in the marketing groups. She was on the team that would have to implement whatever they came up with. She needed the plans to be something she knew about and wanted to do, so she had a turf, too. They all worked as evening came and went, as midnight came and went. Sandwiches and fruit long ago replaced pastries on the food table, but there were no breaks to eat. People grabbed something while they worked.

As the hours went on, folks got punchier, crabbier, and more frank with each other.

Rosa changed from not shy to pushy. "Unless we come up with a system for stores to order non-standard local items, localization won't work. You're the experts on our inventory systems. Figure it out. That change is fundamental. Without it, don't count me in."

The guy in charge of the Rex-Aid inventory objected. "We're supposed to work together, but you just laid down an ultimatum."

"Ultimatum? You mean like, 'Localize the inventory or your plan is screwed?' It won't meet the goals Lou said we have to meet, so yeah, I think you're right." She moved on to the marketing display group.

They worked on store displays, sounding like most of them had never seen one. Rosa had to sit with them a lot longer. "Three types in every store. First, we've got the contractors, the people who do the snack food, the refrigerator cases, the cosmetics, the magazines. All that. Their displays are usually better than ours, but some of them don't give a damn. You have to fix that from here. The stores don't have any control over them."

"We don't have any mechanism to do that." One of the women.

"Well, make one and put it in the plan. Second we've got the regular Rex-Aid displays. You ought to know those, right? Big, bright, attention-grabbing, lots of variety to choose from. Keep the customers in the store as long as possible. The only new element is making room for one or two big displays of locally attractive items. Near the seasonal goods, probably, since the rest of the store is so standardized."

Apparently there was one marketing guy who knew about displays, but there was no way to teach it to the managers.

"The way I understand this, training is not your problem. Your job is to tell somebody what to train about. Have I got that right? Didn't Phil tell us that?"

Most of them nodded.

"Okay. Somebody else's problem. Third, we've got the check-out displays. The opposite of the main displays. Customers won't hang around the store once they're in line. One last impulse buy. Few choices, big displays of the same item, lots of local material."

Rosa and the group worked over the three-type display framework and began to fill in some specifics under each category.

Jim bought the whole charrette plan, with one exception. "The cost. We'll have to spread these expenses over more quarters than you planned for—fewer total work-hours, fewer new staff, and a longer timeline for the full implementation. Otherwise, great job."

By the time he was finished, the coffee counter had become a bar, the sandwiches had become appetizers. Strangers from different departments when they started, they had come to know each other well, in an unbalanced work-only way. Now they stood around and talked about families and backgrounds and the normal jobs they'd all come from.

Because Rosa had been introduced as the woman behind the charrette, and because she was such an HQ exotic—no college, ethnic, younger, new, maybe still benefitting from the therapy glow—men crowded around her. As much as possible, she turned their questions back on themselves, still mapping the headquarters terrain, who was who. Especially, she tried to understand what the hell HQ did that needed so many men making so much money.

People drifted off to head home. Phil and Lou came to pull her out of the remaining crowd. They took her out to eat at a seafood restaurant.

Lou had been up all night because he was in charge of the charrette,

101

so he went home early. Rosa was tired, too, but Phil wanted to hang around and talk. She thought he was making a move, but fortunately that wasn't it.

"You know Lou's hands?"

"Sure."

"I forgot. You were in the Hilton with him. I'll bet it didn't go very well, did it?"

"No, it sure didn't."

"Let me tell you his story."

Phil squirmed in his seat. "It's not a pleasant story. Lou's house exploded—a gas leak. He was outside mowing the grass, and his wife and kids were in the house. He ran into the flames, rescued his two children, laid them on the lawn, and ran back to get his wife. He found her on the living room floor, pinned down by flaming rafters."

Phil paused for a minute. "Sorry. I get emotional. He was in there, on fire himself, struggling to get the burnt wood off her, when the first firefighters arrived and pulled him out. Flames had burned his hands, arms, and the whole front of his body from his hair down to his feet—second degree burns under his heavy pants, third degree everywhere else."

Phil pulled out a handkerchief and wiped his forehead, as if the heat got to him too. "The super-heated smoke damaged his lungs, just as it killed his children and his wife."

Rosa guessed he talked so softly because of his lungs.

"Drugged for the pain, he was in the burn center at New York Presbyterian Hospital for seven months while they worked to create new skin. He almost died of infections. Even after he got out, he went back for repeated surgeries."

Phil said, "Lou used to take a week off to have plastic surgery, then return to work same as normal, except his head looked like a mummy. Recover and repeat. The doctors had to use cartilage from his ribs to build new ears and a nose."

Rosa couldn't see the scars from any of that, but Phil said he had them. He wore those fashionable glasses with thick black frames to hide the most visible scars that ran from his eyelids to his ears.

The eight-person implementation committee took three weeks, until two days before Christmas, to accomplish half as much as the charrette had done in two days.

On the last day, Rosa summed up her new role to make sure she understood what everybody had agreed. "Some trainer person and I will take a tour of a couple dozen stores, training the managers and testing how it works. And teaching me how to train. Right?"

The guy in charge, Lou's number two man, said, "That's just the beginning."

"I know. Let me finish. Then this trainer and I start holding sessions in hotel meeting rooms, twelve or fifteen managers at a time. After we do that a while, we train other teams to do the same, and by some far-away day we've covered the whole country. Okay. Is that all?"

"I think you've got it."

"Good. Christmas is two days from now. I haven't bought any presents yet, and I have a big family. Are we ready to adjourn?"

The man in charge looked down at his notes. Somebody said, "I second the motion."

He stopped looking at his notes, since everyone else had stood to walk around and shake hands good-bye. "This committee is adjourned."

Rosa got in the new car Rex-Aid leased for her, a Toyota Camry, and headed for Staten Island.

Chapter 17

They drew Rosemont High for their first-round game. The Tournament would start with four games on Friday. Their game was scheduled for eight o'clock, the last of the day. The winner of the second game would be their opponent in Saturday's semi-finals, if they got that far.

The girls all sat together, watching the second game intensely, studying the girls they'd match up against. If they won their first one that night, because if they didn't, nothing mattered.

Tony sat at one end of the twelve-girl row. He kept his eye on the three DeAngelo girls. They'd know if their aunt showed up. She had some big new job in Connecticut, but she'd said she get to the game, leave work early if she had to.

In the second game, their whole team rooted for Holy Family, who'd only won one game so far. They should be easier to beat. Jacked up already, the girls became fervent fans.

Jojo showed up during the game, at the end of her McDonalds work shift. "Is it a good idea for them to get so energized over who they might play tomorrow?"

Tony stood, so she could get past him to her seat. "Why, because they'll be worn out by the time of our game?

"Exactly."

"Maybe they'll be more psyched up."

"Okay. Let them watch. Then get them out of here so they can rest up, eat a little, and have our team meeting."

Tony considered. Jojo's plan was sound, except for one flaw. He might not be here when Rosa showed up. But the point was to impress her, not to be a loser. "Okay, Jojo, good idea."

Holy Family put up a decent fight, but ultimately lost to New Dorp. A tougher game for them on Saturday, if they got to Saturday.

"Come on, girls. We can't watch the next one. Too much prep to do." Tony started down the stands and out of the gym.

Jojo handed out food from by-now-cold Happy Meals she picked up at her job, a couple of little hamburgers apiece with extra apple slices and bottles of water. It was important to eat an hour or more before the start. She believed in guided meditation before a game. Tony was dubious, but he didn't think the process did any harm. Nobody meditated when he'd played.

"Finished eating my delicious MickeyD food? Everybody take a place on the floor. Roll a towel under your neck."

What the hell. Tony lay down, too. God knows he needed to dump some anxiety, if this crap worked.

"Breath in, breath out. Pay attention to each breath…."

Ten minutes later, after noticing all the parts of their bodies, Tony meditating on whether that was a good idea since everyone was banged up somewhere, Jojo took them back to their breathing. "Inhale 'win.' Exhale, 'now.' Win…now. Win…now. Silently. Deep on the inhale, long on the exhale. Your mantra, Win…now, win…now."

She gradually brought them back. Tony felt woozy. This helped?

Jojo stayed in the locker room while the girls dressed. After ten minutes or so, she opened the door and waved him in. Fifteen minutes 'til game time. He started his talk, "Win…now." Raising his voice, "If we don't win now, we won't win tomorrow. We won't be here. I intend to be here…."

Should he refer to their hero Rosa? No, better not.

Time to go. They ran into the gym. He didn't want to look for Rosa, so he watched her nieces again. They'd find her.

A woman screamed from the stands behind him. "Let's go, girls. You can do it!" The voice from Rex-Aid. Maybe the meditation worked, because his hands didn't tremble.

Chapter 18

Rosa had gone too long without a man. She originally zeroed in on Lou, back at that dinner with Phil and Ella. He seemed like a good candidate. He dressed like a model for some high-class men's store, he was polite, and he spoke in a quiet, self-confident voice.

Then she discovered his skin and she loved the textures. Now that she knew his story, she must have seemed rude, wanting to touch him like that.

When she'd learned what he'd been through, and saw he could still function as a leader, she wanted him more. What a man. The feel of his burnt skin was sensuous to her. He wouldn't find any other women who liked his wounds so much.

After the charrette, Rosa and Lou had casual no-Hilton conversations, but she wasn't in his department, so she didn't see him very often. She couldn't get anything started.

As the implementation committee wrapped up, she saw him more, because he was responsible for the training side. If she got the chance, she'd decided to ask for a date, in an innocent, family-disguised way.

Early one morning, she came across him standing in the hall outside the committee conference room, drinking coffee from a cardboard cup and looking over some notes.

They talked about the implementation plan, as little as Rosa could get away with.

She touched his arm. "Lou, I want to invite you to my family for Christmas Eve. It's a big deal with Italians. We have all kinds of fish, course after course. Pasta with clams, calamari, eel, pulpo, bacalao, you name it."

"Yes, Rosa, I know. I go to my sister's in East Haven."

"You're Italian?"

"I look Irish? Don't answer that. I look like a man who's been burnt."

"You look real fine to me."

"Yes. We both know you're strange about burnt guys. Let's not get into it again."

"If you're Italian, how come your name is Bates? Are you half-Italian?"

"No. My name is Luigi Batesorio, or that was my name once. I got a scholarship for an MBA at Tuck, the business school at Dartmouth, and I went up north to check it out. I hear it's different now, but back then they had no black people, no brown people, no tan people."

He hesitated, looked aside for a few seconds. "I changed my name to Lou Bates before I enrolled there. That's what it's been ever since. I regret I did it, but back then... I was on scholarship, I was poorer than all those ruddy New England types, and I didn't have any confidence in myself."

"Oh..." He was embarrassed, so she dropped the subject. "Where's East Haven?"

"In Connecticut. There's New Haven with the big university. There's a town full of Italians just east of that and, surprise-surprise, it's called East Haven."

"You're busy Christmas Eve. I'm happy for you. I was afraid you might need to be with a family, but you have one of your own." He was Italian!

"I appreciate the offer, but we have family traditions too and, frankly, it helps me to be with relatives. I almost wasn't."

"I know. But I'm not going to give up yet. I have three nieces who play on my old high school basketball team. They're in a tournament the first weekend in January. Can you come watch that with me?"

"You used to play?"

"Yep. All-City. New York City, which was a big deal."

"When are your nieces' games?"

"Friday at eight p.m. Then after that, it depends how far they get. The finals are Sunday afternoon."

"On Friday, will you take me out to dinner first?"
"I'd love to."
"Okay. Let's go out to eat and then watch the game. Two things though."
"What?"
"No creepy stuff with my skin, and find a better restaurant than that pricy joint you dragged us to last time."

A handful of young teens looked after a crowd of younger kids. The teens talked among themselves while the younger ones ran around shouting to each other. Cooped up in the shelter for their safety, the running and yelling burnt energy.

The shelter, a converted warehouse, consisted of a main room downstairs with an open kitchen, and stall-sized bedrooms upstairs. On this visit, child-made Christmas decorations hung from the ceiling, the walls, the stairway banister.

Sister Mary and the shelter's women cooked and chatted in the kitchen area. Sister Mary was a tiny woman with wispy white hair, probably in her seventies. Dressed like a homie kid, she wore shapeless black pants and a hooded gray sweatshirt. Black work shoes protected her feet. A white sweat band, a cross pinned in front of her ear, held down a thin tangle of gray curls. From under the hoodie, wooden beads looped into a bulging pants pocket, like a trucker with his wallet chained to his belt.

She darted around, talking loud and giving orders, sometimes disguised as suggestions.

Mary gave Rosa a big hug. "You came back! We're so glad to see you. Merry Christmas!"

Carmella hurried from the kitchen, wiping her hands on an apron. "Merry Christmas, Rosa. Wait here, I have a present." She ran up the stairs.

Rosa listened to Mary, which is what people did when they conversed with the woman. Actually, she only half-listened, preoccupied because she was about to receive a present and had nothing to give in return.

Carmella returned with a plastic bag containing misshapen Italian cookies, the common should-be-round kind with the chewier outside and the soft, sweet inside.

If they tasted right, Rosa doubted their shape would make much difference. She tasted one. They weren't Mama's, that was for sure. "Delicious. Thank you so much."

"I'm glad you like them. I never made them before."

Rosa offered a cookie to Mary, who said, "No, these are for you. We ate some already."

Sister Mary had almost no budget, so she had become a skilled scrounger of things and recruiter of people. If a woman graduated from St. Rita's, a middle-class woman with money or a car, she would be on Mary's volunteer staff for the rest of her life.

"Rosa, Carmella tells me you are some kind of therapist who can make beaten-down people feel again. Like a faith healer?"

"No. We can't heal anything, we help people renew their sense of touch. Everybody's touch sensitivity runs down over time, much more so if they've been beaten, especially by someone they had trusted. We can help with that."

"Look around. We have a house full of women who've been hit, and some kids, too. When can you start?"

"I just got a big new job way out in Connecticut. With a lot of traveling. I'm sorry, but I can't do that. I'm only an apprentice therapist, anyway."

"Okay. Later then, after things at your job settle down. What's the job?"

"Mostly training store mana—"

"You're a trainer?"

"Not yet. I guess I will be."

"That's who we need. Our women need all sorts of training. You'd be a double-double volunteer. You let the corporate types teach you how to be a trainer, then someday you'll feel a tornado reach out of the sky and suck you down to the shelter. That'll be God. I'll start working on Her tonight. Sometimes She doesn't respond right away, but if I pray on something long enough and hard enough, I can usually bring Her around. You stay alert, because someday you're going to feel a breeze start to kick up."

"God is a She?"

"No, Rosa. God is God, but we have to use human terms to describe the creator, the teacher, the savior of us all. He or She. To me, She comes closer to God than He, so that's the word I use."

To Rosa, God was maybe not anything at all. If Rosa felt a wind kick up, she'd step inside before the rain started. She doubted she'd decide to make her way to the Bronx.

Chapter 19

Every game, when Tony or Jojo needed to speak one-on-one with a player on the bench, their voices competed with loudmouth fans sitting behind the team. The DeAngelo cheering section filled three or four rows. From the direction of her voice, Rosa sat there with the rest of them.

Tony refused to look behind him until after the game, when he hoped to talk with her. Rosa would hang around afterwards, because Jojo had played on her championship teams and they were close.

Richmond ran up an early lead. They had two tall, wide-body girls playing under the basket, and Tony's girls couldn't get through without committing a foul. The whole Richmond team played a rough, physical style that his team hadn't seen before. Sometimes his girls retaliated.

As always happened, the refs saw the second push and not the first. His girls got the foul. Especially Tessa, of course. Tony had to pull her out of the game temporarily because she already had three fouls.

At halftime, they were behind 19-30. Tony had seen this style of play many times in the men's game. "Stand up. Stay in front of her, stand up, and take the foul. If it's a rough hit, let it show. Let the refs see what's going on. There's a lot of body contact. So what? That's what your body is for."

He paced, slapping the backs of his knuckles into his other palm. "Outside shooters, you have to take the pressure off the girls under the basket. Take the three-point shot, make the defense come out to you."

Again, one minute before the halftime break was over, "You want to win? Take the hit, draw the foul. Don't move, don't fight back. Stand and take it like a ma— woman."

He sent in Aggie's daughter, their best three-point shooter, but young, and weak at the rest of her game. "You're in there to shoot." He snapped his fingers. Snap-snap, snap-snap. "Get the ball, take the shot. No passing off. None of that. Move around just outside the line to get open, take the pass and shoot." She was young. All he could do was hope.

Halfway through the last period, behind 48-42, Tessa fouled out. Tony called time-out. "We lost our center. Outside shots. Rebounders, with the long shots, look for a farther bounce off the rim. Set up outside your opponent. Keep 'em boxed in under the basket. If you get the rebound, pass to an outside shooter. Let's go."

They pulled ahead for the first time in the last minute. Richmond ran out of time. His girls won, 56-53.

Aggie's daughter got twelve crucial points, four long set shots that reminded him of Rosa. Behind him, as the game clock ticked down, and even after the game was over, he could hear the elated shouts of Aggie and Rosa—shrill, hurt-your-ears yells.

During the celebration, Aggie came down from the stands to hug her daughter. Rosa came down to hug Jojo. He stood alone, watching his team hugging and jumping with excitement.

"You know what Vince Lombardi said," he shouted to his girls. "Act like you've been here before." He waved his arms back and forth over his head until they turned his way. "This is just a game. This one's over. Think tomorrow. Think New Dorp."

Jojo brought Rosa over to him, as if he and Rosa were strangers. "Rosa, this is our new coach, Tony Prezzi. Tony, this is Rosa DeAngelo."

"We've met," he said. I'm Pete's—"

Jojo continued, "And this is her friend, Lou Bates."

Tony shook his hand, which was injured somehow. Like a mechanic who had his hand in the wrong place when someone turned the motor on.

Tony didn't hang around.

The girls headed for their locker room, and Tony followed them. He faced the hardest job a coach could do – take a bunch of celebrating kids and turn them into a team seriously focused on the next game. While his mind was outside with Rosa.

When he came back into the gym, the rest of the DeAngelos were still there, but Rosa was gone.

"Left with her new friend," said Aggie, still excited about her daughter's performance.

They had reached the finals and lost in the New Year's Tournament. In the League play-offs at the end of the season, same story. Second place. A second place year. A better record than the coach before, but disappointing. Second place was the worst. They made it to the end and they lost.

No, "Yay, we made it to the playoffs!" Instead, "We could have won it all, but we lost." The final game created two reputations, the champions and the losers. Twice, they were the losers.

Needing a drink or three, Jojo and Lee climbed into Tony's 4Runner and headed for the tavern to hash over the season.

He and Jojo focused on next year. With seniors gone, like Tessa, who did they need to step up? What would the team look like? Any of those three girls on the practice squad going to help?

After Tony bought the third round, Jojo switched topics. "Tony, I always wanted to ask. What's your deal with Rosa, anyway?"

I don't have any deal."

"Well, obviously you don't. That's why I'm asking. Why not? I mean, as far back as when we played ball, thirteen, fifteen years ago, we all knew you had a thing for her."

"Who all knew?"

"Well. Not Rosa. All she could see was Joey DiFalco. But the whole rest of the team saw you in the stands every game. Not that many people came to the women's games, but you always did. You cheered when Rosa scored, you watched her, not me or Lilia or any of the rest of us. We didn't know who you were. We called you her secret admirer."

"I can't believe this. You knew?"

"Yeah. Some of the girls thought the whole thing was romantic. You watched the games and dreamed. That's some of the girls. The rest thought you were a stalker. We didn't say anything to the coach, because Rosa had Joey to protect her. We thought he'd protect her. Young and stupid. There's a reason that phrase exists."

Stalker? Tony fought to hide his feelings.

"Want to know what I thought?"

"What?"

"I thought she was your forbidden love. Because of your age, you know?"

"You win the prize. That's what she was."

"I had a forbidden love, too." She put her arm around Lee, who let herself be hugged while ducking away from Jojo's beer breath. "That's how I could tell."

He looked at Lee. "Did her forbidden love know about a secret admirer?"

"No. I wish I did. It's better now, but in 1993 I knew something was horribly wrong with me. I was a lesbian. I couldn't tell anybody, not even my best friends. People would know what a sicko I was. I was lonely and all the time scared. Yes, I wish Jojo said something."

Jojo hugged Lee again. "I didn't have it so bad. My mother guessed, because her sister was a pervert, too. That's what Mama said, 'pervert,' just normal like 'my sister is an electrician,' which she is. She lives in Manhattan, and Mama used to let me go visit her, after she knew I was 'one of those.' My aunt said I should let people know; it wasn't so awful. No way, not in high school. Not back then."

Jojo went to the bar and came back with beers and a couple plates of the tavern's garlic bread. "Okay, your turn. Did anybody know your secret?"

"I think Pete knew deep down, but he was my friend. If he didn't know, then he didn't have to do anything like stop being friends or beat me up. So he decided not to know."

"The funniest thing was you were a stalker and you had a stalker of your own. That's what the girls on the team used to say. You were watching Rosa while half-pretending you weren't, and Lucia was watching you while half-pretending she wasn't. It was pretty funny."

What could he say to that? He drank some beer, that's what he could say.

Jojo took a slug, too. "Sorry I got off topic. I meant to ask, why didn't you make a move? She had some pretty lonely years until this guy Lou showed up. She and I are friends. We talk."

"Joey moved in so fast. She was engaged on her 18th birthday. She was still too young for me before that. I married Lucia, and we fell in love. Rosa divorced Joey, but I didn't care because I was with Lucia. Then they killed Lucia. That's how I think—her own cops let her die, same as if they killed her. That was hard. That still is hard. It took me a long time to get over that." He looked up at the ceiling, wiping his shirt cuff across his eyes as he looked back down.

Jojo let him get settled. "I know, and I'm sorry—You okay?"

"Yes. Thanks. Go on."

"But you did get over it. When—four years ago? Where have you been since then? I'll tell you where you've been. In different girl's beds but not Rosa's."

"I never asked any of them out. It's the tavern. You know. They kept coming after me. I think it was pity. Help out the poor widower."

Jojo laughed. "Boy, are you out of it." She left their table, went up to the bar, and picked up two dark-haired, thirty-ish women.

Tony looked at Lee. "Are you okay with this?"

Lee shrugged her shoulders, so he relaxed.

Jojo shepherded the wobbly women back to the table. They both sat down. They had a little trouble aligning their butts with the chair seats, but they made it.

Jojo asked them, "You know who this guy is?"

They both said, almost in unison, "Tony." One added. "Tony what's-his-name... Tony Prezzi."

Her friend said, "That's right. Pretzel."

They looked familiar, from the neighborhood, but Tony certainly didn't know their names. How did they know his?

"Just pretend he's not here." Jojo draped a napkin on his face. "Tell us what you know about him, what you think about him." The napkin slid off.

The girl on the left shrugged her shoulders. "First thing, I guess, his looks—you know, big shoulders, no gut, hunky. And the Elvis hair."

"And the second thing?"

The one who hadn't yet said anything hunched down in her chair. "Well, I don't know. We're married women. The only reason we're here is the men bowl tonight."

She looked at her friend and her friend gave her a nod. "Well, if you really want to know, all the girls say...."

Jojo lifted her hand a couple of times, like keep going, out with it.

"They say he's good in bed." She put her hand over her mouth.

Her friend leaned in. "No they don't. They say he's a good fuck."

Jojo put her arm around Lee. "What does that mean? The two of us wouldn't know, if you get what I mean."

"Oh, you're you," one woman said. "That McDonalds woman."

"Yes, I am. Don't change the subject. Why is he such a good fuck?"

"This is just what I hear. I wouldn't know personally. I'm married."

"Of course you are," Jojo said.

"What I hear.... It's hard to explain.... He doesn't care about his own thingie. Like he's not worried it will do what it's supposed to. He's going to be happy, if you know what I mean. He wants to make me go two or three times, too. Not me. You know what I mean. The woman he's with."

Yeah, that's what he liked to do. Didn't every guy? That's how you make it more exciting. Meg sure thought so.

Her friend finished off her beer. She had begun to slur her words. "Why don't you tell it straight? With most guys, I mean before I was married, it was 'Blow job, blow job, give me a blow job.' My husband, too."

She pointed at Tony. "He's different. He has a—how do they say it? An equal-opportunity tongue. I don't know personally. I'm married. But I've heard."

Jojo grinned at Lee. "His tongue, eh."

If you wanted to get a woman excited, nothing worked better. Wasn't there a saying—men come out of a vagina and spend their whole lives trying to get back in? Well, there were two ways to get back in, and Tony liked them both. This was a big deal?

After the two drunks and Jojo discussed his supposedly great tongue longer than Tony thought necessary, Lee pointed at the clock. Their husbands might get home any minute. She and the owner got the women into a cab.

Jojo studied his face, her body slumped sideways against Lee's shoulder. "You really thought all your women were pitying a widower?"

He honestly did. They came for a little while and left. No commitments, no split-up drama, everybody happy. Like it was their turn to do him a favor. What else was he supposed to think?

Chapter 20

The restaurant was right on Long Island Sound, somewhere in Connecticut. A wall of windows would have looked out at the water, but it was a wind-whipped, wet evening in January. Tonight, the windows looked out on blackness. If she listened for them, Rosa could hear the crash of the waves. They'd been thunderous out in the parking lot, but the restaurant's walls muted them to background music. A march, maybe.

The night before, Rosa had taken Lou to a Greek place on the Island, like an overgrown diner. They sat in a back booth, away from the noise and bustle, and the food was fine. Not fancy, but good.

"Good restaurant, Rosa," Lou had said. "Let me take you to my favorite place after the game tomorrow. It's just over the line into Connecticut, but the semi-finals are in the afternoon, so we'll have plenty of time to get there."

"Okay. I'd love that. But what about tonight? Are you driving all the way home to Connecticut?"

"I'm staying in the Hilton, and no, you can't."

"After the last time, I'll pass. Let me express my sorrow for you, though. I never got the chance."

"Thank you."

So, here they were the next night at his favorite restaurant, in Connecticut. They'd come in two separate cars, so they could spend the night in their own places, she in the Residence Inn, and he in wherever he lived. The final game wasn't until mid-afternoon.

Though the location was great, or would be in better weather, the seafood place was more of a joint than a restaurant. No wine, just beer, and everything fried. He had to walk up to the counter to order their beer and food. She had the fisherman's basket, and he had fried clams. He said they were the best fried clams around. If she ever wanted a pile of fried clams, she'd remember that. They drank some beer brewed nearby, darker and bitterer than anything at the tavern.

"There's a marina next door," he said. "I used to bring my boat over and we'd come here to eat, before...."

"I know about before and after, Lou. Phil told me."

"I don't think it's any of his business."

"Does it matter?" I know about your loss, why your skin is the way it is, how much pain you must have gone through to survive. I know."

"I don't know what to say. I never do. That's why I don't talk about it. There's a group of us who've been through.... I talk there."

"You don't have to talk. I'm sorry I touched your skin when you couldn't feel me. I was thinking only of my own pleasure."

"That I'd like to talk about, if you don't mind. Do you have some kind of a fetish? Wait, don't answer that yet. I have to go see a man about a horse. I'll be right back."

Rosa went to use the ladies room, too, as long as they were taking a break. The word "fetish" made him have to pee? Talk about a fetish.

When Rosa got back, he was lounging against the back of his chair as if he'd never left. He got up to pull her chair back, then went back to his seat. He sat and leaned on his elbows, waiting to hear about her fetish.

"No fetish, Lou. Sorry. I'm a touch therapist. We can make skin, especially traumatized skin, returned to the sharpened sense of feeling it once had. My finger tips are unusually sensitized and the feel of different textures gives me pleasure, like if you saw or tasted something fun or pleasurable."

"I don't see or taste like I used to, because of heat and the smoke."

"I know, and I'm sorry I mentioned it. I can't help you there. I can't help you either on the burnt places, where the new skin has no sense of touch at all, where the nerves are gone. That's what I was touching before, right?

"Right. Do you want another bottle of beer?"

No, she didn't. Too bitter. But she said yes.

He went up to the counter and came back with two beers. He went back to get more paper napkins.

Once he'd stretched out his interruption as long as he could, she continued.

"The place where they harvested skin to cover your burns, they're traumatized, and I can help. The areas of untouched skin, too. All the parts of your body that weren't actually burnt and patched over, I can wake up your sense of touch there."

"The second-degree burns?"

"Sure."

"The places where they transplanted a full layer of skin, like the plastic surgery on my face?"

She'd never heard of that. "If it has its nerves intact, sure."

"How do you know so much about burnt skin?"

She had a ten minute talk with Birgit? Not going to say that. "Because I'm a touch therapist."

"What is that? What do you do?'

"Touch every inch of your unburnt skin, different techniques for regular and traumatized skin." With his skin, she wouldn't have to worry about feeling some residue of trauma from long ago, like Aggie's bump. The areas of harvested and transplanted skin were visible. Even an apprentice could do it.

"You mean all of my skin? Like nude?"

"Afraid so. Yes."

"Thanks. That was educational." He stood and went to the counter to pay the bill.

Outside, he ran her through the rain to her car. After she slid into her seat, him still out in the downpour, he shook her hand. Like they'd just come out of a business meeting

As he left for his car, he turned and shouted over the crashing of the waves, "See you at the game tomorrow. Two o'clock, right?" He climbed into his big SUV.

Chapter 21

Busy spring. Three months left to graduation, and Tony had fourteen seniors who needed jobs. Twelve were his problem. The other two had signed up for military service, promised training in heavy equipment and airplane maintenance.

Working from his teaching plan, Tony created a list of skills his seniors knew. Most days after school, he visited a dealership—they paid best—or a repair shop, to schmooze with the service managers, show them his list, and find out if they needed apprentices. He made dozens of contacts, found some who said they might be hiring and he should send a kid over for a talk.

Two days in early June, he trained the seniors about how to land a job, starting with handing out his list of their skills. "Two most important things. One, don't be cocky. You know a little bit about a lot of things." He waved the list. "Emphasis on the 'little.' Two, act confident you can pick up new skills. You already know some things, and you're sure you can learn more."

He pointed at his own blue uniform shirt, his pants, his steel-toe shoes. "For the interview, dress like the job you want. Look like a mechanic. Nothing dress-up, nothing high-school cool. Like a mechanic. If you have to buy work clothes, wash 'em a few times. Make them look like you've worked before. Tomorrow, wear your work clothes. We'll role-play an interview, and then I'm sending you out. Good luck."

By the end of the school year, nine had jobs. The other three, he had to call his new contacts and beg, but they got jobs over the next few weeks. He had done what Mr. Forte used to do. He placed all his graduates in decent jobs. Next year, he'd know what he was doing and teach even better.

He had loved being a mechanic, diagnosing and solving problems with the cars. He helped customers, but he never met them. In this job, he helped kids he came to know well, almost like sons. He gave them a start on a good life. Fresh out of high school and they had interesting, good-paying jobs and maybe life careers. No minimum-wage work for them, ever. How many other teachers did that for their students?

Tony had gained confidence that he was a decent shop teacher and would be a better one next year. Two drunken women had given him second-hand reports that he fucked women fairly well.

"Fairly well for a man," Jojo had specified. "You guys never get a chance to practice on a woman's equipment before you're thrown into the dating pool. Watching porn and beating off doesn't count."

Since Jojo had dragged those two drunks over to their table, he had stopped letting women take him home from the tavern. Most guys would find that strange. Hell, he found it strange. It didn't make him any friends, either.

Take the scene with Gianna a few weeks back. "What, I'm not good enough for you? And Lia was? Are you kidding me?"

"No, I'm just not dating right now."

"Who's talking date? A hook-up, we're talking. We say hi, we have a drink, we go back to my place and you screw me blue. I hear you're good at it. Maybe I am too. Why don't you come find out?"

"I'm sorry, Gianna. Nothing personal. I don't hook up anymore."

"Well, fuck you." She went back to the bar.

Jojo and he had become friends, the only woman friend he ever had. They had come to respect each other, each discovering how good a coach the other was. They got together once or twice a week for pizza or something, with Lee along of course. He had begun to avoid the tavern.

At the pizza place, Tony sucked down a beer. "I'm a good teacher, I think. I'm a good coach. Apparently I'm a good screw. How could I ever know that, by the way? Guys brag. I don't. I know a certain percentage of the bragging is BS, but why believe I was any better than average? All the girls say it was great, afterwards. That's just what girls believe they're supposed to say."

"Where are you going with this? You want Lee and I should try you out and give you a score? No thanks."

"No. I always knew I was a good mechanic. That's all. In the last few months, I learned I'm good at three more important things. People things. Teaching, coaching, fucking. That takes getting used to. Like I'm a whole different person. But a skill I'm missing—is this okay? I'm blabbing about myself like you don't have anything you'd rather talk about."

Lee put down her pizza slice. "I think Jojo would agree. I never once in my life heard a man talk about his feelings. I want to hear it."

"I never learned how to find love, to have a family, to be a father. I noticed Lucia, she already loved me, I finally loved her back, and great. But then the damned cops…"

He paused for a minute, until he was ready to talk again. "I've loved Rosa. I never had the confidence to tell her because she was so incredible, so that option has never been real. I've never succeeded, never even tried, to find a love on my own, like Lucia did. That's the one thing I'm still no good at, and it's the most important thing." He grabbed a napkin, turned away to blow his suddenly-runny nose.

Lee squeezed Jojo's hand. "Yes, it is the most important thing. Uh, maybe not the father bit, but the rest of it."

Still holding Lee's hand, Jojo reached across the pizza and grabbed his hand, too. Not the one with the napkin, the other one. "Please, Tony, please. Lee and I have talked about this, a lot, and it's still a mystery. Help us out. What's so great about Rosa?"

"You should know, you played with her three years. She's the best basketball player our school has ever had. She's beautiful. The shape of her body, her long dark hair, her black eyes and black lashes, even her eyebrows. The way she walks, straight ahead and confident, no girlie butt waggle."

"I don't want to tear her down, just give you a little dose of reality. She was a great basketball player. That was thirteen years ago. She's thirty-one. I'm thirty-one. Because of my coaching and her never touching a basketball, I'm a better player than she is. Not then, understand, but now."

"No offense, Jojo, but you're a mediocre basketball player now, just like me. Just like I've always been."

"If you say so. Want to talk about her looks? Have you ever seen her naked?"

"If only."

"I have. In the same locker room for three years. I'm a lesbian. I looked."

"So, tell me." His underwear tightened uncomfortably.

Jojo described Rosa, in enough detail so Tony had to adjust his mechanic's pants.

She looked at Lee. "You okay with this, that I checked her out?"

"Hey, remember I played too. Different school, different locker room. Similar bodies, I bet."

"Okay. Her beautiful eyebrows? She plucked them into shape, just like everybody else. Her lashes, mascara, just like all the girls back then. Like most of us dark Italian beauties, she had a little hair above her upper lip. That turn you on? We all have to wax. My Mama did mine. I don't know who did hers."

"As I remember, I thought she's incredible and you were trying to convince me she wasn't. You've done a lousy job so far. Even with the upper lip thing."

"Look at her job. All these years, and she got up to Assistant Manager. Just like me"

"Yeah, but she's some kind of executive now."

"Big deal. You're a teacher and a coach now. Around here, that means a lot. Around here, being off in Connecticut doing who knows what, that doesn't mean so much."

"Okay. Good try. I still think she's incredible. You tell me what she looks like naked and you think that was supposed to tell me, 'down boy.'"

"You mean your boy's not down? No. I wanted to tell you, on a scale of incredibleness, she's not as high as you have built her up to be, and you're higher than you believe yourself to be. You don't have to so fucking intimidated."

Lee leaned look-at-her-face low across the table and punched him in the shoulder. "You want her, go get her. In high school, she was a star, and you weren't. That's long gone."

Jojo leaned low across the table and punched the other arm. Like they both wanted to show him Rosa wasn't the only one with boobs. "Plus, you're not giving yourself enough credit for loving and losing Lucia. Every woman in the neighborhood could see how much you hurt. That your emotions were so obvious, and yet you stayed a man of respect, women admired you for that. They still do."

She held her palms out toward him—you got it yet, dummy? "On top of that, you're the neighborhood's greatest lover—greatest straight lover, I mean. Wait till I see Rosa and tell her about that."

She and Lee stood up. "You know your reaction to all the talk about women naked? Us, too. We're heading home. See you next time." They left the pizza place holding hands.

He sat there, ordered another bottle of beer. That new friend of Rosa's? He didn't even have a whole hand. He'd see if Pete knew where she lived these days. Maybe take a ride to Connecticut.

Chapter 22

To earn her eighty thousand, Rosa and her training partner, Harry, traveled Monday through Thursday, two stores a day, and gave their display-training spiel to the store managers. Phil and Lou had chosen the neediest managers, in stores scattered through Massachusetts, Connecticut, New York and New Jersey. Finishing the second store of the day at six or so, they stayed in a hotel that night, and hit the next store at eight in the morning.

They used Rosa's Camry. She was newer to the job, and so was her Rex-Aid car. Rosa drove and Harry talked. He was forty-three, divorced with three kids, and not shy enough about sharing his personal life. Or his interest in visiting Rosa's room some night. Short, wide, with dandruff hair, he did not inspire interest. Rosa hoped to God she never got that desperate.

It had been a while, and she was horny, just not Harry horny. Lou had made clear he wasn't going to help. When Harry brought it up, she was initially polite. After a while, she just said, "Down boy," the minute some comment seemed headed in the same old direction. He was persistent. A role model for how she should work on Lou.

Thursday night they'd return to their homes. Rosa leased a one-bedroom condo fifteen minutes from headquarters. On the second floor, one flight of stairs lower than her old place on Staten Island—she was moving down in the world. Her unit viewed the parking lot. She could step out onto her one-chair balcony, peer to the right, and see her car in its assigned space.

Fridays, she and Harry went to HQ. They wrote a report covering the week, and polished their paperwork about each store. Late in the afternoon, they sat with Phil and Lou to discuss their week.

After two months, she and Andy switched to group sessions, fifteen store managers gathered around a conference table in some anonymous hotel meeting room. Each training lasted two days, and by Friday each week, they were back at HQ again, analyzing the evaluations and reporting to their bosses.

If Lou wasn't going to East Haven, he and Rosa would have Friday dinners together.

Rosa figured a therapy session with a nude Lou might turn into something more satisfying. Even if it didn't, she could get her fingers on his tortured, wonderful skin. "Why don't you want to have a better sense of touch? Are you worried the pain would increase with the greater sensitivity?"

"No. I can handle the pain."

"Then why?'

"I've never shown anyone my skin. I don't even loosen my tie. I'm going to show you my nude body? My front was burned, and my back was carved up. That's all you need to know."

Rosa wanted to ask about one particular piece of his front, but the question would be wildly inappropriate. "I don't understand. Your face looks normal enough."

"Do you really need to know all this? Look it up online or something."

"I know about skin and burns. I don't know about your skin and your burns, about what you went through. I'm interested in you and your skin, not burns in general."

"Marron'. Okay, plastic surgery. They take whole skin grafts, down to the tissues underneath. It looks more normal, if they manage to put the scarred edges in the right places.

He wiggled his ass and rubbed his back on the booth. "Just so you know, talking about it makes it feel worse."

"I'm sorry. I didn't have any idea."

"Do you feel guilty?'

"Yes. We don't have to talk about it."

"Good. As long as you feel guilty."

He stopped squirming. "The transplant creates a new spot as bad as the original burn, on my inner thighs or my ass, which they have to patch over with half-skin, like they did where I was burned. So they only do it if I tell them I want to. I stopped at my face and neck."

"Whole skin. Can I do touch therapy on your face at least? It would help a little."

"Some other day. I don't mind, by the way."

"You don't mind what?"

"Making the pain feel worse."

"Why?"

"Because I deserve it. If I was in the house, maybe I could have saved them. Or died with them. Either would be better. I was outside, because riding my little tractor, making the lawn pretty, was more important than being with my wife and kids. I worked long hours. I hardly saw them, but still the damn lawn was more important."

"Dying with them? Don't say it. Don't think it."

"Yeah, I know. Notice the thought and set it aside. My shrink. She's probably right, but I can't just decide to move them around in my mind and—poof, magic—the thoughts are gone, you know? You do that kind of therapy, too?"

"No, but I know your sister, the people at Rex-Aid, and especially me—we're all glad you're still around. Your life means something. You mean something. To me."

Lou pulled out his credit card and let the waiter know he wanted the bill. "Rosa. You've become a friend. But go find yourself a less choonka lover."

Rosa sat silent.

As the waiter approached with the bill, she put her hand over Lou's credit card. "No, Lou, I don't think I'll let you run away again."

The waiter left the bill on the table, inside a worn-out vinyl folder. Rosa handed it back to the young man. "A good meal needs a digestivo. I'll have an Amaro. Avena Siciliana, please. No ice cube. What'll you have, Lou?"

He looked at the bill in the waiter's hand, then at Rosa. A moment's silence. "I'll have the same."

"This is important, Lou. Give me your tie. I'll take good care of it in my purse. Would you rather I folded it or rolled it?"

Lou stared at her. "This is none of your business. You have some nerve."

"Yes, I do. You should discuss it with your therapist. Meanwhile, take off your tie."

He hesitated so long, Rosa was sure he wouldn't do it, but he touched his hand to the knot. The server arrived with their two Amari. He waited until the server left, then unknotted his tie, folded it carefully, and put it in the inside pocket of his suit jacket.

He held up his little glass. "Cin, cin."

She did the same. "Cin cin." She took a sip. "You look ridiculous, Lou. Unbutton your top button."

"I've never let anybody see this but a doctor. I don't want to do this, you can't know how much."

"Maybe I don't. But you're special and so am I. This is a breakthrough moment. We need to take advantage of it."

He unbuttoned his top button, gave her a 'damn you" glare, and unbuttoned the next one down. He spread open his shirt.

A wide scar ran horizontally across his neck line, as if someone had tried to kill him with a garrote. The light in the restaurant was not bright, but Rosa could make out striated pink and white skin below the scar, quite different from Lou's tanned face.

She resisted her urge to reach out and touch it. "Why the fuss? Your skin below the scar is different, but it's beautiful. To make sure I understand, the skin above the scar, you can feel things, the skin below you can't?"

"Yes. You've seen it. Happy? Can I put my tie back on? People will stare."

"Lou. My ex-husband beat me. He left scars and bruises on my face. I had to have two plastic surgeries. It was more than a year before my face got back to normal. Your scars will never go away. I know they're worse than mine were. But, you got your scars as a hero, a story we all know whether you want us to or not. I got mine as a pathetic victim, another story everybody knew."

His fused fist lay on the table. She put her hand over it and he didn't pull it away. "I wish you could feel proud of your scars. Let people stare. You earned them, through heroism and through pain."

"Your husband beat you?"

"My ex-husband."

"Do you have any marks that still show?

"No"

"I've been beaten, too. My marks show, scars on top of scars. Nothing heroic. Shame."

He switched his stare from his shot of Amaro to her face. "You understand why you will never give me your nudie therapy?"

"Not really."

"Because you will never see those scars. Never." He had raised his voice to a gravelly growl, a tone she'd never heard before.

Taken aback—no, scared—Rosa didn't answer.

"Good. Let me take you to your car." He threw down three fifties and headed for the door.

A week later, Rosa got a message at work.

Before she could look at it, the woman behind the lobby desk unloaded her opinion about the man who left it. "A workman, tough looking, blue work clothes, asked if you were here. Big shoulders, big hands, 50's hair, like a guy out of the Godfather."

Looking proud, the bitch said, "I told him to use the warehouse entrance from now on."

When she finally got a chance to read it, the message was from a guy named Tony Prezzi. "It's important that I see you. Here's my cell number. Give me a call. If you don't remember me, talk to Jojo or your Mama. Like I said, it's important."

The new basketball guy who coached with Jojo. Why would he come to see her? She called Mama.

"Rosa, dear. Is something wrong? It's not Sunday yet. Whatever you heard, Papa and I are okay. Are you?"

"Yes, Mama, I'm fine."

"Us, too. Why the call?" It's Friday. Aren't you at work?"

"Yes. I just got in."

"They let you make a personal call while you're supposed to be working? Won't you get in trouble? Maybe you should call later."

"Mama. One more time. I'm not like a worker who'd get in trouble. I'm like a boss."

"Well, I know that. You were like a boss at the Rex-Aid store, too. But that didn't mean you could decide to make a personal call and the hell with your work."

"Never mind. Tony Prezzi came to see me. Said it was important. He said I should talk—"

"Tony Prezzi came all the way up there to see you? What a hunk. If I were your age, he could see me any night he wanted. We don't see Pete's daughter so much, because of his situation, you know? But Dino's and Aggie's—they love him. I told Aggie she should watch out, because her daughter has a crush on her coach. Teen girls, you know, they can get hurt so easily. Because they have no sense. Remember you and that porca DiFalco?"

Yeah, she remembered. "Why would this guy want to see me?"

"I don't know. His wife, that cop who was killed? That was a long time ago. I hear lately he's been tomcatting around the neighborhood. Maybe he wants to take you out. If he asks, say yes. It will be well worth it, that's what I hear. Women my age talk about him. Your papa's always been fine, but—"

"Mama, I don't want to hear about it. Maybe I'll call him."

"You do that. Too bad you weren't there to see him in person. You could have rubbed up against him by mistake. Something. You know."

"Right, Mama. Bye. I'll see you on Sunday."

She called Jojo.

After small talk, not much small talk, because Jojo was in a hurry to tell her something, Jojo said, "Dummy. Like I told you in high school, but you couldn't hear because of the DiFalco creep, he loves you. From afar, obviously. If he knew you like I do...."

Rosa heard a voice in the background, probably Lee. Talking away from the phone, Jojo said, "Don't worry, I'll tell her. I am telling her."

Back to Rosa. "He's a teacher and a coach now, he was a terrific husband till he lost his wife, and any woman he dates comes back babbling. Lee and I told him to stop mooning around and go after you. Maybe he is."

"You told him to…"

"Damn right. And if I were you…. Let me put it this way. You know when you played defense on the court, legs and arms spread so your opponent couldn't get by? Well, if he comes running at you, assume that position, emphasis on the legs spread, and stand your ground. Don't let him get by."

The guy had been around forever, Rosa never heard one word about him except when his wife died. And now she had an old lady and a lesbian assuring her he was a women's wet dream. She couldn't take Aggie's daughter's word for it either. Rosa put his number in her phone, and waited to let him come running at her, as Jojo so delicately put it.

She already had Lou. Sort of.

Chapter 23

"Mid-April, folks. Nothing's worked out and we're out of time. Personally, I never heard of her—"

Several of the older faculty spoke up. They quieted to let Mrs. Delana speak. She'd taught American History since Tony was a kid. "You're relatively new, Meg. I assure you everybody in the community has heard of her."

Tony couldn't stay silent. "Look at our sports trophy display. She's the best athlete this school's ever had. All-City. How many other school's biggest star was a woman? Plus, she has some big executive job at Rex-Aid headquarters."

Mrs. Delana added, "Don't take this wrong, Meg, but we've never had a woman graduation speaker since before you came. It's about time our female seniors had a role model."

"Great." Ms. Gennaro reached behind her to pick up a phone and waggle it at them. "Who's going to call her? The Principal usually does, but she doesn't know me and I don't know her. Whoever makes the call better close the deal, because we're out of time."

Bob Berreto, the gym teacher who'd talked Tony into coaching, pointed at him. "Tony can do it. His assistant coach was on Rosa's team. They're still friends."

Meg turned to him. "Can you pull it off? We're out of options."

"Yeah. I can do it. No worries." How could he do it? She didn't even call back when he drove all the way up to Connecticut and left a message.

The three of them were at Lee and Jojo's apartment, in their living room decorated with sports equipment and two yappy dogs. "Hi, Rosa, it's Jojo. Yes, I know you can read it on your phone's ID. That's why we used this phone. Sorry the sound's so bad. I have it on speaker. My friend, Tony Prezzi, is here. He's got a question for you. If you're wonder—"

"The basketball coach? The guy you told me about—take the defensive position?"

The speaker worked well enough. Rosa's voice came through clear and lovely. Take the defensive position? What did that mean? He remembered Rosa playing defense and got a hard-on.

"Yeah. Him. Forget the defensive position until later. Remember he's a teacher at the high school? I'll let him talk in a minute. Most important, he needs to ask you a question, but not that kind of question. Your friend Jojo is telling you the correct answer is yes. For our high school, for you, for all of us."

"Then, how is it a question?"

"Oh, bullshit. Tony, just ask her."

Tony blurted in a rush. "We need a graduation speaker, a role model, especially for the girls, so we want you. Will you do it?"

"I'm a role model?"

"Because you're the biggest sports hero we ever had, and because you're a big executive success. The girls need to see both those things."

"Just the girls?"

"The boys, too, of course. But we've had men speakers seven years now, and the girls should have a woman. We should have a woman. We should have you."

"I don't know…"

Jojo had been holding the phone out so Lee and he could talk and hear. She put it close to her mouth. "Yes. You do know. No need to think. I already told you the answer."

"When is it? What if I'm busy?"

"Then change your plan. When is it, Tony?"

"June seventh. Saturday in the afternoon. Same as it was when we all watched you graduate."

"You watched me graduate? Why did you watch me graduate?"

Jojo put the phone back near her cheek. "Because of his thing for you, dummie. I already told you. You and he can talk about it some other time. Right now, we got the "yes," correct?"

"His thing…"

"You heard me. He says you have his number. Did you keep it?"

"It's in my phone."

It's in her phone! Tony pumped his fist. Lee rolled her eyes and the dogs barked.

"Good. I'll put yours in his phone. You can talk sometime on your own. If you make him unhappy, I don't want to see it. If he gets too earnest like he does, I don't want to hear it."

Before Jojo could hang up, he stuck his mouth up to the phone, inches from Jojo's face. "Terrific, Rosa. Thanks—from the whole school."

Jojo said, "Bye," and pushed the button.

"Thank you, Jojo. You were great."

"Thank you for what?"

"Everything." He kissed her on the lips. Lee laughed and the damn dogs attacked his legs.

Chapter 24

Rosa spent Memorial Day back in the neighborhood, sleeping in her old room. Mama, the aunts, and Aggie stuffed everybody with azit' and meat balls, sausage and peppers, long-boiled attrip' with sauce, the good bread and pastries from the bakery.

She had come for the food, and to order dresses from Mrs. Billetski and her daughter. The pair made every prom dress and bridal gown in the neighborhood. Despite her name, Mrs. Billetski was Italian. There'd been a Mr. Billetski thirty years ago, but he'd died in Vietnam.

Rosa got plenty of food. Mrs. Billetski loved her ideas for dresses.

Since her skin got sensitized, Rosa had always longed for loose, silken clothes with no pinching belts, or straps that dug into her shoulders. Now she had the money. If Mrs. Billetski could do it in time, she hoped to wear the first of her new dresses for her graduation speech.

Rosa's order was big, but Mrs. Billetski said her dresses were simple and fun, so different from a bridal gown. Rosa knew what she wanted in general, long silky things with no pressure on her skin, but she left it up to the women to know how to do that.

They showed Rosa pictures of wide sleeves: angel, bell, kimono, batwing. She picked two bells and two angels—at least she'd heard of them—and ordered one each of the others.

The Billetskis decided an ankle-length A-line would work best. To avoid bra straps and elastic panties pinching her in sensitive places, they recommended an old-fashioned dress-length chemise, designed with cap sleeves, a bodice, and a slip that hung almost the length of the dress.

Both the dress and the chemise should be made out of light, silky polyester. Silk was too expensive and not as durable. The double layer would prevent any see-through. Well, maybe a silhouette in the right light, just the thing for a single girl like Rosa.

They promised they'd make her first outfit before graduation day.

The Billetskis gave her the first dress in only three days—warm blush white with angel sleeves. In the mirror, she looked transformed, a beauty from another planet. The angel sleeves were enormously wide at the wrist. When she held her arms out straight, the sleeves draped so far down they looked like angel's wings. The blush color brought out the warmth in her tan face, magnifying the effect of her touch therapy.

Rosa hugged Mrs. Billetski. The one dress cost almost as much as her whole closet full of Walmart and store-sale clothes. But so what? She made eighty thousand.

She picked up the dress on Thursday. On Friday she wore it to work at HQ. She worried about wearing such an unusual dress to work, but if she was going to wear the dresses every day, she might as well start.

The dress caused an uproar. She entered the building and the receptionist asked, "Oh, is this a religious holiday?"

As far as she could tell from the questions, the main guesses seemed to be she'd joined some religion where women couldn't show their skin, or she had to please a new boyfriend from one of those religions.

The big to-do was among the women, which in HQ meant mostly support staff. Men stared, sometimes visibly shrugged, greeted her the same way they always did, and moved on. The little office where Harry and she prepared their report had become a storeroom of newly important items. Every five minutes, some woman needed to come into the room, find an item in the credenza, and ask Rosa a question about her dress.

Harry, who had shown no more curiosity than any of the other men, wrote "Do Not Disturb" on a blank piece of copier paper and taped it to the door. "They'll get used to it. Later. Right now, we have a report to write."

Lou acted as blasé about her dress as any of the other men. Nevertheless, after dinner he invited her to see his house for the first time.

Rosa blessed her angel dress. If only she'd bought it weeks ago. His old house was gone. She wondered how he lived now. Persistence paid off—for her, if not for Harry.

She followed his car through a neighborhood with huge houses set at the end of long driveways. Even with her windows closed, she could smell the salt air. This was the season for azalea bushes to bloom, and gaudy patches of red and white decorated the lawns. Apparently, his new house was in a super-rich neighborhood.

Lou signaled, then abruptly turned right into a driveway whose pavement ended at a burnt-out ruin, or maybe a memorial, a foundation and chimney covered with honeysuckle vines. The asphalt turned to dirt and detoured around the ruin. They both bumped downhill to stop in front of a long wooden building perched at the edge of a tidal inlet. His house? On the other side of the building, upper levels of a big fishing boat towered over the shed's roof, the boat's top bristling with poles, antennae, discs and radar dishes. A big boat. Maybe he lived on that.

Nope. Inside the door, she could see the building was laid out like a narrow mobile home, bedroom and bath at one end, living area and kitchenette at the other. The ceiling slanted like the roof, old nautical paraphernalia hung on the walls, and glass double doors led out to the dock and the boat.

Lou waved his arm around in a half-circle. "Home, sweet home. I tried living on the boat, but after the first winter I had this built. The zoning commission thinks it's a boathouse. If it was a real house, it would have to be a mini mansion like the one we used to have. You want a drink?"

Without waiting for an answer, he opened a trap door in the floor, kneeled down to pull out a bottle of red, and poured them each a large glass. "My wine cellar. They stay cool down there." Sipping his wine, he turned to look at his boat through the double doors, his back to Rosa.

She stood watching him, his curly hair in particular. Why was he being so rude?

The hair nodded once. He swiveled. "Do you remember when you wanted to do your touch-whatever on my head?"

"Yes. I still want to."

"This might be a good time."

Once in position with his head hanging over the arm of his red leather sofa, Rosa began the touches, His whole head was traumatized, so she used the soft twisting technique, repeated over and over.

"This hurts. You never mentioned that."

"I'm sorry, I'll work on another spot."

"I don't mind pain. We're old friends. We've been together for years now. I'm so used to it, sometimes I like a little extra. Touch away. Don't worry about pain."

Working so close up, she noticed new things about his face. A big scar across his head, hidden in his hair. Lips and eyelids lightly outlined in medical tattoos, the lip color probably a tattoo also. A web of narrow scars everywhere, hidden in wrinkles under his eyes or alongside his nose. His face looked like a man who'd endured a hundred top-notch plastic surgeries, which he probably had.

She declared the session over, ninety minutes and one ruined wrist later. He needed more sessions for that much trauma, but she had hurt him enough, no matter how casual he pretended to be.

He sat up and patted his head. "Should I feel any difference?"

"No. I'd have to touch more of you, like I said."

Not offering her any, he poured himself the rest of the wine and gulped it down like he was chugging beer. He opened his mouth to say something, but changed his mind. Indecision changed his face into something she'd never seen before. At work, he was decisive, and he looked it. Whatever he was struggling with, she saw him make up his mind. His face returned to normal.

He said, "You can touch me more, if you let me touch you."

"Deal." Before he could chicken out, she fumbled with the few buttons that closed the neck of her dress.

"All but my back. I said you'd never touch it. It's still not going to happen."

"Okay."

Rosa's only clothes were the dress and the chemise. She pulled her dress over her head and folded it carefully before laying it over the arm of his recliner. She looked back at him and all he'd removed was his suit jacket and tie. She went to help him unbutton his shirt.

He grabbed her hand between his thumb and his fist. "No. No back, remember." With just the thumb, his grip was stronger than she thought possible. He undid his belt, unzipped, and his suit pants fell to the floor. They wouldn't come off over his shoes, so she kneeled down to untie and yank them off his feet. She flung each one over her shoulder. His pants too. He wore black calf-length socks, thin and silky. She rolled them down his leg, enjoying the feel of them. One at a time, she tapped his toes, and he lifted his feet so she could slip them off. The rolled-down socks looked like giant black condoms. She tossed each one toward his face.

All he had left to remove was his boxer shorts. She was still completely covered in her chemise.

"I'm down to my underwear, and you're still totally covered."

With one hand, she lifted her chemise up to her waist and gave him a flash. "By the time I get this thing pulled over my head, your boxers better be off."

They were.

His rear end and his thighs were quilted with scars between patches of harvested skin. If his lower body looked so bad, she couldn't imagine what his back must look like. She turned her attention to his little stub with skin like cracked leather.

He whispered, "You *are* an angel. You looked beautiful, but I figured there must be something wrong underneath, or why would you be so interested in a guy like me? You can have any man you want. Why me?"

"I can have any man I don't want. A man I want has been hard to find. Until you, Lou." She touched his penis. "Does it work?"

"That was blunt. No it doesn't."

"I'm sorry. Maybe your tongue?"

"You know Italian men don't do that. Too demeaning."

"Well, then, your fingers will be fine. But what are you going to enjoy?"

"Looking at you. Touching you. Kissing you."

"Me, too. I mean beyond that. Have you ever had any kind of therapist look at your penis?"

"Not until you stared at it a minute ago. And you still are. Let me give you an overview, before you do any more touching around. See the burnt skin? It's got little elasticity. I can't get any wider, longer, shorter, or skinnier. It is what it is. When blood rushes in, expecting to pump it up, it hurts like hell."

"Does it hurt now?"

"Are you kidding me? With your finger on it? But I'm used to pain. Right now, it's worth it."

"Would it hurt more if I examined it?

"*Stugatz*. What's a little more pain?" He lay on the sofa again, like when she'd touched his head.

Rosa lifted his penis with a finger. The burns weren't as bad on the underside, and the skin looked almost normal. On the top and sides, though, the second degree burns were bad. She imagined a hot dog on a grill, when the skin hardened and crackled. That's what had happened to Lou.

She touched near the tip, twisting her finger. "Do you mind if I give it therapy?'

"No pain, no gain."

Rosa touched the whole area, not a hard job because of its size. She concentrated on the less damaged underside. Lou moaned at first, then clamped his jaw together. She decided she'd hurt him enough. She stopped touching and leaned over to give it a little good-bye kiss.

He batted her head to the side and let loose a shot the length of the sofa. Gasping for breath, he pulled her head to his chest and tried to speak. Not letting go of her, he lay back on the sofa arm, his fist over her left ear, his fingers combing her hair. She turned her head inside his tight embrace to look up at his face, reddened now, its white scars visible.

He pulled her higher, their faces level. Hugging her, he kissed her cheek and nibbled on her ear.

Her breasts naked against his shirt, she felt pride and warmth. Especially warmth.

He leaned back to look in her eyes. "Worth the pain? Unbelievable." He kissed her. "I think it's your turn."

Damn right. "Maybe we should move to your bed." She didn't mind a wet spot, but the leather sofa was a puddle.

"I don't know, the sheets aren't clean."

She glanced at the mess on the sofa.

"Okay. Bedroom it is. Let me straighten up." He ran into his room. She could hear sheets rustling. By the time she came in, a blanket covered the dirty sheets of his double bed. They both sat on the blanket side by side, sipping wine.

Her outer warmth retreating from her skin, Rosa felt a chill. She wasn't used to sitting around nude, drinking wine with a half dressed man. If she had her way, they'd both be snuggled under the blanket, warming her again, inside and out.

"You were incredible," he said. "In eight years, I've never been able to do what you just did. And I've tried. To mix some pleasure with all the pain."

He turned his face away from her, talking to the bureau. "This is the first time I've ever been unfaithful to Kate. Eight years of fidelity exploded by an angel with the skills of a pros—"

He turned back to her. "Ready?"

A prostitute? Unless his fingers were incredible, after all those months Lou had just turned himself into a one night stand. "I'm cold." She lifted the covers and snuggled in. "Come in where it's warm."

With no choice, he slipped into the other side of the bed. They turned on their sides. Out of the corner of her eye she noticed the sheets were dotted with brown spots, but she focused on his face. She took from him a long kiss, advancing with her tongue every time he tried to withdraw his lips.

To pull him closer, she wrapped her top leg over his thigh, and put her arm around his shoulder. Her fingers fell to his back.

He jerked away, pulling his shoulder blade past her fingertips.

She whispered, "Oh, my...."

Chapter 25

After school, on the second day of finals, Tessa came looking for Tony. She was their center, the tallest girl in the school, yet she managed to look like a little child—a woeful, teary, angry little child.

Seeing him, more tears streamed down. He wanted to hug her, and she tried to hug him, but he stood back. The school system came down hard on two kinds of faculty-to-student touches, hitting and hugging. Coaches could hug players on the court, coaches-turned-teachers couldn't hug students in an empty classroom.

She stood unhugged and put her hands over her face. "Where's Jojo? I need to talk…Jojo. They say I can't…graduate." She took her hands away to wail, "And he started it."

He called Jojo.

He held his phone toward the girl, who had slumped onto a shop stool.

Jojo said, "Ten minutes. I'm coming."

He guessed what happened. The familiar pattern. Some "he" did something, she retaliated, and she caught the foul.

Jojo arrived, hugged her until she was recovered enough to stand up straight, and asked her if she wanted Tony to leave. She didn't say anything for a long while. He got up to go.

"No. He can stay. He knows about asshole boys."

Jojo looked over her shoulder, fighting to suppress the smile. "You're right. He does."

True. Him in high school.

Before they'd heard thirty seconds of the story, Jojo said, "We have to get this on video."

The shop had a couple digital cameras on tripods. Tony set one up and they started over from the beginning.

"We fooled around sometimes. He was on the men's team. We were friends. But he wasn't my boyfriend or anything. Besides, he was with his creepy little kiss-ass buddy. We were in that narrow hall that goes to the computer labs. 'School's almost over,' he said, 'and you haven't given me a blow job.' He wanted me to go in the Media Room with him. I told him, 'Not unless you brought a roach clip.'"

"He laughed, and said if I wouldn't give him a BJ, I should flash him. He squeezed my breasts, then yanked my top up over my bra. While I was fighting him off, his creep friend grabbed my arms from behind. I swung sideways to get my boobs away from the asshole's hands and I guess his little buddy had to let go of one arm. I must have swung back the other way and elbowed the bastard into the wall. He let go of my bra and I yanked down my top. He got knocked out, I think, and fell down. A little blood on the side of his head where he scraped against the wall. His creepy buddy ran away. I could tell the asshole was just groggy, like happens all the time on the court, and I left."

"End of story?" Tony asked. "What was the business about not graduating?"

"Somebody called an ambulance. The guy was hardly hurt. Ms. Gennaro called me in, told me I was suspended, and she was notifying the police. I might get arrested for assault. Then I came down here."

Jojo grabbed a piece of paper and started writing on it legal-sounding stuff about when the tape was made by whom. Tony and she signed as witnesses. She hugged the girl again.

Tony called Meg. "I have an important, legally important, clip I need to show you. I'm coming right down. Yes, I'm sure you are. I'm busy, too. I promise you, you'll want to see this piece. Or, if you'd rather, we could just let the school get sued and its principal fired."

Jojo took the girl to McDonald's to buy her some comfort food. "You need us, call me."

Meg was Tony's boss, and annoyed. He was nobody's boss, and angry. They balanced each other out. She fumed while he ran a thin cable from the camera to her computer.

Set up and ready to go, he said, "Remember orientation last August? Not a word about teaching or anything like that. Half the time on the school system's sexual harassment policies, discrimination policies, hostile environment, etc. Teacher are responsible for behaviors in our classrooms. Administrators are responsible for the school as a whole. Remember that?" He double clicked the mouse and the video appeared.

Together, they watched the video. It was only two minutes long.

At the end, Meg looked at him. "He said, she said."

"More like—he said, she wasn't given a chance to say, and she got suspended. Or, he sexually assaulted her, and the school suspended the victim for defending herself."

"I can see how it might look like that."

"What the hell were you thinking, Meg"

"I was thinking…. I'm busy as hell. I don't need this right now. One kid had to be taken away in an ambulance. The other kid had been in trouble for her temper before. Handle it. Get back to work. That's what I was thinking."

"In other words, you were thinking about it as little as you could."

"Maybe. Anyway, her statement is not proof of anything. It's just her view of the situation."

"Which she was suspended without ever getting the chance to present. If she tells her story to the press, what kind of shit-storm do you think will smash down onto this school? Smash down onto you?"

"Okay, Tony. You just clinched your case. Do you still know where she is?"

"Why? What are you going to do?

"Un-suspend her, apologize and grovel, though I don't do either well, and launch an investigation. We won't have time to finish it before they graduate, when it will become moot. If either of them wants to file a criminal or civil charge, that's their business. We're out of it. That's what I'll do."

"She's with Jojo. She'll be here in less than fifteen minutes. Practice your grovel."

Not that he didn't trust Meg, but he disconnected the shop's camera and took it with him.

Half an hour later, Jojo and Tessa came into the shop and hugged him. He decided the rules might allow a student to hug him, as long as he just grinned and didn't hug back. He couldn't shut down the grin, even after the two of them left.

Chapter 26

The skin under Lou's T-shirt felt like gravel. Where Rosa had dragged her fingertips, dots of blood traced a trail.

"Lou.... What have you done?"

"You nosy bitch. You couldn't stop yourself. I gave you everything you wanted. My attention, my affection, my skin. One thing I asked. One last piece of privacy."

He rose to his knees, his back toward her, and pulled his shirt off over his head. "See, bitch. Is this what you needed to know?"

The gravel stones were crusts and scabs, rising from a background of half-formed scars. Diagonal intersecting paths crisscrossed his back. His skin was a horror, drawing her in with the fascination of its texture, repelling her with the ugliness of what he must have done to himself. She turned her head away.

She rose to her hands and knees, edging away from her pillow, edging away from him.

"Where are you going? Don't you want to see it all?" His voice was the loud husky scratch which had scared her in the restaurant a millennium ago.

He leaped off the bed and yanked something off its hanger in his closet, in plain sight if she had cared to see. Holding its handle between thumb and fist, he whacked her with it. A broad path of pain started at her ear, neck, and shoulder, then raced down her back.

The shock buckled her knees and elbows, dropping her flat on the bed. She lay there stunned and hurting, her mind whirling through the possibilities. How do I escape? Do I run naked? Where? Can I get beyond the reach of that...that thing?

He yanked her hair straight up, pulling her neck back as far as it could bend. "Sit up. I want to show you something." He kept tugging her hair upwards, the pull forcing her to scramble up into a kneeling position. He let go and she slumped back, sinking her butt down onto her heels.

He splayed out his whatever-it-was on the bed before her. Rawhide strands, some with knots, some with bits of crimped metal. Stiff rawhide, smelling of blood. "Not pretty to look at," he said, "but beautiful in a way. It does its job so well."

He snatched it up and slashed it over his shoulder, with more speed, more force, and more awful noise than when he hit her.

She slid off the bed, rising from a crawl to scramble toward the door. This time, he whipped her legs so hard, her knees buckled and dropped her to the floor.

"You're right. Not in here. Let me show you how it's properly done." Hauling her by her wrist, both of them naked, he dragged her out onto the dock. He only had his thumb and fist to grip her with. She couldn't believe she couldn't get away. She jerked her arm around, trying to slip her wrist free.

"Stop, bitch." He stretched out her arm as long as it could go and slammed her hand and his fist down into her pubic bone, doubling her over with pain.

A folded chair stood tied to the side of his house. He used his finger stubs to untie one end of the line and tossed the chair away. One-handed, he tied some weird knot with a big loop, shoved her wrist through the loop, and pulled it tight. She worked on the knot with her free hand, but she couldn't loosen even one strand. She was tied to the house.

Stepping a few feet toward the dock's end, he pointed to a dark red stain surrounding a length of chain attached to the deck, and kneeled down on the chain. He whipped his back over his right shoulder, then over his left, teeth gritted against the pain.

After he'd recovered enough to breathe normally, he talked as if they weren't naked outdoors, he scourging himself, she beaten and tied to the wall. "Penitence. Atonement for sins. You probably never heard of the concept. Because you think you're innocent, a blameless victim."

He reached out and struck bloody stripes across her hip, circling around to her rear.

She cried out and curled into a ball, her left arm protecting her face, her right arm still hanging from the wall.

He whipped himself, not her, twice again, and each one harder than he whipped her. Recovered after a few seconds, he said, "All of Rex-Aid knows you're a whore, picking the only VP that no other woman could look at and pretending to be in love with his loathsome skin. I listened as you deceived me into believing your ridiculous story about that bullshit touch. Then, tonight, you looked like an angel. I said, 'Maybe.' Fool."

He hit her again, across her forearm and the side of her breast. He smacked himself, twice, and leaned forward, gasping.

Rosa saw the rivulets of blood running down his back, until he managed to raise himself upright again and put his back out of her sight. Another wait, her body too enveloped in pain for her mind to wonder what he'd do next.

"Then you worked on a dry well and made it flow. Only a pro could do that—a top-notch, high-skill pro. You're a whore, one of the best. I don't know why you're not working for some pimp, training other whores."

By the time he'd finished his speech, his voice had declined to a breathy whisper. Hope lumped her throat. Maybe he'd hurt himself so badly, he'd slump down and quit.

Instead, he knelt up straight and began to flog continuously—her first, then himself twice, her again, himself twice. The blows grew weaker, but so did she. She keeled over into a fetal position. He lashed her back, her bottom, the soles of her feet. Her pain was less. Everything was less. She felt her body shut down. At last. She couldn't feel the whip's awful hurt, she couldn't cringe away from the next blow, she couldn't smell the blood, she couldn't....

Chapter 27

Saturday, at ten in the morning, Tony and the rest gathered at Jojo's house. Lee had a new HP computer, a word-processing program, a laser printer—plus, she knew how to use them all. Tessa, the group's only graduate, brought cookies from her grateful mother. Jojo was Rosa's friend and supporter. And Tony was the faculty member who'd recruited her to speak. Together, they'd help Rosa write her speech. She'd have a week to practice, because the next Saturday would be graduation.

Everybody gathered, that is, except Rosa. Jojo called her cell, repeatedly. It worked, rang, and took her messages. She simply didn't answer her phone. She had no other land line at her apartment. But maybe she'd forgotten her phone at home when she left to meet them. Tony did that all the time.

After eleven, they stopped joking about her lateness. Lee had to leave for work at two. Their graduating senior planned to meet her mama in the afternoon, to buy clothes for Tessa's new job. If Rosa showed up late, none could hang around except Jojo and Tony. They knew nothing about this new WordPerfect program that Lee and Tessa used.

Jojo called Rosa's mama, in case she knew anything.

"No, she's not here. We only see her on Sunday afternoons. Unless she snuck in late to sleep in her room."

"Probably it's nothing. But she was supposed to be here at ten, to work on her speech. I don't think she would blow us off."

"Well, maybe she came in late. Sometimes she does that if she wants to be in the neighborhood the next morning. Let me check."

They heard her drop the phone and clomp up the stairs. They heard her clomp back down. "Nope. Not here. Why don't you check with that Tony hunk? Maybe they finally got together. A night with him, she probably couldn't remember her name, let alone some meeting."

Tony reddened.

Jojo laughed. "No, I'm looking at him right now. They haven't gotten together."

"Porca vacca. Damn. Maybe that man from work. The guy with the screwed-up hands. It's possible. She's a smart girl, but when it comes to men, she's a stupad with the brains of a squirrel. I don't remember his name, but somebody ought to know it."

Jojo said, "Lou Bates."

"Yeah. Like in the *Psycho* movie."

Jojo pointed at Lee, who was already typing his name. "I'll try to get his number. Meanwhile, if she shows up, have her call me."

"You're with Tony Prezzi?"

"Yes."

"No offense, but I'll have her call him."

Lee took less than a minute on the internet to find where he lived.

Jojo stayed home to call police stations and hospitals. Tony left for Connecticut.

As he headed for the door, Jojo called out, "She drives a blue Toyota Camry."

A mailbox in front of a burned-out house marked the address. He followed a dirt driveway downhill to a small building, a big boat, and a parked Camry.

His 4Runner was big, almost a truck, and not quiet. Nobody came to the door to see what was going on. Her car was here. If they were both still asleep after a long night, how could he explain driving all the way out here to disturb her and her boyfriend? He'd feel like a stalker, for sure. He'd be one.

It was after noon, though. Late to be still asleep. What if there was some kind of trouble? Undecided, he sat for a few minutes. He needed to know. Better to stalk. He got out of his car, slammed the door, and walked to the front door. He stomped his heavy shoes on the little wooden stoop. Still no noise from inside.

No doorbell. He put his hand to his forehead to block the reflections in the noon sun, and peered through the door's window. Nobody. He knocked tentatively, then loudly. He banged on the door. No response. The door knob wouldn't turn. He looked through the two windows flanking the door. No longer stalking, he'd become a peeping tom. He saw a living area, a bedroom with an unmade bed. No sign of Rosa or Bates. At one end of the building, a wooden walkway led to the building's water side and the boat.

Still stomping his feet, he stepped onto the walkway. A window at the building's end gave another view of the living area. A sofa, a recliner. Still nobody.

He stood and looked around, listening. Seagulls cawed. The boat creaked against its dock. Small waves lapped the shore. Otherwise, silence. The clean smell of salt water and seaweed. None of Staten Island's harbor smell of oil and polluted mud. Another odor instead, wafting on top of the salt. Sharp, tangy, coppery.

He hurried down the walkway, turned onto the dock.

Two bodies lay on the decking, naked, covered in blood, surrounded by red stains. Rosa lay in a fetal position, one arm sticking up in the air, tied to the side of the house. He knelt to look at her face. He heard tiny breaths pumping air, thirty or more a minute. She was alive! He felt her untied wrist. A faint pulse, too fast to count the beats. Her skin was cold, so cold.

He called 911.

"Police, fire, or ambulance?"

"Ambulance. Two people covered with blood, at least one still alive, barely. Police, too." For the first time he looked at Bates, knees and face on the deck, back covered with cuts and blood, whip in one hand. "One guy whipped himself and Rosa almost to death. She's alive. I don't know about him."

"Help is on the way, sir. You are?"

"Tony Prezzi. She's tied to the house. Her skin is freezing cold. I am going to untie her and cover her with a blanket."

"Leave that for the professionals, Mr. Prezzi."

Fuck that. He hung up, took some cellphone pictures for the cops, and untied her. He took her into his arms and carried her through the open back door to lay her on the bed. He noticed the bed was already splattered with dried blood, but he wrapped her in the sheets and blanket anyway. He had to get her warm. He sat on the bed with her head in his lap. She still made her sped-up little dog-pant sounds, breathing through her mouth. Her eyes seemed blank, yet they followed his face when he moved.

First Lucia. Now Rosa. If she died, he couldn't see a way to keep on going.

As soon as the ambulance arrived, the EMTs called for a helicopter to take Rosa to the nearest trauma center. They said Bates was dead. Good.

Tony called Rosa's mama, to tell her where they'd taken Rosa. Jojo, too. He didn't tell anyone about the whipping, or how bad Rosa looked.

The cops pulled up, several cars. He was the top suspect, cuffed at once. Obviously a love triangle thing. How many guys committed suicide by beating themselves to death? Tony wouldn't have believed it himself. He told the cops about his phone's pictures, and that his wife was a cop killed in the line of duty. They calmed down and waited for the detectives.

He didn't get out of the police station until early the next morning. He headed for the hospital. All the DeAngelos were there, from Aggie and Al down to the youngest. Jojo waited, too, but only family members could see her in the Intensive Care Unit, two at a time for five minutes, four visits an hour.

Mama tried to get him in. "He's the man who saved her."

That didn't work.

Aggie whispered to Mama, "Tell 'em he's her fiancé."

Mama brought Tony over to the nurse's station. "I didn't want to say anything in front of the family, because it hasn't been announced yet, but this young man here, he's Rosa's fiancé."

The nurse smiled. "Not family yet, but let's bend the rules."

Even if it was just pretend, Aggie and Mama had given him a dream he could hold onto for a long time. However long it took until it came true. Rosa was so hurt and he was happy. What a stroonz'.

The next time Mama went in, she brought Tony with her. Rosa slept, sedated, with blood and drugs dripping down two tubes into the back of her hand. Bandages emerged from under her covers, across her neck and the side of her cheek, up to her ear lobe.

"I don't think I believe in this," Mama said, "but why take a chance?" She knelt beside the bed, held Rosa's hand, and recited in a sing-song voice, "Hail Mary, full of grace, the Lord is with thee. Blessed art thou among women, and blessed...."

Tony knelt beside her, and held Rosa's arm, but his prayer was different. He thanked God Bates was dead. If he were alive, Tony would have to kill him. Killing Bates would destroy Tony's life. Thank you, God, for helping the bastard kill himself.

While Mama and Tony were in Rosa's room, a doctor came in. "Hello, I'm you're hospitalist." Their hospitalist? They'd never heard of that before. They rose off their knees to talk to him.

"Let me explain. She's in hypovolemic shock, caused by exsanguination."

Mama said, "English, please. Or Italian."

"She lost so much blood, the exsanguination, she didn't have enough volume left to feed oxygen to all her organs, the hypovolemic shock. That's why her heart pumped so fast, and she breathed so rapidly—the body's attempt to circulate more oxygen. We estimate she was in stage three shock, with loss of a third of her blood volume. Mr. Bates was deep into stage four, and expired. In layman's language, he bled out."

Rosa almost bled out, the same way Lucia died. Tony's own heart bled.

Chapter 28

After two days, her blood stabilized by transfusion and the painkiller drip switched to pills, Rosa rode an ambulance to a Rehab Hospital on Staten Island. She told Jojo and Tony she planned to give her graduation speech. She could see Tony didn't think it possible.

Rosa asked Aggie to see if Mrs. Billetski could make a new dress. The first one was held as police evidence. Tony should notify Ms. Gennaro, she said, that the head of the English Department could stop preparing a speech, because Rosa would do it after all. She asked Jojo if Lee could find statistics on the internet and print Rosa a list. Tony could please arrange for a wheelchair.

One last request of Tony. "Come get me Saturday noon. I'll give my speech and you can bring me back here when the graduation's over."

"But we were going to help you write your speech. What'll you say?"

"Don't worry. If Lee gets me the numbers, I know what I'm going to say. I'm a trainer now. I know how to talk without a script."

After the Opening, the anthem, the valedictorian's short address—"Now is our time. We are the future, etc."—Rosa's turn came to speak. As planned, she had Tony roll her toward the podium. As no one knew she'd planned, she grabbed onto the podium and pulled herself upright. Her slash marks hurt like hell, the unhealed gaps in her skin trying to open up again. Barefoot except for the bandages that swaddled her feet, the gashes on her soles stabbed with pain. She stood on them for the first time since her beating.

Standing behind the podium, both hands gripping tight, she swayed as she waited for her head to clear, the dizziness to recede. Not only her feet, but her blood pressure objected to standing upright. Her light mauve kimono-sleeve dress, with its ample width and the deep lavender scarf Mama had wrapped round her bandaged neck, hid most of her sway and tremble. She looked around the gym, the parents in the stands, the graduates in folding chairs on the floor, hoping to look like she intended a dramatic pause. She needed to recover from standing up, and to accustom herself to the new level of pain.

She pulled Lee's piece of paper out of a sleeve and set it on the podium.

She greeted everybody, thanked them for the opportunity to speak, and launched into the obligatory graduation BS she'd heard at her own graduation, and at the ceremony of every brother or sister. "This is not the end...this is the beginning...commencement means beginning..." Blah, blah.

Then the twist. "The commencement of what?"

She paused again. "Personally, I commenced an engagement, a wedding ceremony, marital adventures that brought me great joy" Students and parents alike smiled at the "marital adventures" bit.

"Less than four years later, I joined a large group of women in our country and our neighborhood, women who think they are alone, but who are linked together by the bonds of common experience."

She winced, at her pain and at her coming announcement. "My husband beat me. With his fists. I was assaulted. Like one third of all women in the United States will be physically or sexually assaulted by their husbands or their boyfriends. One third! A horrible number. But those are other people, you say. Not us. Not our neighborhood. The numbers are so high because of the violence in whatever ethnic groups you feel superior to. You are right. Some communities experience more assaults than Italian-Americans."

A short pause. "But most communities experience fewer assaults. We Italians are pulling the percentage up, not down. Our men assault our women more than the U.S. average. Only a little bit more. Should we feel proud?"

She looked around the parents in the stands. "What are your children commencing into? I have just told you the statistics among Italian Americans. A little over one third. Unless our neighborhood is different from Italian-American neighborhoods in other places—and from my experience, it certainly is not—one third of the women in these stands have been assaulted. One third of the men in these stands have assaulted the woman they claim to love. Let me say it another way. An assault is a felony. A felon is a criminal. If caught, a criminal goes to prison. Not a little misunderstanding, not a few slaps. An assault, a crime, possibly prison."

People rustled in their seats. There was a scattering of boos. Whoever heard a commencement speech like this? She leaned into the mic and, in a low, firm voice like Lou used to use, said three times, "Quiet, quiet, quiet," and the noise subsided. She wondered. Were the objections coming from the one third or the two thirds?

"Let me address the graduates. More than half of all women assaulted by husbands or boyfriends are between the ages of eighteen and twenty-four. If we don't change, almost twenty percent of you, one out of five—that's right, look around you—will become criminals or victims in the next six years." The percentage seemed so high, she checked Lee's paper again. Verified.

"In her excellent speech, your valedictorian..." She turned toward the girl. "She said, 'Now is our time. We are the future.'"

She turned back to face the graduates. "Your time to do what? You can guess what my suggestion is. Now is the time to make this problem public, for women to speak up, and for men to stand up and act like men. People think this is a women's problem, and there are programs for women to deal with their beatings. But men too must solve this problem, because it is mostly men who must change."

She tested whether she could grip the podium with only one hand and still stay standing. Maybe. "Why do I talk of this subject at a graduation, a time of celebration and hope? Two reasons. First. I have hope that we can end this horror."

She prepared for her next move. It needed to be quick but also smooth enough not to knock herself off balance. "Second, because I had no other choice."

She unfurled her scarf, revealing the bandages that it had hidden. "As some of you may have heard, my boyfriend," though he wasn't really, "almost killed me last Friday. You don't need to worry about this speech going on much longer, because this is the first time I have been able to stand on my feet since that day, and I can't stand for long."

She looked over Lee's paper one last time. "Let me close with an inspirational example from history, an example my friend found on the internet. In rural China, not very long ago—about the time the grandparents of our graduates were eighteen themselves—it was normal for men to beat their wives. A national association of women formed chapters in every village to stop this. When a man beat his wife, the local chapter warned him. If he did it again, the village women's association gathered at his house. To beat the crap out of him. Wife-beating ended almost at once."

She signaled Tony to bring back the chair. "As I said, not a suggestion, just an inspiring example."

She raised one hand to wave good-bye. "Sons of Italy, if any other man assaulted your wife, you would kill him. Maronna Mia! You know what it means to be a man of respect. Be one."

Her remaining hand lost its grip on the podium. She fell backwards. Tony caught her and eased her body into the wheelchair.

The graduates leaped up to give her an ovation. One by one, the parents in the stands stood up.

Tony wheeled her to the front of the stage, she bowed, and he wheeled her back through the stage door. She slumped in her chair, took her pain meds, and escaped into unconsciousness.

Chapter 29

Tony wheeled Rosa to his 4Runner. She was too woozy to help him move her into his car. He slipped his left arm between her back and the wheelchair, his right arm under the back of her knees, and lifted her up. The hem of her long, loose dress dragged on the ground. Gently, he set her down in the car, arranged her dress so it wouldn't get caught in the door, and buckled her in.

Before they got to the hospital, she began to talk, her speech a little slurred. "I am so grateful, Tony. For everything."

"Forget that. You were incredible. Just like you used to play b-ball. Take it to the opposition, get in their face, then score the big shot. I am so proud."

"I could do it because I wasn't dead. Because of you."

"Anybody would have done what I did."

"No. But my brain isn't working well now. We'll have to talk later."

We have to talk? Oh, God. The four words a man feared most. They were not in a relationship, despite his phony fiancé status. Maybe she didn't mean, "We have to talk," like Lucia used to.

Back at the hospital, a hospital assistant wheeled her to her room. Two nurse assistants ducked in front of him and closed the curtain around her bed. When they opened the curtain, she lay under covers, the head of her bed raised.

She waved at him, whispered "Thank you," and shut her eyes.

Tony sat in the six-seat waiting room of Rosa's hospital unit.

An old women was already there, dressed in a weird outfit—a gray hoodie, a cross, big wooden beads. The old lady stopped fingering the beads. "Out of it, eh? She always like that?"

"No. She just gave a speech and it wiped her out."
"Gave a speech? Good for her. I'm Mary. Who are you? Family?"
"No. Just a friend. Tony Prezzi."
"Just a friend. Right. I've got eyes. I can see."
"O...kay. Who are you?"
"Just a friend. When Rosa wakes up, tell her Mary was here. I can't wait now. I'll be back."

As soon as Mary left, Mama passed by. She went to Rosa's room for a few minutes and walked back to sit with Tony.
"Asleep in that hospital gown, she looks like she couldn't get out of bed. Amazing she could stand and give that speech. Did you like it?"
"I thought she was incredible."
"Yeah, but did you like the speech?"
"Of course. After what DiFalco did to her, and now that guy Bates, she stood up and fought back. That's what I love about her."
"Me, too. I was wondering if a man would like it."
"Depends on the man, I guess."
"Yes. It's so hard to tell. Not this last guy, I don't think. He was strange. But Joey? Did you know he'd do that? Can men tell?"
"No. I was jealous but I never thought he'd hit her."
"Women can't tell either. It's like a lottery. A lottery the young ones don't even know they're entering. Unless they saw it in their own family. With Italians—except for Rosa, of course—it's always a family secret."
"Did she know about Pete?" He didn't. Not till Paola left him.
"Some of it. But young kids—they think bad things will never happen to them. At least Rosa didn't think it was normal. She left. A lot of women hang around."
"She's a strong woman. What I love about her."
"Sometimes she is. I'm so tired of worrying about her. Worrying about all my daughters, I didn't worry about my sons so much, even with Pete. Now she tells me I should. It never stops. The grown ones, you worry more. You can't help much. They're on their own"
"Sounds hard."
"Not always. Let's talk about something better."
"Okay. What?"

"You. Thank you for saving her. You love her? You said so three times in the last five minutes."

"Yes. For a long time."

"See. That's a problem. You hung around and didn't do squat. But that's over, right? You grew up or something."

"I think I did."

"Okay. This fiancé thing? I'm telling her you're permanent. The rest of the family, too."

"Please don't do that. The pressure. She'll fight back."

"Stugatz. She picked her own man twice and she blew it. In Sicily, her Papa and I would have picked a man and that would be the end of it. Course, a lot of women got beaten there, too. Anyway. You're picked. By her family. She might fight for a while, but when it's a family thing…." She stood up, so he did, too. She reached up to pinch his cheek and left to go sit with Rosa.

Un-fucking-believable! Her Mama! Some Italian women, Mama's orders might mean wedding plans. Not Rosa. She was tough. Still, to have Mama on his side….

He sat there in the waiting room. His butt knew everything there was to know about the black vinyl chair. He tried to plan for his next school class. His mind kept leaping back to Rosa and her mama.

An hour later, Aggie waved as she went by to see Rosa. A minute later, she returned. He stood up, waiting for her to sit, but she didn't sit. She held his shoulders and pulled his face down level with hers. She looked into his eyes, their faces a foot apart.

She nodded, released him and sat down. "Do you know what Mama is doing in there?"

"I think so."

"And this is all right with you?"

"You mean do I want to marry Rosa? Yes. You mean do I want her mama to tell her she has to marry me? I don't think so."

"Oh, I think she'll marry you if the family assumes it's a done deal. Eventually. I worried about resentment, but she's too strong for that. She won't do anything until she gets over Mama trying to force her."

"That's for sure. Maybe years. I think I could have won her faster on my own. Maybe."

"So what happened? Mama just up and proposed?"

"Almost. We were talking about men hitting women. About one minute after that, she announced I was the fiancé for real."

"I guess you said the right things."

"Really? Just that?"

"No. You saved Rosa's life. Mama already named you the fiancé temp. You must have passed the interview and got the permanent job."

Mama came back to the waiting area. She turned to Aggie. "I'm sorry you'll have to wait some…. Hey, guaglion'. You still sitting here? That's been your problem all along. Get in there."

Tony leaped up and strode down to Rosa's room. Nerves slowed him down by the time he reached her door.

Rosa was sitting up with her magenta scarf draped around her neck.

"Hi, Tony. Pull the chair closer. Sit down."

"Rosa, it wasn't my idea."

"I know. The whole thing has a nutso Mama tinge."

"I love you, though. If you say yes, I'll be back with a ring in an hour."

"Okay. That answers one question. Jojo always said you did, 'from afar,' but I never heard it from you. Never heard much of anything from you. You saved my life. I'm grateful. But I'm not marrying you over it. I hardly know you."

"I understand. You'll get to know me. I'm not going anywhere."

"That's nice. You seem like a good guy. I don't have any men friends. I told Mama this already, and I'm telling you now, first chance I've had. I'm not marrying anybody. I'm not dating anybody. Maybe I will someday. Probably I will. But not soon."

She laid her hand on his elbow. "We can be friends. Maybe when I've had enough time, we could be friends with benefits. Jojo and Mama say you have a lot of benefits. I can't see how either one would know. Friend, not boyfriend. I don't know if I will ever want a boyfriend."

Rosa started to say something, then shut her mouth. Her eyes looked at the ceiling for a second. "Okay. As a man once said to me— I should have listened—'We're becoming friends. Go get yourself a less choonka lover.'"

Rubbing her knuckles on his cheek, she said "Bye, Tony. Come back and visit anytime."

"Bye, Rosa."

He left and rushed by Mama and Aggie, shaking his head at them. As soon as he was out of their sight, he stopped. Ducking his head down, he used his left thumb to push his shirt up into the inside corner of his left eye, then his right thumb and his right eye. He straightened up again and hurried out to his car.

Tony drove aimlessly. He didn't want to go sit alone in his apartment. He didn't have anywhere else to go. He'd stayed away from the tavern because of his hassles with hook-happy women, but he decided to head over there. He'd have people around and he could drink away some of the hurt. He'd found a place to park when his phone made its "Ahooga, ahooga" hot-rod sound. Lee, the caller ID said.

"Tony, are you with Rosa?"

"No."

"Something happen? You okay?"

"Yes. No."

"Can you come over? We can talk about it if you want. Jojo and I want to show you something. You'll have to see it to believe it."

"Do you have any beer? I can pick some up if you don't."

"Just a minute." He listened to Lee ask Jojo, but he couldn't hear the answer. Lee came back. "Is a case enough?"

"Ten minutes."

At their apartment door, Jojo handed him a bottle, Lee pulled him by his sleeve, and the two little dogs yip-yipped around his ankles. She led him, dogs prancing behind, through the living room into a bedroom-turned-office. Three chairs crowded in front of a computer monitor. They sat him in the middle. With a few keyboard clicks, Lee brought up a YouTube video of Rosa's speech.

"There were only eight uploads when we first looked. They're up to fourteen now. Some have thousands of hits, some many more." Lee flicked among the different videos, from different angles, some zoomed-out to get him and Meg and the Valedictorian in the picture, others tight on Rosa.

"Check this out," Lee said. "I put together a medley for you." One clip after another, Rosa fell backwards and Tony caught her. At the time, he thought he'd just caught her and guided her into the wheelchair, no big deal. From the audience perspective, he watched her dramatically collapse and him scramble to catch her.

Lee held up an empty beer bottle. "This is the best one. We'll need a drink after this one."

Jojo ran to get new bottles.

Everybody back in their chairs, Lee pulled up a clip titled, "Speaking for me at my daughter's graduation." Unlike some others, it didn't start until mid-sentence when Rosa said her husband beat her. From there on, it focused tightly on Rosa all the way through her collapse at the end, then caught the students leaping to applaud.

Lee stopped the video. "The best part is next."

She backed up to when Tony caught Rosa and turned it on again. They watched the catch, the loud applause, the camera turned around to show a woman's face filling the whole frame, tears ruining her graduation-day makeup, shuddering, her voice catching as she repeated, "Come out, come out, come out." Paola. Tessa's mother. Pete's ex.

Lee pointed at an ever-rising number along the border of the screen. "Hundreds of thousands. This one's going viral."

Jojo said, "The Harvey Milk of abused women. I think she's right. It worked for us."

Tony had been trying not to cry since he left the hospital because he was a man and he shouldn't feel like weeping so often. What with Paola crying and the beers, he let the tears leak out. The dogs nuzzled his knees.

Chapter 30

The trauma doc had passed Rosa on to a dermatologist and a psychologist. They were both in the business of minimizing scars. The psychologist was pleased with her graduation speech.

The dermatologist was really pissed. "You tore half-healed wounds, dislodged scabs, and guaranteed wider, thicker scars. We'll do our best, but the damage is not fully fixable."

"If I'll have scars, does it matter whether they're wider?"

"With proper compression now, plus laser treatments later, we can make scars almost unnoticeable. Usually we work with a single surgery scar. The sheer quantity of your wounds is challenge enough. If you keep pulling apart the healing wounds, we won't be able to do our job."

"The neck and cheek scars matter to me. The others, who cares how noticeable they are?"

"Bikinis and attractiveness to partners. That's what my women patients usually say."

"Oh. Okay." She hadn't worn a bikini since high school. Hadn't even been to a beach. Textured skin was fine with her. There probably weren't many men who liked scars, but she wasn't looking for a man anyway.

Still, she resolved to be a good girl. Stay in the bed. Pee in the plastic thingy instead of using the bathroom. Let the nurses move her into a chair instead of hopping out of bed on her own.

The day after her speech, Jojo showed up. She carried a heavy laptop computer. "Hi, Rosie. How you feeling?"

"They've got me doped after what I did yesterday."

"Yesterday? That's what I came to talk about."

"I gave a speech and wrecked my wounds. You were there. I was there. What about it?"

Jojo sat down and opened the computer.

Rosa craned her neck to look. "Where did you get that thing?"

"Lee borrowed it from somebody. I've got to be careful with it. I want to show you something. Do you know about YouTube?"

"Yeah."

"Wait till you see these." She showed Rosa some video bits of her speech. "People in the audience. Fifteen people uploaded these from their cameras. More than a million have watched them. So far."

"Why? It hurt me to give it, but it wasn't really a graduation speech."

"Let me play this one. It's the big hit. Lee's and my favorite, too."

It started up when Rosa talked about Joey beating her and ran to the end. Rosa was surprised to see how she almost fell over before Tony caught her. She didn't remember that. The students gave her a big ovation. She didn't remember that, either. Then the camera turned around to show Paola crying, ruining her makeup. She said "Come out, come out, come out," and the video ended.

Paola got beat up, too, more often than Rosa because it took her longer to get away from Pete. Rosa could see why she cried. "What was that "come out" stuff at the end?" I mean I know about lesbians being out, but Paola has a second husband. I don't think she's a—

"I can see why you don't get it. You've never been in the closet. Most beaten women hide. She's telling them, don't hide anymore."

"Good. Good for a woman who comes out and good for the rest of us, too." Rosa stopped turning sideways to see the laptop. "I'm not supposed to twist myself like that. Plus, it hurts."

"Lie back. I don't have to see your face to talk. I know what it looks like. The other fourteen uploaded videos. Who do you think did that?"

"Some of the one third, I guess."

"I think so. And all the people viewing these, they're probably in the one third too. You're making a big splash."

"That's good."

Jojo closed down the computer. When she was done, she looked over at the bed. Rosa watched her through half-closed eyelids. Jojo blew her a kiss and tip-toed out of the room.

Rosa sat uncomfortably in the clunky hospital recliner. Now that wounds had closed, new tight bandages kept her skin from moving, but they also itched like hell.

Dr. Eleni was back. Her name badge said Dr. Eleni H, followed by about twelve letters. She was Greek, and she preferred people didn't butcher her last name. Just call her Dr. Eleni, she said.

"This is our final rehab session. You can always come see me at my office, but your rehab is over. You'll be released in the next day or so. To start with, any questions from last time?"

"No."

"I've got some questions. But I'm not asking for facts. We'll never know the facts. I'm asking for your thoughts. Okay?"

"Okay"

"Why do you think he did it?"

"I don't know. He never seemed crazy before then. He was a nice guy. Smart and confident. Great dresser. I knew he had issues with his burns but I liked him. I liked him a lot. He was a hero from trying to rescue his family."

"But he didn't succeed, did he? Do you think he felt guilty?"

"Sure. Who wouldn't?"

"I don't think I would, if I were in his place. He did everything he possibly could. He almost died trying. As you say, a hero. Why would he feel guilty?"

"He told me he felt guilty because he wasn't inside the house to help. He was outside doing something less important, mowing his lawn."

"Is that why he whipped himself, do you think? He felt guilty?"

"I think so. He called it, 'penitence.'"

"There's such a thing as functional equilibrium. Maybe he was in one, not a healthy one, but it worked for him. As long as he whipped his guilt away in private, in public he could be nice and competent and all those things you said."

"That's scary."

"Yes. We call what he did to himself NSSI, non-suicidal self-injury. Cutting is a lot more common than whipping, but they're both self-injury. There are many risk factors for NSSI, and who knows how many Mr. Bates had. One is obvious—PTSD, post-traumatic stress disorder."

"Like soldiers get."

"Yes. Like anybody who survives trauma can get."

Uh-oh. Rosa saw where she was going. "But only some of us trauma people get it, right? Not everybody."

"Right. Some are more likely than others. Do you mind if I change the subject?"

God no. By all means, change the subject. "No. You're the Doctor. Go ahead."

"We talked about why he whipped himself. Why do you think he suddenly lost his equilibrium? Why did he switch from non-suicidal NSSI to attempted murder and suicide?"

"Well. He called me a whore."

"Why? Did you have sex with him?"

"Sort of. I used touch therapy on his prick and he came. He didn't give me any sex."

"Was he happy to come?"

"He was at first. He hadn't come since he was burnt, since his wife died."

"You said 'at first.' How did he change?"

"He said he'd been unfaithful to his wife, and that only a really skilled whore could have made him come. He said that's what I was. Bastard."

"That's what set him off?"

"It didn't help. But what really did it was I touched his back—his big secret I wasn't supposed to know about." She looked at her fingers and remembered the feel of bloody gravel.

"People with NSSI sometimes go to great lengths to hide their injuries. Cutters often wear long sleeves in the hottest weather."

"Yeah. His deal was we could get naked, except he wouldn't uncover his back."

"So back to my original question. Why do you think he changed from NSSI to suicide? Do you have a guess?"

"I made him come? I touched his back?"

"Did he want you to make him come?"

"No. He didn't think he could." Rosa looked around for the hospital's little box of tissues.

"Did he want you to touch his back?"

"No, never." She gave up on the tissues and pushed the heels of her palms into her eyes.

"But you did it anyway?"

A wheezing moan escaped from Rosa's trembling lips. She rocked back and forth, her shoulders shaking, tears trickling down her wrists.

Dr. Eleni let her cry for a while. Then she bumped Rosa's arm with the corner of the tissue box. "Here. Use these."

Rosa used the tissues. She stopped rocking and moaning, though she still leaked a little. She kept a balled up tissue in one hand to pat her eyes dry.

Dr. Eleni leaned forward and touched her knee. "Ready to continue?"

Rosa nodded.

"What if I were to go out in the hall, get some guy, and bring him back in here so we could offer to masturbate him? Would he like that, do you think?"

"Sure, unless he was gay." Rosa smiled for the first time.

"Okay. Say I interview him first. 'Are you straight?' Then I bring him in here."

The doctor was so transparent – why drag it out. "Any straight guy but Lou, if I touched his back or made him come, he'd be happy about it."

"You're right. Let's go a step further. Lou went through a terrible tragedy. Was he was responsible for what happened? What do you think?"

"I don't think so. No."

"Even if he was mowing his lawn?"

"No. Of course not."

"A guy you liked lost his psychological equilibrium and whipped himself and you, so badly you almost died and he did die. Do you think you are responsible for what happened?"

"No?"

"Even if you helped him ejaculate and you touched his back."

"Well…. No."

"He felt he was guilty for the death of his family. Does that change anything? That he felt guilty about it? Does that make him responsible for their deaths?"

"That he felt guilty? No."

"He felt you were so guilty, he had to punish you and himself. Does that change anything? Does that make you responsible for his death and your injuries?

"Because the bastard thought I was guilty? No."

"If you yourself felt guilty for causing him to punish you and kill himself, would that change anything? Would you be responsible for his death and your injuries?"

"I guess not."

"Remember that. We're almost done. You bear no responsibility for what happened. Even if you feel partially responsible, you're not."

"Even if I feel it was partly my fault?"

"Right. Two things are true and you should feel free to accept both of them. First, you may feel guilty. Right now, we both know you do feel guilty. If that's your feeling, it's a true feeling, a perfectly acceptable feeling. Don't try to force it away."

"I don't understand."

"Feeling guilty is fine. It's your feeling. Believing it's true, believing that in fact you are guilty—that's not fine." She leaned forward and touched a finger on Rosa's knee. "Again. One, you may feel guilty, that's okay. Two, you are not guilty, that's true. Can you separate the two—feelings inside you, and reality outside you?"

"I think so."

"How would you know so? What would you have to do?"

"Um. Decide?"

"Can you do that? Without the question mark?"

Rosa looked away from Dr. Eleni, off into space. She sat silent in her recliner. She turned back to the Doctor. "Yes, I can. I just did."

"Just checking. Did what?"

"Decided feeling guilty and being guilty are two separate things."

"Good. It's important you remember that. When you're feeling guilty, remind yourself of the difference. We're done. As I said, you can call me anytime. I'll probably be in a session, but I'll call you back." She hugged Rosa and kissed her on the cheek. Or rather, kissed her on the bandage.

Rosa said good-bye, smiling.

Chapter 31

Summer school had begun in the auto shop. Once again he smelled like grease, and like lanolin from the gritty waterless hand soap. Because Tony didn't want to repeat what he taught during the year, he came up with his three-wrecked-engines curriculum. For their cost as metal scrap, Tony bought a GM V-6, a Ford in-line four, and an ancient Subaru boxer.

The students tore the engines down, to learn the operating parts of three engine types. They discovered the principles of internal-combustion engine design, the different cam configurations and how they worked. By the end, they had to figure out what caused the three fatal flaws that turned the engines into scrap.

Tony liked his summer course because it emphasized the mechanic's work he loved to do most—figure out what had gone wrong. The students liked the class too, at least so far. Twelve kids had signed up to spend their summer in the grease with him. Best of all, three of his basketball players had joined the class. Twenty-five percent girls!

His life followed the pattern of years past—great relationship with his work, nonexistent relationship with his love. Tony couldn't be friends with Rosa. He loved her. To be a friend, he should pretend he didn't? No. He couldn't, and anyway he didn't want to. He wasn't going to make a friend's visit to that hospital, where Mama had pumped him up and Rosa had shot him down.

His relationship with the DeAngelos was nutso, as Rosa had said. Mama invited him to their next big family function. "As a member of the family," she said. On Sunday, July 20th, they held a special celebration. Centered in the patio-sized backyard, the eating and talking went on all day.

Rosa's mama had eight brothers and sisters with who knew how many children and grandchildren, seven kids, fifteen grand-kids, a small row house and a smaller yard. People filled every space and children played in the alley. The kitchen, packed with chatting women preparing food, was the only passage from the backyard to the rest of the house. The room was jammed like a subway car in rush hour.

Upstairs, the bathroom had a line of impatient adults and small kids holding their crotches. Children played with toys in every bedroom. Young girls sat on Mama and Papa's bed, talking of boys and trading secrets with their cousins. Men sat on folding chairs in the backyard, watched the Mets game in the living room, or played cards down in the basement. Tony ended up in the backyard.

The party featured the public debut of Aggie's first granddaughter, Mama and Papa DeAngelos' first great-grandchild. Following her mother's example, one of Aggie and Al's oldest twins had given birth right after graduation. Tony wondered what was keeping the other twin from following in her mother's footsteps. They weren't identical. Maybe that was why only one of them got pregnant. The baby wasn't the reason for the celebration, though. The date was Rosa's thirty-second birthday. The family celebrated because she was alive and doing well.

Five weeks had limped by since her graduation speech. Mama had hoped the doctors would let Rosa attend her birthday party, but no. She wasn't healed enough, the dermatologist said.

Tony had not enjoyed a family party for a long time, not since he was married to Lucia. His own family had disappeared—his father in the cemetery, his only sister in Alaska, and his mother living with a widower whose grown kids didn't want her around, let alone her son.

His three DeAngelo ball players were at the party, of course. They waited on him, bringing him each new round of food and drink. On special occasions like this one, Rosa's papa mixed ginger ale with his Italian Table Red, the kind of wine that only came in gallon jugs, so he could drink all day. Tony followed his example, because he didn't want to fall asleep, and because he wanted to get in good with Papa. Anyway, Papa's wine came from a New Jersey bottling plant and tasted best in a glass of mostly ginger ale.

Everybody had already heard he was Rosa's fiancé. Each welcomed him to the family. The first few times, he mentioned that Rosa wanted no part of Mama's idea. They all acted like that was irrelevant—"She'll come around"—so he stopped mentioning it. Rosa might never let the family's fantasy influence her, but it had already started to work on him.

To Tony's surprise, Jojo and Lee showed up, even though they weren't even pretend family. "We're here because one of Aggie's twins invited us. She plans to come out to her mother today. If she does it today, her sister's baby is the big deal, not her news. Plus, the whole family will hear about it in five minutes. They won't have to text and call each other, none of that hassle."

Tony had an "ah-ha" moment. "So that's why she wasn't pregnant like her sister."

Jojo tapped her head twice. "Good thinking. For birth control, nothing's more reliable than sex with another woman."

Tessa brought him another red-tinged ginger ale. She asked the three of them if they knew about Rosa's Angels. Jojo and Tony didn't know what she was talking about, but Lee had been following them on line.

"They're growing fast, aren't they?" Lee pecked at her phone. "Almost forty websites."

"I just put my mom's site on line yesterday. She was number thirty-six."

"I'm glad to hear she has a website. She's the star whose YouTube video got the whole thing going."

"Mom would say Rosa got the whole thing started."

"Rosa didn't say anything about, 'Come out, come out.' It was your mom that inspired all these sites for survivors to tell their stories."

Tony was gradually putting it together, but Jojo didn't have the patience. "Pretend Tony and I are here. Pretend we're interested in Rosa and Angels. Tell us what the hell you're talking about."

"Women coming out," Lee said. "Local sites all over the country where women can name themselves and tell their stories. Paola is running the first one on Staten Island, but there are already a couple others in the City."

Tessa was the only one of them who'd actually set up a site. "The stories are from survivors like mom, who were abused and got out of the situation. It helps the survivors to share, but mom hopes it will inspire other women to get help or get out."

"Sure." Lee tried to take a sip of wine, but her plastic glass was empty, "If a woman is still being abused, how is she going to come out? She'll get beaten or worse."

Jojo handed Lee her glass. "Like when LGBTs first came out. They'd get fired. Or gay men would get arrested for gay sex. And people beat up gays just for fun. Dangerous shit."

"So far, Mom's site and all the others have links and info about the help lines, like 800-799-SAFE. But what Mom really wants is for each site to have a group of volunteers, an Angels Squad that can go make sure a woman gets to safety. Same as the Chinese women, but for modern America. Wouldn't that be great?"

Tony wanted to be part of this. It might help with Rosa, too. "Would you let men be on those squads? I mean, maybe they could confront other men better."

"I don't know. I'll ask Mom. Sounds paternalistic to me."

"Pa.... Father-like? Why? Not my father—he was a drunk."

Jojo took his elbow. "She'll ask her mom. We can talk about it later."

Mama came over carrying her great-grandbaby. "Watch it, Tessa. Those two might be contagious."

"My cousin told her mom already?"

"Yeah. Big whoop. All her 'friends' have been girls. Since junior high."

"I've been her cousin all my life. Does that worry you? I mean if lesbians are contagious?"

"True. You may have built up immunity. No matter. Jojo and Lee have been off the market too long. I doubt they remember how to recruit. It's not purely one way or the other, anyway. Back when I was young, I.... Well, never mind."

The great granddaughter started to kick and squall. Mama lifted the baby up to her face and wrinkled her nose. "I think she wants her mama. So many years of diapers, I'm retired. Tony and Tessa, I came to tell you you're in the group with me and the other two basketball girls. Tony, can we use your SOB?"

"SUV?"

"Yeah. We'll leave for the hospital in a half hour."

The baby was yelling by now, a loud cry anyway. Best a four-week-old could do. "I've gotta go find her mother." She scurried toward the back porch.

Tony asked Tessa, "What was that about?"

"Nona organized a few groups to visit Rosa. The baby and her parents and grandparents. You with Nona to protect you and us b-ball players to give you cover. Are you really going along with Nona's freaky idea that the family gets to pick you as Aunt Rosa's husband?"

"I asked her not to do it."

"Well, you better do more than that. You're going to be on Aunt Rosa's shit list so long all you'll share in bed is arthritis."

Everybody laughed but Tony.

"I wouldn't let Nona force me—and Aunt Rosa's tougher than me."

Chapter 32

Dresses, dresses, dresses. The Monday after her birthday, Mrs. Billetski showed up at the hospital with Rosa's whole order. Almost white, all of them, but each with a different tint of violet or lavender or rose.

The seven dress-and-chemise sets cost about half what she had in savings. After she paid for the dresses, she was almost as poor as the old days, before she moved to Rex-Aid HQ.

Rex-Aid had taken back their Camry, "for now." She was on disability leave, but she and Phil both knew she'd never be back. Rex-Aid offered decent severance pay, but it was on hold, wrapped up in the lawsuit.

A woman named Jenny Barret had shown up at the hospital. Short with an emerald pantsuit, she wore pumps that probably cost more than one of Rosa's dresses. Per shoe.

From her recliner, Rosa watched her walk by the room in the direction of the nurse's station, her heels tapping on the hallway floor.

She reappeared. "Are you Rosa DeAngelo?"

"Yes. Come in."

"Hi. Mary sent me. I'm a St. Rita's grad, so my law firm does all her *pro bono* work. We'd take your case on contingency, not for free, because you are not a charity like St. Rita's."

"What case?"

"Your case against Rex-Aid." She sat on Rosa's bed. "Do you mind if I take off these shoes while we talk? My feet are killing me."

"No. Go ahead. Rex-Aid is suing me?"

"Ah, that's better. Other way around. It looks to be an easy case.

A Rex-Aid VP invited you from work to dinner, and then to his home, where he almost killed you. The company knew or should have known Mr. Bates was violently unstable."

"But I wanted to go to dinner and home with him. He wasn't seducing me or anything."

"The case is not about what you or even Mr. Bates wanted to do. It's about the company's negligent retention of a violent supervisor. I doubt we'll even have to file in court."

"I don't understand. Why would Mary—"

"The average settlement is a half mil, but that's for an employee peer and a lesser injury. A VP and your injuries? Rex-Aid will be thrilled to get away with three million. Our firm will front all the expenses and take the standard one-third contingency fee. You'd get two million, give or take."

"Two million. That's crazy."

"Maybe. The law often is. It will take many months to reach the settlement. Maybe a year or more. If you feel the money is too much when it finally comes through, you could share it with a certain needy charity."

A familiar sound came down the hall. Wooden beads clacking rhythmically with every step. They clacked their way into her room, "So Rosa, when do you bust loose?"

"The day after tomorrow. That's what the Hospitalist guy told Mama and me."

"Where to? Connecticut again?"

"No. I have to get my scars rubbed down with lotion. To stay soft and keep them flexible. Thirty days. I'll go to Mama's and she'll do it. Trouble is, she's trying to force me to marry this guy she picked. He seems okay, but I don't want a man right now. Or a marriage. Especially a marriage."

"Force you? That's not right. Come to St. Rita's. We've got women can rub you down."

"But Mama and Tony—that's her husband pick—are coming to get me."

"Does that Greek shrink know about the forced marriage?"

"No. It's not really forced. Just pressured."

"Pressured, forced—same difference. Family abuse. You

obviously have to enter an abused-women shelter like St Rita's. For protection. The shrink has to release you. Before the family's new firín takes possession of you. Tomorrow. Urgent. Your safety is at risk. Call her up. You tell her your problem and I'll take over the arrangements. Got it?"

"Okay."

"By the way, you a trainer yet?"

"Yes, I am."

"That touch thing, it still working?"

"I don't know. Probably not, but my fingertips may still have a little zip to them. I don't know. I haven't tried to use them."

"Well, think about it. We've got plenty women can rub your scars. We still need your training skill. We need your fingertip magic. That's laying on of hands, I'm sure. God gave you those fingertips, even if you don't believe in Her. To make beaten women feel again, that's a calling."

"I don't know about a calling, but it's a good thing. I need it, myself."

"It's settled. You're coming home to St. Rita's. You'd be good in the therapy group, too, and the other women would help you."

Rosa rubbed the scar on her neck. "I have to tell you. Besides Mama and Tony, there's another problem. The reporters."

"What reporters?"

"All of them, I think. They've been following the fuss on YouTube. Mama said I'd talk to them when I got out of here. But St. Rita's location is secret. I couldn't have them come there."

"I've got an idea for that. We can handle it. In fact, it'd be great. There's a house for women in the East Village, more convenient for news people than the Bronx. Great poverty atmosphere, too. In the house, I mean. The neighborhood's yuppie city now. TV will love it, and it would help us. Another way you could make a difference. You're an abused-women goldmine."

"Okay. How do I get to St. Rita's?"

"Oh, a volunteer will chauffer you. Same way I got here today. See you tomorrow?"

"All right."

Mary rubbed Rosa's cheek, touching the scar. "Not bad, considering. Bye."

175

Rosa looked at her facial scar in the bed tray's mirror. "Not bad" was another way of saying "not so good."

Rosa's room at St. Rita's was the size of the walk-in closet in her Connecticut rental. Lalique, a big woman who used to work as a nurse assistant, massaged Rosa, kneading her scars and applying the lotion.

Since she had scars from the soles of her feet to her head, they closed themselves inside Rosa's room, where Lalique worked on her nude body to the sound of children chasing each other up and down the hall outside.

After the rubdown, Lalique joined the rest of the women in group therapy. Mary put on her angel-sleeve dress and went downstairs to meet Mary and a woman named Brenda.

Mary waited at the foot of the stairs with a tall woman. With broad shoulders and big boobs, she was an older, browner Jojo.

The woman shook Rosa's hand. "Brenda, PR. I'm here to backstop you with the reporters."

Rosa didn't know why she had to announce she was Puerto Rican first thing. Maybe people thought she wasn't, because of her height.

Mary smiled. "Public Relations, not Puerto Rican. Make the same mistake myself. Brenda's one of our grads. Long time back."

She ushered Brenda and Rosa into her tiny office. They all stood because there was space for only one desk chair. "We have a half dozen women here who don't mind being on TV. We might get another few abused street women from Mary House, where we're going. They've got a room for the press conference."

Brenda took over. "The women will stand behind you. Your visual. Can't have a good press conference without a visual to background the speaker. Like the American flags behind every politician."

She counted off on her fingers. "Number one, decide on your boundary before we get there. Draw the line between public witness and your private life. The more open you are, the more effective your witness. But if they pry too hard, just say, 'I'm sorry, but that's personal. Next question.'"

Second finger. "Decide what you want to say most. Say that before we let them ask their questions. That's your statement."

Third. "Relax and let them see the real you. Like you did in your YouTube speech. They're all here because of that video. Give them more of the same—speak from your heart."

Mary looked at her cell. "Time to go." She loaded everybody into a beat-up old van and clambered onto a thick cushion sitting on the driver's seat. She said, "Your turn, Donna."

A woman in the back said a rambling prayer about a safe trip and bless Rosa.

Mary said, "Amen," cranked the engine a few times until the van started, and bashed into the stream of traffic. Rosa saw the need for the "safe trip" part of the prayer.

Chapter 33

Tony loaded the wheelchair in the back of his SUV. He doubted that Rosa would need it, but he'd feel awful if he didn't bring the thing and she couldn't get to the car. He drove over to Mama's.

She came out the door talking on her cell. "Of course you're coming. Rosa will want to see the new bambino first thing."

He walked around to open the passenger-side door and stood waiting for Mama.

She pointed at the phone with her free hand, then waved the hand upwards—See what I have to deal with? "Just put a baby blanket over his head and your front. I swear to you he's seen a boob before."

By now, Mama stood next to him. He could hear both sides of the conversation.

"He's never seen my boob before. He hasn't even seen Aunt Rosa's. No disrespect, Nona, but if you want him to see a DeAngelo boob, why don't you.... No. I'm not coming. It's not a good time. I'm not bringing my baby to a hospital full of sick people. I'll bring the baby over to show Aunt Rosa soon. I promise."

Mama sighed and hung up. "Looks like it's just me and you, guaglion'. In my day, we used to birth a bambino, wrap it in a scarf, and go on with our lives. Girls these days, one baby and their normal life comes to a stop."

Tony wished she would stop calling him guaglion'. He was 37, too old to be a "young man." He didn't know whether a woman should mother a new baby like a seven-kid woman used to, or like a one-kid woman now. Whichever way Rosa wanted would be okay with him.

Touch

Mama had never told him anyone else was going to the hospital. As he got to know Mama better, he learned she liked to make any simple activity into a big chaossa. Like picking her daughter up from the hospital with a baby and a nursing mother along for the ride.

Papa was probably at work laying a sidewalk somewhere, or she'd have dragged him along, too. No. If she did that, she'd have no excuse to bring Tony. If Papa wasn't working, she probably sent him to spend a couple hours at the corner bar where the old men hung out.

Tony and Mama headed into the hospital lobby.

"They'll have one of their own people roll her out, because they worry we'll dump her on the floor and sue. Our job, Tony, will be to cart out the stuff she's piled up, the plants, magazines, the hospital swag like the little tub and the liquid soap. Especially those dresses she got delivered while she was here—they're the big thing."

She looked around the lobby and spotted a herd of wheelchairs in a corner. "Grab two of those. We can use them to carry her stuff."

Sorting through the wheelchair pile-up, Tony eventually found two with wheels that rolled freely and swiveled well enough to steer. With difficulty, he ushered them both back to where he'd left Mama, but she was gone. Looking around, he spotted her through the window of the hotel gift shop, waving a bouquet at the volunteer clerk. He couldn't get two wheelchairs through the gift-shop door, and if he left them in the lobby he'd lose the primo chairs he'd worked so hard to find.

Fortunately, Mama stopped waving the flowers around and carried them into the lobby, "Look at these. They're almost passed and she had the nerve to try and sell them like a decent bouquet."

She pointed at brown edges on one rose petal. "I told her she was going to have to throw them away soon. She might as well give one to me. She tried to be a gabbadost' about it, but she finally saw the light."

Mama held out the bouquet. "Here. You brought these for Rosa. I've gotta do everything?"

Rosa wasn't in her room. Nothing was in her room. They must have moved her. Mama and he pushed their wheelchairs to ask at the nurses' desk.

"Miss DeAngelo? I believe she's been moved. Let me get some people who know the story. You can talk to them." She said a few words on her phone, and flashed them a phony smile, as her colleague had been doing since they showed up.

They waited at least five minutes. Mama sat in her wheelchair and Tony leaned against a wall. Four security people appeared, two walking down the hall from one direction, two from the other.

A little guy, hair short and uniform sharp like a miniature Marine, seemed to be in charge. "Are you here for Rosa DeAngelo?"

"Yes." Mama stood up out of the wheelchair. "What did you do, hide her?"

"Are you her mother, ma'am? And you, sir. Are you her fiancé?"

With Mama there, Tony couldn't say he wasn't really her fiancé. He had to say, "Yes."

Mama said, "Who wants to know?"

"Come with us. We'll explain."

They started to push their wheelchairs down the hall.

The little guy said, "You can leave those here. The nurses will guard them for you. He turned toward their desk and said, "Won't you?" Big-eyed, they nodded.

Tony grabbed his bouquet off the seat of his chair and followed the men to the elevator. They rode down to the lowest underground level.

Mama got a Kleenex out of her purse. Speaking low, she said to Tony in Italian. "Something's wrong. Some boss is going to tell us she took a turn for the worse." She dabbed her eyes. "We're way down in the basement. You know who they keep down here."

Mini-Marine opened a door and let them into a room crowded with a half dozen desks and two cops, one who looked Italian and a black one who did not.

The security guy told the cops who Mama and Tony were. He said, "They communicated in Italian in the elevator. We don't know what about."

The Italian cop said. "We'll take care of it. Thank you. You can go back to your jobs now." The little guy, looking disappointed, led his crew out the door. The cop told Mama to have a seat at the nearest desk. He left the black cop with her and led him—"Please, follow me, sir."—to the desk in the farthest corner.

"You're the fiancé? Any idea why your girlfriend requested the doc to release her to a secure women's shelter rather than wait for you to pick her up?"

Damn Mama and her nutso idea. "No, but I have a good guess." Tony nodded his head in the direction of Mama.

"Me, too. She just recovered from serious abuse, and she doesn't want to go back to the guy who still calls himself her fiancé, even after he put her in the hospital. Good for her. We run into women all the time that won't leave their abuser."

"Right. I found her barely alive and called 911. Her abuser killed himself, if you want to call him an abuser. The Connecticut cops called him an attempted homicide and a suicide. Don't you guys communicate at all?"

"Not much. We're down here slogging around in the real world. They're doing drive-bys to check on the vacant houses of rich people who spend their summers at the beach house, or their winters in the Caribbean."

"You have no idea what happened. That figures. When it comes to fucking up, you guys are the champs."

"What guys? You have something against cops? You got a record? What's your name again?"

"Prezzi. No record. But I have a couple of medals, or I did. I couldn't stand to look at them. My wife caught a shots-fired domestic, saved her partner's life, the victim's life, the baby's life. And then a hundred of you bastards stood around and watched her die on the street. Too chicken to do what she did, or too stupid to come up with a safe plan, or too callous to care. Yeah. I have something against cops."

"Calm down, sir. You're thirty seconds away from wearing cuffs."

He called to the other cop. "Joe. What was the name on the LOD death we had over here a few years ago?"

"Pizza. Piazza. Some guinea name like yours. You ought to know better than me."

Tony said, "Lucia Prezzi. Ten thousand cops you had lining the street here, to make her family feel better. To make you assholes feel better, after you as much as killed her. And now you can't remember her name?"

"One more time, Mr. Prezzi. Calm down. Maybe you got a legitimate beef. Maybe not. I don't know. If Officer Prezzi was your wife, I don't want to put you in cuffs. But you have to shut up and let me do my job. Capisce? Have a seat." He pulled back a chair next to the nearest desk.

Tony sat down, just as Mama started swearing at her cop in Italian.

Tony's cop said, "Wait here," and crossed the room to tell Mama in Italian the same things he had told Tony in English. Calm down. Don't want to use cuffs. All that. He was more polite this time, either because of Lucia or because Mama was putting on a confused-old-lady act.

The other cop left his Italian partner to deal with Mama and came over to Tony. "The family picked you to marry her? Isn't that kind of old country?"

"The family didn't pick me. She did." He pointed at Mama. "Yes. She's either a little nuts or a little old country. Both, I guess."

"I need confirmation of her story. Especially if she's nuts. Her daughter was married once before?

"Yes. And the guy hit her, so she left."

"Okay. Then this last boyfriend almost killed her and killed himself because of it?

"I don't think he meant to kill himself. But, yeah."

"And you found the girl and rescued her. You're the hero."

"Yeah. And my cop wife died dealing with a domestic abuse situation. So her nutso Mama—that's what Rosa calls her—named me her fiancé. Somebody who's safe and nonviolent. Rosa ran away, as if the fiancé nonsense was a real thing she'd be forced into, not some fantasy of her mother's."

The cops let them go. Sent them to talk to one of Rosa's doctors.

A shrink named Dr. Eleni told Mama that Rosa had requested admission to a shelter for abused women. She had been beaten twice, the last time almost fatally. Now Mama wanted to force her into a marriage with a man she hardly knew, at a time when the last thing she needed was a marriage.

The shelter's location was secret, to keep abusers away. As far as the Doctor was concerned, Tony was a potential abuser. One of the warning signs was pushing for control over the victim, and that's what Mama and Tony were attempting to do. Rosa was afraid to go home to her mama's, for good reasons, and she found a shelter. She was lucky, because there were never enough shelter spaces to meet the need.

Rosa would come out of the shelter in a few months. The two of them should consider therapy if they wanted to see her then. Dr. Eleni could recommend someone. She couldn't take them because she had been Rosa's therapist.

Mama said the idea that Tony and she needed therapy was completely pazzesco, Italian for Rosa's word, nutso. Which it was, because the idea came from believing Mama's nutso nonsense in the first place.

Tony wasn't going into therapy. Not the doctor's kind. He had decided to sign up for touch therapy at Rosa's Le Salon de l'Amour. That kind of therapy might be nonsense too, but the touch business was important to Rosa, and he wanted to be therapy-touched by the time he saw her again.

Chapter 34

Brenda arranged Rosa's human backdrop. She posed the women like props on a stage set. Rosa remembered her sister's wedding when the photographer physically pushed the family around until she had a composition she liked. When Brenda was done, the six St. Rita's women, some wealthy and dressed in their tailored outfits, some not wealthy and dressed in their Walmart sweats, stood behind four homeless volunteers sitting on folding chairs, their grocery carts or trash bags alongside.

Brenda's audio tech pinned a mic on Rosa, powered up the mixer box, and told Rosa to talk while she set the sound levels. Satisfied, she went back to her cup of coffee.

Brenda chalked marks for the St. Rita's standees so the women could walk around before their stand-there job began. The seated women sat in place and guarded their goods. They were tired from sleeping on a shelter's floor, surrounded by women who coughed their illnesses or cried out their nightmares. They saw no need to move from where they were.

Rosa sat in a hallway, to collect her thoughts and jot down reminder notes. An obviously Irish red-head, another Mary, handed her a page like Lee's, statistics on abuse. In bold letters, she had written, "At least 90% of all homeless women were abused before they became homeless, either as children, as adults, or usually both." Rosa looked at the new sheet, circled some numbers and put the paper in her sleeve, where she already had Lee's page of statistics.

Brenda pulled up a chair. "Ten or fifteen minutes. Reporters are filing in and the TV crews are setting up."

"I guess I'm ready. I won't be any readier in ten minutes."

"Rosa, if you need me, I'll be in the front row. Just give me a signal or say something. If you can get along without me, try to do that. This event is designed to look like it's just you and a handful of abused women in a shelter. You're the spokesperson, because you're the one the press wants to hear. That viral video made you the news. But you're just one of millions of women like yourself."

"If another one of those millions wants to answer these reporters' questions, I can live with that."

"Don't worry if you look nervous or make mistakes. This is a sincere, amateur event. No polish attempted or accomplished. No prompter, no podium. No attention drawn to the PR person sitting in the front row. You haven't had days to prepare, because the more you prepared a speech, the worse the press conference. Talk about your experiences, say what you think. You're better off with emotions than the statistics which I saw you stash up your sleeve. I'm not saying don't use them. I'm saying don't emphasize them. Reporters can't fact-check emotions."

"I won't need many numbers. Don't worry. It's like running a Rex-Aid training session. I say a few things, throw out a few stats about how lousy we're doing, and get everybody involved by answering their questions."

"Good. Sounds like you can handle the one big difference from your graduation speech. No podium. No fixed mic. You can walk around. You can walk toward a reporter to hear her question. If you use those notes," she pointed at the paper Rosa had been writing on, "you'll have to carry them in your hand. You won't have a podium to set papers on."

"If you'll be in the front row pretending you're not there, how do I know when to start? I just walk out there, say who I am, and talk?"

"Red-headed Mary, who just gave you a sheet of paper? She's on the staff here at Mary House. No relation. She'll welcome people and turn it over to you. You and your scene-setting women will be left out there to run with it. If I were you, I'd say something about the other women first, or the reporters will spend your whole talk wondering who they are."

"...wounds mark your body and they mark your soul. Do you see this scar I have on my cheek?" She walked forward and stuck her cheek out at the cameras. "I have scars like that all over my body, to the soles of my feet. He tied one arm to a wall. When I fell down and lost consciousness, he kept going on the back of my legs and the bottom of my feet." She lowered her head and fought out from under the shower of self-pity that splashed over her.

"I-I loved my husband totally, from when I was fifteen until I was old enough to get married until he started to punch me. All I wanted was to have a husband, and a family, and children to love and to raise. I couldn't."

She left Joey behind and moved to the other side of her space. "When I'd recovered, I went out to dinner with a guy ten times. He finally invited me to his house—you know what I mean—and then this." She pointed at her visible scar and waved her arm down her body to point at her feet.

"Now there's this other guy who says he loves me. My family all think he's Mr. Wonderful. Maybe he is. But I have this scar on my soul. I'm scared. I don't dare try. At this rate, I'll never have a family and children. My time will have come and gone."

"...share my experience. One out of three women. Nine out of ten homeless women. One out of five women between high school and age twenty-four. I'm not even talking about the abuse of female children by family members. I don't know that. It wasn't my experience. But the statistics are even worse."

"...left my husband. I had a job, at least. Not much over the minimum wage, but a job. I could afford to share a shabby one-bedroom with one of the girls from work. Or my parents would have taken me in."

She went and stood next to one of the women in a chair. "Let's say I didn't have parents—death or divorce, like people I know. Let's say I didn't have a job—if I was a fulltime wife and mother like I wanted to be. I wouldn't have a place to live. I would have been homeless. If I had children and no place for them to live, they might have been taken away—"

The woman sitting next to her began to sob, loudly. Rosa crouched down and put her arm around the woman's shoulders, brushed a hand over her greasy hair. She glared at Brenda. She couldn't treat people like a painted theater set. They wouldn't stop being people. She hugged the woman harder and whispered, "Thank you so much for being here with us, for sharing yourself with us."

As everyone knew if they ever watched politicians on the news, if the mic was on, it didn't matter if she whispered. Rosa realized that and shut up. She didn't want to use the woman's pain as part of her backdrop. Rosa looked at the nearest St. Rita's resident and nodded her head toward the woman in the chair. The woman's crying had subsided, but someone should still be there to give her comfort.

"…why soul-scars cover over your self-confidence, your sense of who you are as a person. Soul-scars…"

Brenda caught Rosa's eye and tapped her wrist. Rosa looked at her watch. Oh, my God. She'd talked for more than half an hour. She would have guessed five minutes. She finished her point, stopped talking and asked for questions.

"Well, of course it hurts. It may be healed. I may have scars instead of scabs. I may not be in agony. But my skin lets me know it can't move like it used to, and I feel the old hurt. Where it doesn't hurt, it's shut down, like my skin can't feel, and that's just as bad or worse. Why bother trying to find a lover, even if I was ready, if my skin couldn't feel him? Next?"

"Yes. There are early warning signs. If he wants to move you away from everybody, even your family. If he pushes you to do things you're not ready for, in your bed or in your life. Google 'early warning signs of abuse' and a dozen sites will come up with twelve or eighteen warning signs. But my two guys didn't show those signs, or maybe I didn't look hard enough. Next?"

"Yes. Men are abused, too. Everybody wants to say that, to minimize abuse of women. Just a minute. I have the numbers." She shook her sleeve and her statistics papers fell on the floor. Everybody laughed as she bent over to pick them up.

"Ten percent of abused people are men. Some of them are gays abused by men. Gays and lesbians have the same abuse problem that straight people do, but somebody else will have to give that press conference." More chuckles. "Next?"

After a couple more questions, Rosa stopped saying, "Next?" She began pointing to reporters sitting at the back or along the edges of the rows of chairs. She figured they must represent less important papers or channels or whatever. The whole corps of reporters sent to cover her were women, but the ones on the edges were younger and not as good at shouting out the loudest question.

As a result of trying to be fair, she got the fashion question.

"No. It has nothing to do with my religion. I used to have a skin condition that made me extra sensitive to straps, elastics, rough touches, and minor abrasions. I had these dresses made that gave me full skin coverage without binding anywhere. After my injuries, I need these dresses more than ever."

"If your skin was unusually sensitive, wouldn't—"

"Yes, whipping would probably hurt me more than somebody else. Until we lost consciousness. After that, we'd probably both hurt about the same."

"No elastic? How—'

"Oh, for God's sake. Don't you think that's a little too personal? Never mind. Women wore underclothes before the invention of elastic. So do I. Satisfied? Any serious questions? Ma'am?"

"You gave your graduation speech days after your injury. Yet you were in the hospital for many weeks afterwards. Could you talk about that?"

"Let's see, why did I do it? I was crazy? It hurt a lot, even though I was in a wheelchair except for the actual time I spoke. My doctor said I did permanent damage, making more prominent scars. Mainly, I wanted to talk because that was my high school. Those graduates were from my neighborhood. Most were either my relatives or relatives of people I knew. I wanted to warn those girls. It turned out many of their mothers knew exactly what I was talking about and posted the speech part of their graduation videos on YouTube."

"A follow-up, please?"

"Okay."

"Who was the man who caught you as you fell at the end?"

"His name is Tony Prezzi. He is the auto shop teacher at the school, and he was on the faculty's graduation arrangements committee. He was responsible for asking me to speak and brought me to the school from the hospital."

"He's the one, isn't he?"

"What one?"

"Mr. Wonderful."

"I believe that's all the questions we have time for. Thank you very much for coming out. The Mary House staff tells me they have provided the same snack their residents sometimes enjoy. In the back of the room you'll find past-date muffins and coffee. No cream, I'm afraid, but plenty of sugar. Enjoy. Again, thanks for coming."

Chapter 35

The high school cranked up for the new year. Teachers had come early for the two-day training session and to set up their classrooms.

Meg called Tony into her office. "Welcome back."

"Glad to be here."

"Good. You do know the limit for shop classes is twenty, right? You've signed so many special-exception forms, you've got twenty-six juniors and twenty-three seniors. All the new exceptions are girls. What the hell are you doing?"

"All of a sudden girls want to take shop. Great! They didn't sign up at the end of the spring semester, so I had to use the exception forms. Don't you want to train girls for high-paying jobs?"

"Why do you think they're flooding in?"

"Word of mouth from the three girls in summer school?"

"You're so sweet. Dumb but sweet. They want in because you're a stud. They watched you catch Miss DeAngelo, a hundred views apiece. They've seen the press conference video about Mr. Wonderful. They have Mr. Prezzi fantasies."

"That's ridiculous. I'm their father's age. In fact, I was in school with half their fathers."

"Right. A sexy version of daddy."

"You're getting carried away, Meg. It's become acceptable for a girl to be a mechanic. That's all."

"I asked you in here to give two warnings. One – no more special exception enrollments. The shop can't safely accommodate any more students. And you can't responsibly teach any more students. You got that?"

"Yeah, I already knew. I stopped handing out the forms."

"Good. Here's the second warning. Listen hard. All those girls will throw themselves at you. Don't catch one. Don't even think about one. In these situations, men let their dicks do the thinking."

"C'mon, Meg. Give me some credit. I'm not that dumb."

"As I remember, I gave you the slightest encouragement—"

"You mean, you leaned in to show me your boobs. Twice."

"That's what I said. And you came jumping into my bed."

"You practically pushed me into it. And leaped on top."

"You were a great screw. Fuckworthy for sure. On my all-star team. If I can't screw you anymore because I'm your boss, you can't screw any hot little thing either, because you're her teacher. You'd lose your job, and maybe go to jail."

"This is offensive. You really think you have to tell me this?"

"Yes. You'll be facing a parade of seduction attempts. They're too young to be good at it. But they don't have to be—their boobs are younger than mine. I have personal experience of what an easy target you are."

"I've given up the kind of casual sex we had, Meg. It got in the way of my long-term life goal."

"Good luck with your 'long-term life goal.' You picked the one woman who doesn't want to leap into your bed, I mean arms. Now, get out of here. I have work to do."

"Hello! Anybody here?"

"Just a minute." A man emerged from the waiting room's only door. Older, buzz-cut white hair. Broad shoulders and bulging biceps. He reached out to shake Tony's hand—a surprisingly gentle handshake.

"Tony. Tony Prezzi. Good to meet you."

"Karl. Just Karl. Rosa's famous Tony Prezzi? The one chasing her?"

"Right. You mean the Tony Prezzi that Rosa is running away from."

Karl smiled. "Maybe. If that's the way you see it. What can I do for you?"

"That touch therapy you guys do? I want one. Are you a toucher? Therapist? Whatever you call it?"

"Therapist. Yes."

"That's good news. I thought the therapists were all women."

Karl ran his hands over his own flat pecs. "Nope. No breasts. Apparently we're not all women. But let me ask you something. Did you happen to read the lettering beside the door when you came in?"

"I guess not."

"It says, 'Exclusively for female clientele.' Do you think you qualify? Personally, I'm in favor of gender bending."

"No." Damn. His disappointment kicked him in his disqualifying parts. "Does the therapy only work for women?"

"It works for anybody. The city's paranoia about massage parlors means we're only licensed to give therapy to women."

"Sometimes when city regulations create a problem, construction guys will take a job after hours—off the books, if you know what I mean."

Karl kept a poker face. "Yes, I do. The subject has come up before. May I ask why you are so interested?"

To get closer to Rosa? No. Not what Karl would want to hear. "I've had a lot of stress in my life. My wife was murdered. I think my skin sensitivity could use a tune-up."

"Do you mind if I touch you? Your wrist, your forehead. Nothing embarrassing."

"What for?"

Karl touched the inside of his left wrist. One finger, several different spots. "To see if you're right, if your skin could benefit from the therapy."

Tony smiled. "Okay, go ahead and touch. You already have. What if I'd said no?"

Karl touched Tony's forehead, bouncing his finger around. "I'd lose a non-client I'm not allowed to work on. Not a big risk. Yes, you do need the therapy. Stress, mostly. A little intimate contact with desensitized people. Take my word for it, sex is better with two sensitized people. Or three or four. I don't judge."

"I don't have 'intimate contact' with desensitized people. Unless you count me and my hand."

"Too much information. I don't care who or how many."

Those years at the tavern, until he shut down the merry-go-round. "My lifestyle has changed."

"I still don't care who or how many. My only point, you could benefit from the therapy. And it would improve your sex life. Though I hear you—you're not interested in that aspect."

Karl hesitated. "Back when I knew her, anyway, Rosa was quite interested in that aspect. You and she will have to work that out. I'm sure she needs a touch-up, after what I saw on the news. If you see her, tell her she'll get the same discount she got last time."

"Believe me, I won't see her. I mean, she won't see me."

"Sorry to hear it. Maybe she'll come by here. You want the therapy?"

"Definitely."

"Tomorrow night, after we close. Eight o'clock. Okay with you?

"That'll work."

"Come to the back door."

September rushed by. Sensitized skin and an auto shop didn't go together well. He had always worn heavy cotton work shirts and pants. They protected the skin okay. He wore his shirt cuffs unbuttoned as often as possible. His belt chafed the skin underneath. He bumped into tools and parts, or kids bumped them into him. A series of small hurts—nothing he couldn't live with. On the plus side, his workspace was a garden of grease and oil, metals and textures. He could tell a cheap socket wrench from a good one, just by touching the metal.

The shop was crowded, and the presence of the girls changed things. The boys tried to swear less and flirt better. The girls swore a lot and taught the boys how to flirt.

Rosa's Mama was still in his face, inviting him to family events. One phone call, she lectured him. "If you're going to be in the family, you've got to show up and act like family."

"The more often I do, the less chance I'll have with Rosa."

Silence—unusual from Mama. "Okay. Try it your way. Mine isn't working. You picked my most hard-headed kid. If you catch her, good luck living with her."

Tony made supper in the kitchen of his mother's house. He'd lived there alone since she moved in with her boyfriend, but he still thought of it as her house. Ziti with sauce from a jar and meatballs from the supermarket—an embarrassment. He knew how to cook. Italian men knew how to cook. But why bother? It was just him.

His phone rang more than usual—unfamiliar caller IDs, the kind of junk calls he didn't answer. Finally, a real person called. Jojo. "Do you watch NY-1?"

"Not any more. The local weather's on my cell. I watch it when there's some big news happening. Who cares what the politicians are saying about each other? Twenty-four hours of local news a day. Like a recipe for depression."

"You'll watch it today. Rosa gave a press conference. They have a story about it, repeated every hour. Check it out. Call me when you've seen it."

Instead of sitting at the kitchen table, he poured a glass of wine and ate his pasta in front of the living-room TV.

An anchor reminded viewers that Rosa DeAngelo—Tony sat up in his chair—was the battered woman who'd given the graduation speech at her high school. He introduced the reporter who'd attended the press conference. She said she was at Mary House women's shelter in the Bowery, and went to the tape. Edited snippets appeared. Rosa talked about why she gave the graduation speech even though she was so badly injured. Some stats about spousal abuse. The reporter repeated her name and her live broadcast location. The anchor said, "Quite a woman. In other news...."

She was quite a woman, but the station didn't show anything he hadn't heard Rosa talk about before. Disappointed, he called Jojo and said, "I was glad to see her, but the clips weren't much."

"Lee found the whole press conference on YouTube. Want to come watch it with us?"

Tony ate the last meatball, gulped down the wine, and left the remaining ziti in the bowl. He jogged the seven blocks in five minutes and knocked on Lee and Jojo's door.

At the end of the press conference, Rosa told everybody Tony's name and where he worked.

Both women loved "Mr. Wonderful." Lee called him that ten times in five minutes. "Well, Mr. Wonderful, what did you think?"

He had put his cell on vibrate, because it kept ringing while they watched the press conference. "What I think...." The phone vibrated again. "I think she told the world who I am, then some reporter came out with that Mr. Wonderful BS, and now my phone won't stop buzzing. I bet all these calls are reporters. What do I say?"

Jojo tapped some wine from the box in her refrigerator and gave him a glass. "If you let any reporter assume you are her family-chosen fiancé, you'll be in more trouble with Rosa than you already are."

"Maybe I should just say no comment."

Lee interrupted her Googling of his name. "That would mean, 'Yes. I'm Mr. Wonderful.' Like people think pleading the Fifth means, 'Yes, I'm guilty.' By the way, folks are already writing comments about whether or not you are Mr. Wonderful. Two of them say they have reason to know, and you are him. Anybody who knows the DeAngelos knows you are the designated fiancé."

Jojo snickered. "Maybe they're your tavern women telling the world they have reason to know you're wonderful."

In the end, they decided on, "There must be many thousands of wonderful people all over the city. I'm flattered that a reporter would say I'm one of them. Thank you for asking." He should keep repeating, "I'm flattered…," until the reporter gave up.

He answered his phone from then on, repeating his magic words. He wasn't important enough for reporters to seek him out in person. It took twenty-four hours for his fifteen minutes of fame to run out.

He thought his life had returned to normal.

At mid-term, students stood at workbenches and sat at desks. He required them to write up their work so far—repairing exhaust, suspension, and brake systems. Mr. Forte's similar assignments had taught him how to write. He hadn't been interested enough in English or History to bother with those classes, but Auto Shop was different.

This writing assignment was not a test. He encouraged his students to help each other. He was teaching the kids how to write a memo to a boss, Mr. Prezzi, telling him what they'd done.

He also was writing, filling out paperwork for the mid-term reports. The shop went silent. Looking up, he noticed students had stopped talking to stare at the open garage door. He swiveled his stool to see what was so interesting.

In the doorway stood a short young woman wearing boots, tight jeans, and a white top. Loose and blowing around in the doorway's breeze, the top emphasized her build, though the contrast between her chest and her tiny frame needed no emphasis. Blond hair and blue eyes highlighted a face made of taut planes, each with its own wintry mix of white and pink. Italians came in all shapes and colors, but one glance told him this woman was no Italian.

She waited in the doorway. Tony tensed his chest and shoulders to bulk up his muscles and strode toward her.

"Mr. Prezzi? My name is Tatyana Kozlova. I'm putting together an in-depth portrait of Rosa DeAngelo for *The New Yorker*. Nothing so shallow as 'are you or aren't you wonderful.'"

"There must be many thousands of wonderful people all over the city. I'm flattered that—"

"'A reporter would say I'm one of them. Thank you for asking.' That was a smart answer, Mr. Prezzi. But I am not asking if you are Mr. Wonderful. This morning I talked to Rosa's mother and her older sister, Agata. I need to talk to you and her friend, Jojo. And her ex-husband. Then I'll go on to learn about this neighborhood, and about Rex-Aid, both her store here and the headquarters in Connecticut. Finally, when I know enough, I'll talk to Rosa. That's the kind of story I will write—background and foreground. Complete."

She had to talk to that stroonz DiFalco? "That's a lot to do. How much time do you have to write this?"

"Till it's done, Mr. Prezzi, till it's done. Can we make an appointment to talk? Perhaps after you get off work?"

She spoke foreign-accented New Yawkuh, had a typical from-somewhere-else New Yorker name, and her eyes were the bluest blue he'd ever seen. She held his attention, even though she didn't sound or look anything like Rosa. "How about five o'clock? At the piz…"

No. Better not to be seen eating with her in the neighborhood. Why not? He took a second to figure it out. Rosa. Would it be disloyal to eat with this little blond, so unlike Rosa yet so distracting?

For certain, dinner with this woman was going to happen. Better not to think too hard about loyalty. Still, he didn't want Mama to hear about it. He agreed to meet Ta-something-na at the Greek place on the South Shore.

Chapter 36

Every day, the folding metal chair was hard on Rosa's butt, the discussion hard on her conscience. Joey had hit her a few times. Lou had whipped her once. She was a battered woman. Most of St. Rita's other residents, even the rich ones, had been kicked and punched and raped so often, from such a young age, their spirits had tried to die. They had battered souls.

She did not belong there, taking up a chair. Other women had to rebuild a self and find a place in the world—literally. A home, a job, a new network of friends and family. They were at St. Rita's because they had no other safe place to be. Rosa had a home and a family to go live with. Her "abuse?" Her mama's idea of help was to pair her up with a guy whose only fault might be his ridiculous infatuation.

Even Jojo, her most trusted friend, said Tony was, "a good one—sincere, respecting of women, and straight women think he's hot."

Mary's reason for bringing her here—to hide from him? Every group meeting, she grew more embarrassed. She couldn't talk. She had little insight to share, and if she told of her so-called problems, the other women would laugh themselves off their chairs.

One of her worries, maronna mía, was whether she was really going to get two million dollars, and when, and what to do with it. Her other big problem was should she get her skin resensitized yet, or would Birgit say she should wait until her wounds were better healed. She laughed. Everybody looked at her. She turned carmine and ducked her head, waving off their attention. Women sometimes had private reactions to what was said in the group, and their privacy was respected. Attention turned back to the woman talking.

One afternoon, after a terrible story from a woman whose father beat and raped her until she was old enough for other men to beat and rape her, Rosa sought out Mary. She was sitting in her tiny office on its only chair, adding up columns of numbers without a calculator.

Rosa leaned against the desk and waited for her to finish a column. "Mary… I can't stay here. We're full. You must have some woman who needs St. Rita's more than I do."

"You learning here?"

"Yes, but that's not the point."

Mary wrapped her fingers around Rosa's wrist. "Why not? You don't have things to learn?"

Rosa looked down at her wrist and moved it a little. Mary did not let go. "But I'm taking up a bed."

"So what. I'm taking up a bed. Nobody's hit or raped me since I joined the order. I was sixteen."

Did Mary just say she was raped and abused when she was young? Rosa was still working on that when Mary spoke again.

"I've been a Sister for seventy-one years. Go ahead. Do the math."

"You're eighty-seven?"

"Yes. Unbelievable, isn't it? That's what I think—how can this be? We founded St. Rita's in 1967. Three Sisters and me. We were officially a convent back then, a convent that took in battered women. Two Sisters left the order. Together, if you know what I mean. It was the sixties. Then my other friend passed. A long time back. It's been just me, I've been busy and all of a sudden," she snapped her fingers, "I'm eighty-seven."

"What are you doing? Recruiting your successor? I'm not going to be a nun. I don't even think I believe in God."

"The best Sisters are those willing to wrestle with their belief. But, no. A couple of my graduate volunteers might step up when I'm done. I think I've worked out okay, but our women don't need any old nun. They need someone who understands their hurt, their sorrow, their pain. Only if she knows where they are can she help them move forward."

Mary still clutched Rosa's wrist. Rosa gave it a tentative pull. No.

"Only a graduate can understand all that. I hope you intend to become a graduate."

"That's what I said in the beginning. I don't belong here."

"I assure you. You belong here. But you have to truly be here. Share yourself in the group. You're the one with all the publicity. You told the world, but you won't talk to women who need you."

"I feel silly. They've endured so much—"

"If you share, your belief you don't deserve their help will disappear. Right then. Take that step and you're on the road to becoming a graduate. Then you can do what we need you to do—touch, and train."

"I'm a trainer, but I can't train here. I don't know anything useful to these women."

"You do. You're not ready to see what you have to offer. And you're not ready to graduate. When you see, you'll be ready." Mary let go of Rosa's wrist, and turned back to her columns of numbers.

Rosa stumbled to the office doorway. She held onto the door jamb and looked back. Mary stopped moving her lips, wrote a total with her pencil, and moved on to the next column.

Chapter 37

Tatyana and he had talked for two hours. Or rather, he'd talked while she recorded him and ate. She daintily devoured the Greek lasagna, pasticcio, plus a large Greek salad. Then the remaining half of his salad. After three cups of coffee, she was hungry again and convinced him to split a piece of cheesecake. She couldn't weigh more than a hundred pounds, yet she put more food inside than he could at two hundred.

Whenever his talk tailed off, she put down her fork and gently asked another personal question. And he'd answer it. To a writer with her digital recorder visible on the table between them, he talked about Rosa-feelings he'd never told anyone before.

He'd talked of her looks. And he'd explained about watching her play basketball. Anyone who knew the game could watch a player, subtract out the purely basketball aspect of her moves, and see what was left—her personality, her character, her intelligence. When Rosa was fifteen and Tony was twenty, he fell in love with her strong, intelligent character. And her looks.

From his love of Rosa, he discovered he liked strong women. Lucia was unbelievably strong. He loved her so hard, part of him followed her when she died.

Meg intimidated most of the faculty, but Tony liked her strength and she knew it. He liked Jojo, who was tough and handsome, but....

The tavern women, he'd realized during this interview—yes, he had told Tatyana about the tavern women—may have pitied him or wanted him, but none had strength in her core. If one had a goal and sought it, she wouldn't have been a tavern woman.

Touch

After the cheesecake, which they ate by passing a desert fork back and forth, she asked him about Lou.

"I only met him the one time, after we won the first game in the Holiday Tournament. I was disappointed because I thought Rosa would be alone, and I was distracted because I had to go talk with my girls. His hands were disfigured. He'd obviously survived pain. I thought he was strong."

"Stronger than you? Like with Joey DiFalco earlier, did you think you'd lost Rosa to him?"

"It sounds strange to hear you say Joey's name without "that stroonz" in front of it, like a title he earned."

"Sorry. I'm Russian, not Italian."

"That shit, Joey DiFalco."

"Oh, you mean, that derr'mo, Joey DiFalco. Why didn't you say so? Let's not forget the question. It was about Lou Bates. Did you think you had lost Rosa to him?"

"At first I did. Lee and Jojo convinced me I could get her back from him if I went all out. I did, but it was too late. She went home with him and he turned into a monster."

"What was the attraction, do you think? Why was she so interested? His powerful job?"

"I don't think so. I couldn't figure it out for the longest time. Then I got the same touch therapy she had, where our skin is super-sensitized. I can see the attraction of skin textures. They have a sensuality that people can't feel if they are just looking at the scars, or rubbing against them with a dulled-out sense of touch. She told Jojo she longed to rub her skin against his. I believe it."

"You got this treatment? A therapy, you called it."

"Yeah. Touch therapy. Technically, whole-body skin resensitization therapy. It's supposed to be big in Europe."

"What difference does it make? Show me."

Show her? "Do you mind if I touch your skin? Nothing embarrassing – a wrist and your forehead."

"Okay. What good will that…?"

He rubbed his fingers back and forth on the underside of her wrist. He wasn't assessing her like a therapist, tapping with his fingertips. He was enjoying the feel of her skin. He stroked her forehead, back and forth from one temple to the other, two times. He could feel her tiny worry lines ease away. He swept his fingers back and forth a third time, slowly.

Her skin was polished. Pores too tiny to feel, no micro unevenness from dead skin cells. He had never felt skin like it.

He didn't say anything. He was occupied, appreciating what he'd just felt.

She put her elbow on the table, turned the underside of her wrist toward him, and shook it. He noticed her lowered eyes, looking at him from under her lashes.

How to say it? "You know how paint has porosity? Like on car bodies? Pollution and moisture gets in the little pores and the paint begins to shed tiny particles and corrode. You rub your hand on a car like that and you can feel the roughness even if you can't see it."

Her hand was still up in the air, palm outward. He rubbed her wrist again, fighting an urge to rub down to her elbow. He put his hand back in his lap. "But if a car is polished smooth like glass, the pores fill in and the paint is leveled. Your skin is polished. I've never felt any skin like it. Not just your forehead, like you paid a spa to polish your face, but the underside of your wrist, too."

"I'm like a polished car? Thank you. I think."

He looked at his watch. It was only eight, but they'd been there since five. He had to get up and move his legs. And he had drunk a lot of coffee. He excused himself.

When he got back, she had paid the bill and seemed ready to leave. The evening was over. Relief and regret skirmished in his mind.

Outside in the parking lot, he discovered she drove a little piece of Korean crap that GM used to sell as a pretend Chevy. He tried to understand. She was tiny—why should she need a normal-sized car? But still, that ready-to-rust piece of tin?

Standing next to her car, she pawed through her purse to find her keys. "We have about one hour left to wind up the interview. Do you want to find a place to finish it tonight, or get together another time?"

Hurray. "Tonight. If that's okay with you."

"Let's go for it."

They decided Tony would lead and she'd follow. He knew a couple of bars on the South Shore. Tatyana admired his hulking 4Runner, or did a good job of faking it. Then she slid into her own car and followed him to a bar.

They walked in, listened for a second, and walked out. The combined noise of canned eighties music and drunken patrons made it impossible to hear each other, let alone record his words.

She stood by her car, pawing through her purse again. The keys hadn't been in the thing a full minute and they'd already hidden themselves. Tony had a *déjà vu* from his marriage—all the times he stood next to Lucia as she felt for something in her purse and peered into its darkness.

She came up with her keys. "All the bars will be too loud. Are you sure you want to do this tonight?"

"If we can."

"Maybe we can just sit in your car or truck or whatever it is. The last part of the interview has some of the more sensitive questions—it's standard interviewing procedure to save them for last—so maybe it will be for the best if we aren't sitting across a tiny table looking each other in the eyes."

He had a vision of an old movie, two heads snuggled close on the bench seat of a car from the fifties, silhouetted in the moonlight. "All right."

She headed for his car.

"Not here. Follow me again. We'll go over to one of the parking lots along the shore. We can look at the water instead of the drunks stumbling outside to smoke."

Five minutes later, her car parked next to his, she clambered up into his passenger seat. She set up her recorder on the dashboard under the palm cross hanging from his rearview mirror. Looking at the cross, she said "Just a minute," and climbed back down. She reached into her car, came up with something, and stepped up into her seat. Showing him her own palm cross, she hung it from the mirror next to his. It had four equal arms, beautifully decorated with a pattern of narrow palm strips intricately stitched together.

"It's beautiful. Amazing." Her people had a car cross just like his people, but the crosses were so different.

"The Russian version. My Mama and my Tetya spend days making them for the family. It takes Mama almost two hours to make just one. My Aunt's are fussier and she takes longer."

Tony's Mama made his. A few days after Palm Sunday, his Mama showed up at the house, supervised him as he took last year's crosses off their nails and hung the new ones, one in the living room over the front door, one at the head of his bed, and one at the head of hers, pretending she still slept in it. She gave him a smaller one for his car mirror, kissed him, and walked back to the house where she actually lived.

He had driven Tatyana to a parking lot off the road rimming the Eastern Shore of the Island. They looked out across New York's outer harbor to the tip of Brooklyn, to the lights of Coney Island. Just beyond stood the apartment buildings of Brighton Beach, where Tatyana and most of the City's Russians lived.

He turned the car off. It was a warm night for late November—no need for the car's heater. He sat relaxed, happy with the view, with his car, with a pretty girl in the passenger seat.

"Help me understand this 'Mr. Wonderful' business. I get one meaning, that Rosa was being ironic about her family's view of you. I can tell there's at least one other meaning. Rosa's mother and sister hinted at it, but I'd like to hear your take."

"I can't help much, because my take is, 'It's all bullshit.'"

"You're right. Not much help. What's 'all bullshit?'"

"The whole idea. Some silly rumors...."

"About what?"

He took a pen out of his workshirt pocket, clicked it on and off, then put it back. "About my supposed...you know...in bed."

"You mean 'kiss and tell?' Somebody's been giving you a lover score? That's not right. Think if you were a woman and men talked about you like that."

A good way to look at it. Only a no-class asshole would do that. Those fucking tavern women. Fucking tavern women—he gave a laugh. "Remember the tavern woman?"

"Uh-huh."

"By definition, to be a tavern woman means to sometimes drink too much. Then, I guess they talked about me. I don't know how it happened. Ask them."

"What do you guess they said about you?'

"This whole interview would have gone easier if we'd have found a bar and had a few beers. I guess they said I was worth spending the night with."

"And...."

"I have to spell it out for you? They liked the way I do it."

"What do you think they liked?"

"I don't know. I don't analyze it. Maybe I should give you a demonstration." Tony couldn't believe he'd said that. Like the guys whose idea of seduction was, "Wanna fuck?"

"Sounds lovely. Maybe some other time. Let's assume I know how it works in general, the physics and all. Are they talking about, let me see, physical dimensions?"

"Not that anyone ever mentioned. Wait—why are we talking about this?"

"You're right. Sorry. But the 'Mr. Wonderful' topic is not going away. We can discuss it at a later time, if you want, but—"

"I have to make her happy. The only thing that turns me on is a turned-on woman. I can't even start my engine unless she's already racing down the track, even crossing the finish line. If I help, she can race and finish as many times as she wants. I can't. So why not give her a warm-up run? Satisfied?"

She wiggled herself deeper into her seat. "If you mean, does that answer my question, yes. Well, one more question, if you don't mind. What makes you so confident you can 'get her racing down the track' if you're not there with her? How does she 'make love' if her lover is still back on the starting line?"

"Partly instinct. Every woman is different. Mostly the secret weapon." Tony puckered his lips and sucked in his cheeks. He opened his mouth with a resounding smack.

She turned away and imitated him with her mouth aimed toward the windshield. "That's it? A kiss? That's the secret weapon?"

"It's not what you do. It's where you do it. A French kiss is great. A French kiss thirty inches south is even greater. Nobody told me until it was too late, maybe because I didn't have a father, but it turns out Italian men don't do that. It's my favorite thing in the whole bedroom. Second favorite."

He jerked up straight in his seat. "I can't believe I said that on your recorder thing. End of discussion on this topic."

"No problem. 'Asked and answered,' as the courtroom lawyers say on TV."

Tatyana sat and leafed through her reporter's notebook, apparently

205

not finding what she was looking for.

Tony rose uncomfortably against the part of his pants tightened by his belt. He was happy to sit in his seat calming down until she found something in the notebook. He blushed as he thought back over what he'd said. He rewound the interview in his head until he came to, "He couldn't start his engine unless she's already racing...."

He peeked over at Tatyana. She was randomly rifling through her notebook. Not looking for anything at all. He had liked her since she appeared in his shop door. She was ready, or at least she could be, if he tried.

But the 4Runner had a wide console barrier between the seats. And she had shared nothing about herself. And she seemed vulnerable. His urge to protect her fought and defeated his urge to have her. He didn't even reach across and touch her shoulder. He sat there, looking at the water, his fingers resting on the bottom of the steering wheel, and waited until she was ready to continue.

A half hour passed in the two minutes before she spoke. "Thank you. Mr. Wonderful is a gentleman. You forgot to mention that. It's probably as important as...the other."

Tony stopped looking at the water and looked at her face. "You okay?"

"Yes, thanks. There's only one more topic, and we'll be done. I won't bother you any more after this."

She would be gone. Like Rosa was gone. Maybe he should have touched her shoulder. He sat up straight in his seat and turned toward her. "Go ahead."

"What's your family situation? Where do you live? How come the only family I hear about is the DeAngelos?"

"I live in the house where I grew up. I moved back there when my wife died. My Mama doesn't live there anymore. She moved in with a boyfriend when she was in her sixties. I have an older sister who moved to Alaska as soon as she got out of high school. I had a younger sister, but she died when she was two—something to do with her heart. I was five. I missed her."

He moved his fingers up the steering wheel and gripped it hard. "I had a drunk for a father who died on his construction job. He stumbled over something and fell from the fourth level. I was thirteen and my sister was seventeen. He used to stop at his bar on the way home from work and pass out in front of our TV. There wasn't a whole lot of mourning at his wake, even from Mama."

A blue light started to blink on her recorder. Tatyana took it off the dashboard. "Isn't that always the way. You're five minutes from being done and the battery runs out."

She found another battery in her purse and got her recorder working again. "What about your big family? Grandparents, uncles, like that."

"My Nona died a few years back, my grandfather when I was young. My Mama and Papa both have sisters in the City, but Papa was the black sheep of his family. He moved Mama from the Bronx to here before I was born, and it's a long way north to the Bronx where her family lives, so we never saw them much. Growing up, it was just us."

"Was it hard, just the four of you, and then just you and your Mama?"

"I guess so. My parents used to fight a lot. They'd go in their bedroom and fight, my father yelling in Italian, and my mother loud too, trying to get him to stop. She would eventually shut up. When I was old enough, I thought that was how they worked themselves up to do it. I still think that. Weird."

He talked in a low monotone, so low Tatyana had to adjust the recorder's volume. He must still feel bad about this. He was surprised, because it was so long ago. "Then, when my sister got to be a teenager, she started fighting with my mother. Nothing loud and Italian, like my parents, but she seemed angry at Mama all the time. I think that's why she moved to Alaska. Papa was dead and she didn't get along with Mama. I was a kid. I don't really know why she left."

"You must have some idea."

"No. We talk on the phone—once a year, maybe—but she never talks about that."

"And later. Just you and your mama."

"After my sister left, Mama was quieter. The house was calmer. We got along fine. We still do. She went to work at a dry cleaner, doing the sewing. Repairs, alterations. I had to grow up and be the man of the family when I was only a kid. I got lousy grades, and I'm not that stupid, so maybe I was affected.... But I was good at basketball, and then Mr. Forte.... He was like a father. He straightened me out.

I got a good job. With Mama's and my jobs, money stopped being a problem."

He had his pen out of his pocket again, clicking it open and closed, open and closed, open and closed. "Mama and Lucia liked each other. When Lucia.... I moved back home and, some ways, it was like I never left."

She seemed to wait for him to keep talking, but he'd run out of things to say. She turned off her recorder and dropped it in her purse. "Thank you. For being so cooperative. For...everything."

His hand was on the console. She put her tiny hand on top of it and gave it a squeeze. She opened her door.

He leaped out his side and ran around to open her car door for her, but by the time he got there, she was already sliding into her driver's seat. She shut her door and turned on the engine—no trouble finding her keys this time. Her engine made its tinny rattle. He could hear the clickety-clack of mistimed valves.

She slid down her window.

He bent down to say, more in desperation than in hope. "When that engine loses more power, and it will soon, bring it by our shop and the kids and I will fix it for you."

She said, "You're sweet," and gave him a quick bacit' on his cheek. She drove away, the noise of the tiny engine drowned out by the sound of her tires running over the gravel.

He watched her until she was out of sight and stepped up into his car. Leaning forward to turn his key, he noticed the fancy Russian cross hanging next to his. He made a fist and tugged down an imaginary bell-rope. Yes!

Chapter 38

The woman was tall and model-thin, on the older end of middle-aged. She lived on the Upper West Side and dressed like money. Two days into her stay at St. Rita's, she changed Rosa's life.

In group, she stood up to talk, something nobody else had ever done.

"Roland didn't hate me. He said he loved me, over and over, and I believe he did. He regretted hurting me. He said he was sorry every time, and I believe he was. Sometimes he was so distraught I comforted him rather than the other way around. He wanted to control everything in his life. He couldn't. But I was the biggest thing in his life and he could control me."

She stood erect and wore the same flat smile she'd worn since she arrived, but liquid tracked down her cheeks, as if her eyes leaked but she didn't notice. "He intimidated me, made me nervous—at first because he was older and more accomplished than I was. After a while, when I had a job and babies who loved me, I wasn't so intimidated. Until he hit me. Unpredictably, out of nowhere. Whenever he had trouble with some part of his life, he'd do it again. He only hit me every once in a while, but I was afraid all the time. I became a scared person. I lost my job. I had no way to get out and nowhere to go. He controlled me totally, and he loved me for it. I despised myself. Thank you for listening."

She sat down. Some women applauded.

Rosa stood up like she'd done. "Thank you. I finally know why my husband hit me. He was in control of everything. He owned his business, took orders from no one. He chose me to love him when

I was just fifteen. He was so strong and so confident. When I was eighteen, he married me and I was his. We wanted children and he couldn't make me pregnant. He had weak sperm. He couldn't control his own testicles. Every month, he punched a hole in the wall. He never hit me, but I was afraid. Then one month, he punched me instead of the wall. I tip-toed around our tiny apartment, hoping he wouldn't notice me. One time, he hit me so hard he broke my jaw and sliced my teeth through my cheek. I walked home to Mama's house and she called 911. I went to the hospital and I never went back to him. Thank you for listening."

Rosa bent her knees to sit, then stood straight again. "For years I was afraid to be noticed and stayed in the same crappy job. Finally I let people notice me and got promoted, twice. I met a man who was powerful and pleasant, who'd been through hell and survived. I admired him. On our first real date, I did something he didn't like. He had no control over me, because it was our first date, so he tied me to his house with a piece of rope. That rope was his control. He whipped me and I couldn't escape. He whipped me until I was unconscious and almost dead. He controlled me with that little piece of bloody rope. I'm going to get it somehow and keep it—to remind myself to never fall for a man with a rope. Thank you for listening."

She sat down.

"How do you find someone to love you, if you've been beat up? Especially if you've been beaten by the next man, too?" Rosa looked to Mary for approval.

"That's your training topic? What are your answers to finding love? Write that up and you'd sell a million copies. Never mind. Go ahead."

Rosa took a deep breath. "Number one. We can't be defensive, fighting to keep from giving any control away. The regular guys will pick up the vibes and run. Abusive guys will see the weakness behind the walls and jump right over. Then we're back in the same trouble again. I should know. Number two—"

"How many?"

"Well, eight so far."

"Good, good. Can you explain number one, let them talk about it until the women really get it?"

"I think so. That's what a trainer is supposed to do."

"Then I guess you're graduated."

Graduated or kicked out? Where was she going to live? How was she going to find a job? "Graduation makes me nervous. What's it mean, really?"

"We have a little party, like a birthday, cake for the kiddies. Then you move out, give your bed to some desperate woman like you wanted, and come back here as a volunteer trainer. How about helping women bring their abused sense of touch back up to snuff? You still up for that?"

"I have to get the therapy again myself. And probably more training as a therapist. I have to get a job, too. And a place to live. How do I train the women here when I have to work?"

"Hundreds of women have graduated from here and got a job, a place to live. Pray, if you're so inclined. You're smart, you have skills and experience. Think of the women who haven't worked since their kids were born. You'll get a job. We'll work the training around your schedule. It would be best if you could get a regular Monday-to-Friday job and come here on Saturdays. The group doesn't meet on weekends."

Mary shuffled through the clutter on her desk until she found a lined pad. She gave it to Rosa. "Here. Make a list."

She started to dictate. "Get the new therapy. Get a job – nothing fancy at first. Just a job. Maybe like you had at Rex-Aid, only CVS or somewhere. Find a cheap place to live—reconcile with your mother and live there."

"What?"

"You have family, right here in the city. You have a mother who loves you. A lot of our women have neither. Love her back. Stand up for yourself. Don't let mama or anyone push you around. But love your family back. You need them and they are trying to help."

She pointed at the pad. "I'm dispensing wisdom here. Take notes. Decide what help you need and ask for it—starting with a free place to live. If you don't ask for the help you need, your mama will imagine ways she can help, and you don't want her doing that."

That's for sure.

"In my experience— I have a lot—sometimes reconciling with family can be the easiest thing on a graduating woman's list. Not always. Depends on the family, but usually it's easy. Ask for help. Explain the help you need. And your mama will love you for giving her a chance to help, instead of fighting about it."

"What about my supposed fiancé?"

"I have work to do. You finish your training list. See if it stays at eight or if you come up with more. We'll talk about that. And we'll talk about your marriage problem."

Her marriage problem? Strange way to put it. No marriage, no problem. Period.

Rosa stood next to a teenage girl with a white cast covering the brown skin on her broken nose. Pilar had—bravely, Rosa thought—painted the end of the cast red. She had told the children she was a clown staying at St. Rita's on vacation. The padding under her shirt was also part of the clown outfit.

Rosa stood in her raglan-sleeve dress, shimmery material and a shade of off-white violet. Her fellow graduate wore blue jeans and a maternity top. Rosa was going home to her family. Pilar was going to a room Tessa's step-father had built in the basement of their house. He built it to play scopa in, but the card game never moved to his house and the room had filled with retired things. Paola and Tessa had cleared it out for Pilar, who would become perhaps the only PR in the neighborhood.

Mary gave them each their choice of a gift—either rosary beads or a circle of plain prayer beads. Or maybe they were worry beads. Rosa didn't know the difference.

Rosa already had two rosary beads, one from confirmation and one her grandmother left when she died. She had no worry beads, but she didn't dare tell Sister Mary she wanted the non-Catholic version. She received a third Rosary. Her fellow graduate wasn't Catholic, "wasn't anything," and had told Rosa, "I wish I was something. Especially now." Mary gave her rosary beads. Maybe the beads were a start, if somebody taught her how to use them.

Then the promised cake, the kids shrieking around, the women hugging her, some of them tearful.

Mary announced, "Rosa will be our volunteer trainer from now on. She will be back to start next week. Saturdays like today, we hope. We'll see her often. She'll also give therapy to help cure traumatized skin. Not next week, but starting soon."

A St. Rita's grad in an old mini-van picked them both up. Their destinations weren't more than four blocks apart. The girl had a paper bag for luggage, enough to hold another outfit, maybe. Rosa had one trash bag for her dresses and chemises, each carefully rolled up to minimize wrinkles, and a smaller trash bag for her get-well cards and the hospital junk she'd accumulated when she was there.

As they drove to Mama's house, Christmas lights lined the street because it was already past Thanksgiving. Nearing Mama's they heard a party. Mama's house had no front yard, just a door on the sidewalk, but a dozen of Rosa's relatives stood on the sidewalk, chatting and smoking.

"A party? How did they know I would come home today?"

The driver shrugged.

"Pilar, you might as well come with me. Tessa and Paola will be at the party."

The girl picked up her paper bag and helped Rosa with one of her trash bags. The folks on the sidewalk mobbed Rosa and greeted Pilar. Two cousins, sons of Mama's baby brother, took the three bags and rushed the women into the house.

"Mama DeAngelo, Mama DeAngelo! Rosa's home!"

Mama was in the kitchen, naturally, and Rosa squeezed into the room to give Mama a hug. Mama broke up as she hugged Rosa, laughing and blubbering at the same time. Rosa cried too, feeling her buried affection for her conniving, caring Mama.

An aunt got up from the kitchen table, dragging her daughter out of her chair too, to make room for Rosa and Pilar. Pasta and sausage, braggiol', tripe, salad with olive oil and plain red-wine vinegar, eggplant parmesan on hamburger rolls, plates piled too high to eat it all. More women got up from the table so Tessa and Paola could meet Pilar and talk about her room and her soon-to-be baby and who might have maternity clothes to lend.

Pilar smoked, so she got up after eating to go out front. Out of the corner of her eye, Rosa saw a young cousin carry a folding chair from the living room out the front door, for the pretty teen-age incint' with the clown nose.

Chatting with the other women at the table, Rosa learned the party was for the December birthdays, who always got cheated by Christmas, and for Aggie's youngest daughter, who'd graduated cosmetology school. Nobody had any idea Rosa was leaving St. Rita's that day, or expected she'd come stay at Mama's house.

Rosa made the rounds of the living room and the back yard. She checked out the front sidewalk, where two young men squatted down to chat with Pilar, whose smile showed she enjoyed either the cigarette or the attention. Rosa climbed down the crude stairs to the basement where Papa and the men played nickel-and-dime scopa. She squeezed around the table to hug each one, so they wouldn't have to all greet her at once and interrupt their game. Men pinched her cheek, and told her the scar "wasn't so bad." No woman had mentioned it, as if it would go away if they pretended not to see it.

As she passed through every space, she kept her eye out for Tony, because she'd heard that he came to family parties as her supposed fiancé. She didn't run across him. Too bad, because she wanted to ask him if he'd go to the cops in Connecticut and get her rope. Tony was the only one who'd been there. He knew the rope and he knew the cops. And if she asked, he'd do her the favor.

She ran into Aggie holding her grand-son. Rosa stood next to her, surveying the activity in the back yard. Out of the side of her mouth, she said, "If you tell anybody I asked you this, I'll never speak to you again."

Aggie turned toward her. "Sounds juicy. Prometto. Cross my heart and hope to die."

"Where's Tony? I thought Mama declared him family."

"What I hear, he told Mama that acting like your fiancé hurt his chances with you. Mama admitted you're such a stubborn gabbadost' he was probably right. So he didn't come. And now you're asking for him. I can't believe I promised not to tell Mama. Let me tell her. Pleeease."

"Forget it times three. Me not talking to you will the least of your problems. I'll give you the Eye so bad, you'll have to round up a dozen magas to break the spell."

"Oooh. I don't think there are a dozen magas left in the City. Okay, you win. But you know Mama's going to find out somehow. People have seen you looking around. Even if they don't know anything, they'll tell Mama about it, and she'll decide you were looking for Tony. If that happens, I'm innocent. Send your eye somewhere else."

"Shit. You're right. I can't even go up to my room and pretend to rest. There are a half dozen boys up there playing video games."

Aggie kept her promise not to tell Mama. She told her husband Al, who told whoever, who told whoever else, who told Mama. Rosa went upstairs, kicked the brats out of her old room, and locked the door.

Rosa arranged the folding chairs in a U instead of the group-time O. The open end faced Rosa and her two signs taped to a wall.

"Remember the goal." She held up a piece of paper with the goal written on it. *Get past our defensive fear and learn to love again.* Sticking tape to it, she slapped it against the wall.

Rosa walked over to one poster. She had written a list of things to look for when they met a man, long before any abuse.

"*Potential abusers are often: Angry, Blaming, Hurtful, Entitled, Isolating, Lying, Pushy, Resentful, Superior, Unrealistic.*"

She explained each one: Angry at the world, blaming of people in his past, hurtful in sex or life (supposedly in fun, at first), entitled to his demands, isolating you from friends and family (for instance, by moving you away to a far part of the city), resentful of his life situation, pushing you to move the relationship faster than you want.

She walked over to the other sheet of paper. On it, she'd put the words:

We feel: Afraid, Doubtful, Hurried, Invaded, Nervous.

"Once we're recovered and stop fearing every man, our feelings will come out, the results of his attitudes. We will have to learn to trust these feelings whenever they come up, no matter how hard a man tries to sweet-talk them away."

She walked away from the wall and stood at the mouth of the U. "You each have a pad. We all need to take some time to write, 'I felt—whatever word from our list—when he acted—whatever word from his list.' Then jot down something that will remind you of times when you felt that way. At the end of the session, you can share an incident if you like, but these notes are for each of us, not necessarily the whole group."

Rosa sat down in an empty chair and began to write in her pad.

After a while, she lifted her pencil off the paper and looked around. Many of the women were looking around as well. Two possibilities. They were thinking hard, or the exercise was so boring they gave up on it. Rosa hoped for the first.

She herself was pondering a future question, none from the past. How far along was she in her goal to, "get past my defensive fear, learn to love again?" Progressed enough to spend time with Tony, to know him better, to compare him against the bad-guy list?

Rosa refused Birgit's offer give her the therapy for free again. She had a little money left, and she discovered they were living illegally in what used to be their back office, against the shopping center's commercial zoning. The subject came up because stacks of storage boxes had appeared in the therapy room since the last time Rosa was there.

"We don't make enough to pay the rent here and rent an apartment too. Still, compared to the squatter's digs in Copenhagen, this is luxury."

She showed Rosa the back office. "Hot plate and mini-fridge, plus a little desk where we can eat, and the foldaway bed. It's small, especially for the room my kollasal mand takes up, but I'd rather sleep on a small bed with Karl than on a therapy table without him. Of course, we have the deluxe baths and the washer-dryer we've always had."

It took Karl and Birgit three therapies to get Rosa back to where she was before the whipping. As gently as they twist-touched along the track of each scar, the pain eventually became unbearable. They had to quit, wait at least three or four days, and do it again. And again. Then they followed up on that first lesson so long ago, teaching her to be a therapist.

She was partly trained when she got a phone call.

"You up to snuff yet? With that touch thing? When you going to start? Our women need you."

"I could do a couple people each Saturday after the training, but that wouldn't help much. I can't go back and forth to the Bronx every day. It's hours each way."

"You got a job?"

"Not yet. Still looking." One minute on the phone and Rosa was talking like her. With her experience, Rosa could walk into a Walgreens and be a drugstore clerk any day she wanted, but she hoped to be some kind of a trainer.

"Want one?"

"What do you mean? Doing what?"

"We get interns from the Dorothy Day School of Social Service. Up here at Fordham University. Jesuit joint. Tell you the truth, when they're in session, we're wading through interns. They take care of the children each day. During group. You know."

"Interns? You want me to be one? Clear them out of the way so you can walk around? What?"

"More like clear them out of the way. Babysit them, but they call it training."

"Babysit them?" God, Rosa wished Mary would use an extra few words. You'd think they cost money.

"If you don't have a job, I think it will work. You'll like it. They're nice kids. Good hearts. Problem is, they're too innocent. You'll be the one to messy them up a little. The school would love an abused, homeless, university professor who'll work for a little more than your salary here. Hard to find. I think they might settle for you."

"What are you talking about? You don't pay me a salary."

"Exactly. Come up here Friday morning. I'll explain and you can go talk to them. Spend the night with me, and you can train on Saturday. How does that sound?"

"Confusing, but something might work."

"See you then. I'll tell them you're on." Click.

"On" like coming to see them? Or "on" like taking the job? The second would be ridiculous, except Rosa was talking to Mary, the Mama of nuns.

Before she left for the Bronx on Friday, Rosa had two things to get done. The simple one—get another training session as a touch therapist. The tricky one—find Tony and ask him to get her rope before the cops got rid of it. Lou was dead. The rope couldn't be evidence for anything. No telling how long the police would hold onto it.

Rosa took her therapy lesson Wednesday morning. She could have gone to the high school that afternoon. She tried to come up with some approach—something better than walking in cold and asking Tony for a big favor—but niente.

She procrastinated until Thursday. Driving Mama's old Ford to the shop door at the rear of the school, she found it closed, with kids hanging around a couple cars, everybody smoking, the boys trying to look cool, the girls trying to look like they didn't notice. She remembered, but she had Joey so she didn't play those games. Maybe he was worth something after all.

She rolled down her window. "Have you guys seen Mr. Prezzi?"

The group from the nearest car came over to her window, reeking of tobacco smoke. They wore mechanic's clothes. Sort of. One girl had work boots, white socks, and then bare legs up to her green mechanic's pants cut off two inches below her crotch. In December.

A guy with Elvis/Tony hair answered. "No. Usually he hangs around and lets us use the tools, but today he took off with his new girlfriend. Hot little blonde."

Chapter 39

The kids worked in little groups. Wiring. He could only teach a sample because a modern car ran on its wires, so he had decided on ignitions and audio—ignitions as the serious work, audio as the dessert. His phone vibrated in his pocket. He didn't usually answer during class time, but the groups were all into their work. He flipped open his phone.

"Hello. Tony? Do you still have my cross?"

"Tatyana! Of course. Did you think I would steal your cross?"

"No. I could come pick it up, but I was hoping you had time to talk."

His eyes brightened and he stood taller, almost on his tiptoes. "Sure. What about?"

"Oh, you know. Things."

"Your things? You're interview already sucked out my things."

"I know I did. That's why I want to talk to you, Tony, instead of somebody else. About some of my things, yes."

She wanted to talk to him. To him. "Are you asking me for a date?" Women did that now. Meg did.

"Would sitting in your car looking at the water be a date? If I left the recorder home?"

"Sure. If you call it a date, Tatyana, it's a date."

"If we're dating, please call me Tatya."

"Okay, Tatya. Sure."

"When?"

She wasn't playing it cool, so he didn't have to either. "Tonight?"

"Tonight's fine. Shall we meet at that parking lot by the water? I think I can find it."

"Let me think for a second." His strategy last time, hiding Tatyana, was a mistake. Let the whole neighborhood, especially Mama and Rosa, know he was seeing a beautiful blonde. "How about you meet me at the high school? We can leave your car in the lot and go wherever you want."

"Okay. When?"

"I can get the shop closed by three thirty. Is that too early?"

"See you then."

He closed his phone and clapped it hard between his hands, one-two-three. Uh-oh. He opened the clam shell and the little buttons lit up. Whew.

Most of the kids had stopped work to stare at him. Picking a group at random, he thrust his forefinger in its direction. Everybody turned back to business.

Tatyana settled into the passenger seat, and smiled at her cross. She flicked her finger and it swung back and forth. "Can we go straight to the shore?"

They parked in the same parking space as the last time. In daytime, though, the waterside winter park looked bleak. Gray from edge to edge, the sky pondered whether to loosen its snow. No lights reflected across the water. Sea-gulls cawed, pigeons scavenged. On scattered benches, people lay bundled against the cold. Fast-food bags and coffee cups swirled in the wind.

Tatya shuddered. She twisted in her seat and looked into Tony's eyes. Her face was eye-squinted serious. Little vertical lines in the middle of her forehead. "Remember the gentleman part of Mr. Wonderful? I'd like to talk to him first. Is he here?"

Tony reset his expectations. "I don't think a gentleman can work part-time."

She studied his eyes. "I've never talked to anyone about this before. Well, the Dean, but he doesn't count. I thought maybe I'd be able to talk to you."

Tony nodded.

"Did it seem strange that *The New Yorker* assigned an article to a young writer like me?"

"I noticed young, which was nice, but I didn't notice strange. Is *The New Yorker* a big deal?"

"The biggest."

"Congratulations."

"I got the job because I'm a whore." She studied his eyes.

He blinked. "Uh, boy. That's surprising…. I bet you're expensive."

"Not that kind of whore."

"There's another kind?"

"Yes. I don't take money. I took the jobs my writing coach got me before I graduated CUNY and he kicked me out of his place. Jobs so I wouldn't raise a fuss."

"A fuss about what?'

"That he pretended to love me so he could fuck me till I graduated."

"You were a student and the man who did this was your coach?"

"Well, yeah. A graduate student. My writing coach."

"Your coach should be fired. That's not just what I think. That's the policy. In my school, anyway."

"It's the policy at CUNY, too. Like I said, I talked to the Dean, but—"

"How old is this guy? But what?"

"My father's age, I guess. But he's still there—shacked up with a new first-year student."

"That's terrible."

"Yes, it is. He is."

"Right."

"You're a good man, Tony. I know you're a gentleman, and I hear you're a good—"

"I'm so sick of hearing that. The only one who'd really know was Lucia."

"Okay. Let's put it this way. Will you make love to me?"

Tony sat stunned. There was no women in the world he's rather make love to. Well, maybe one other, but she wasn't interested. He had wrestled with the problem of how to make the leap—from a gentleman who didn't make a move to a stud who made a move. And she'd made it for him.

"Now? You don't want to have dinner first, like a date?"

She put her left hand on his thigh. "No. We can eat anytime."

"That's right." He picked up her tiny hand, kissed the back of her knuckles, and planted it firmly back on his thigh. Jerking the gear into first, he kicked gravel as he left the parking area. On the road, he slowed down to a normal speed

"Where are we going?"

"My house."

She moved her hand on his thigh and he sped up again. Which bed? His room was unimpressive, but it seemed incestuous to make love on Mama's bed.

Better the bigger bed, he decided. Mama never came home, maybe would never know, and probably wouldn't mind anyway. She'll be happy for him, when she meets Tatya.

Opening the door, he grew aware of how stale and unused most of the house appeared. He used the recliner and TV, the kitchen, his bedroom and the bath. Everything else stood where it was, untouched except when he dusted.

After all these years, his mother's bedroom still carried the scent of a woman's space, perfumed powder and sachet. Tony closed the blinds on the two windows that overlooked the sidewalk.

Tatya knelt on the bed and reached up to pull the string that lit the ceiling light. Knee-walking to the edge of the bed, she settled back onto her heels and patted the covers next to her.

"Come sit by me."

Tony sat down.

She took hold of his wrist, put his hand in her lap, and held it there with two hands. "I asked you; you didn't ask me. Do you feel pressured? Like you're a man and you had to say yes?"

"God, no. You're beautiful. And smart. And you need somebody to make you feel better, you know, about yourself."

"That's what I mean. Like you're a gentleman and I'm a lady in distress."

"Another few minutes and I'll be the one in distress." He cupped her breast. The idea of her soft breast and the reality of the silky weave of her shirt fought against the stolid fabric of her serious got-a-job-to-do bra. His thumb found her nipple pressing against the bra.

Tatya pressed his hand against her breast. "Tony, can we pretend?"

He tried to move his thumb back and forth, but she was holding it jammed against herself. "Pretend what?"

"Pretend you asked me. Pretend we're about to make love, not just to do it. Pretend we're lovers, not you helping a needy person in distress."

"I don't just do it anymore. We'll make love. And who knows? Maybe we will be lovers. Maybe we already are." A shiver sped down the back of his neck and across his shoulders. As soon as he said it, he believed it. Maybe Tatya did, too.

She freed his hand.

He massaged her nipple with his thumb, using his other hand to fumble with the top button of her shirt.

Touch

She pushed his hand away from her button and unbuttoned it herself. And the next one. And the next.

While he caressed her midriff, more polished than her forehead, she unbuttoned his shirt. Her hand smoothed his chest hair, little circles. The little circles moved down toward his belt buckle. His stomach muscles tightened on their own.

He had never made love since his touch therapy. He had never made love to such a lustrous jewel of a woman. His hearing and eyesight softened. Touch, only touch. Her caresses left a trail of shivering skin. His fingers barely brushed her body.

Bit by bit, she revealed more of herself. He lowered his head to touch her with his lips. She sucked in a sharp breath and sighed.

Chapter 40

The cold, damp day matched Rosa's mood. Once inside the apartment building, the warmth felt better but she didn't. She trudged up the stairs and sulked her way down the second-floor hall to the last door on the right.

She knocked lightly. Dogs barked. Someone inside asked, "What's with the dogs? Did you hear anything?"

Rosa banged harder. "Open the damned door."

Jojo opened the damned door. "Lee! Rosa's here. Jojo put one arm around Rosa' shoulder and pulled her into the apartment. "She's got a droopy face. Get out here."

"Momento, momento. I'm getting dressed." Lee emerged, fiddling with her sweatshirt—pulling down the cuffs, plucking at its shoulders. She hugged Rosa. "Jeez. Droop is right. Your chin's gonna slide down your neck. What's the matter?"

"I think he's gone."

Jojo helped Rosa take off her coat. "Who's gone?"

"Tony. Who else?"

Lee jumped up to give Jojo a high five. "Free at last, free at last, thank God almighty, free at last."

Rosa watched the display. "I thought you were my friends."

Jojo patted Rosa on the cheek. "We are, we are. Tony's, too. What happened?"

"He has a girlfriend. A blonde little thing."

Lee and Jojo looked at each other. Simultaneously, "The writer."

"The writer?"

"Yeah," Jojo said, "You didn't notice? She was blonde. Little. Young, too."

Lee frowned and shook her head. "For this, you expected sympathy? We've been begging him for five years. 'If you can't get her attention, if you can't break through her blind spot, get the hell out. You're wasting your life chasing after her.' He got the hell out. Good for him. Hallelujah."

"And she doesn't even look like you," Jojo said. "A clean break."

"I can't believe you two have turned so mean."

With her arm around Rosa's shoulder, Jojo led her to the kitchen table, the only place in the apartment that had three chairs. "Mean? Don't shoot the messenger, but let me point out what mean is. Mean is when a guy arranges for a speech that will make you YouTube famous, saves your life—*saves your life*—wheelchairs you over so you can give your speech and be famous, saves you again when you almost fall, wheelchairs you back to the hospital. You desert him, go off to a shelter for abused women, and leave him there to be interrogated by the cops for abuse."

"For abuse?"

Lee pulled her hand back as if to slap Rosa's face. "You talked a doctor into sending you to a shelter for abused women. Why do you think they call it a 'shelter?' Because the residents need protection from their abuser. The cops look around. The guy that sent you to the hospital is dead. Who could your abuser be? You told the doctor you were in danger from Tony."

"I didn't know he'd get in trouble with the cops. Mama made him my fiancé. I was afraid."

"Oh, bullshit." Jojo held out her palms. "On the one hand, a guy who saved your life, on the other hand a Mama who does something silly like she's been doing your whole life. You were afraid of what? Tony might pull out of your blind spot?"

"And when you show up again," Lee said, "you move in with Mama. You must have been terrified of her. And you go back to business as normal." She put on a whiny voice. "I want my rope, but I'm too scared to talk to Connecticut cops. I'll find my errand boy and send him after it."

Jojo reached out for Rosa's hand. "Of course we're thrilled for Tony. Maybe he can be happy at last. And why do you care? What are you drooping around for? You never showed him the slightest interest. At most, he's your friend, like he's our friend. You should be happy for him. If his finding a girlfriend upsets you, wake the hell up and ask yourself why."

The conversation deteriorated into a junior-high discussion of Tony, Rosa's feelings, his good looks, the way he watched Rosa play basketball when she was in high school, his sexy reputation, whether her 15-year-old's mistake with Joey should scare her away from Tony.

Lee said, "Fifteen-year-olds make mistakes all the time, so they won't be so stupid when they turn sixteen." She put her hand over her mouth. Rosa was stupid until she was twenty-two and Joey hit her.

To make up for the insult, Lee hustled around. She set out Italian cookies—some lemon, some almond, both with the same round shape and the same chewy center—and made a pot of coffee.

They chatted while they waited for the coffee. How was Mama? What was it like living with her again, after fourteen years away? What did Jojo think of her and Tony's b'ball team this year? Would they get into the play-offs again?

After serving the mugs, Lee sat down. "I think it's better if we rip the bandage off all at once. What do you think, Jojo?"

Jojo looked at Rosa. "You mean about Paola? Do you think Rosa can take it?"

"Yeah, I do. She's a little wimpy today, but basically she's tough. She didn't use to look it, but now with the pirate scar on her cheek...."

Rosa waved her hand. "Yoo-hoo, I'm here. Mama taught me it's impolite to talk about someone as if she wasn't there. Mama does it all the time, but that's what she taught me."

Jojo turned toward Rosa, folded her arms, and put her elbows on the tables. "Okay. You're fucking over Paola and Tessa. Another blind spot."

"I'm not doing anything to them. I hardly ever see them."

Lee shook her finger, not at Rosa but up in the air, the more polite version. "I couldn't put it better myself. You hardly ever see them. You're not doing anything to them, for them, with them. We're overwhelmed here, trying to get some communication network and website for.... What's the name of the organization, Rosa?"

Rosa whispered, "Rosa's Angels."

"Yeah. But Rosa has more important things to do—train abused women in the Bronx, fix their skin, teach college twits up there. While we're trying to build Rosa's organization, Rosa dances down from the Bronx and dumps a pregnant, abused kid on Paola. Now, we're up to five women stashed in people's houses."

Jojo refilled their mugs. "When the word gets out, we'll have twenty-five, but we're not helping them at all, even if we could find places for them to live. Because the only person around here who knows anything about shelters is screwing around up in the Bronx, helping a shelter that got along forty years without her. Well, we've got abused women down here, more of them needing help than ever because Rosa's Angels urges them to find safety, and there are no shelters for them."

Rosa excused herself and used the bathroom. She sat there as long as she thought she could get away with. She dragged herself back through the living room. She eyed the entry door. No. Not an option. She slouched into the kitchen and sat in her chair. Hopeful, she asked, "Are we done?"

Lee reached toward Rosa.

Rosa automatically leaned backward.

Lee half stood and grasped her shoulder. "I was just winding up. I could have gone on for another hour, but I think you got the gist of it. One last thing. All the women working for the Angels feel like I do. They'd never say anything because you are their founding inspiration, so I had to tell you because I'm your friend." She squeezed Rosa's shoulder. "I am your friend."

"What's that quote?" Rosa slugged down the rest of her coffee. "With friends like these, who—"

"Don't you dare." Jojo covered Rosa' mouth.

Muffled, Rosa finished anyway, "needs enemies?" They were her friends. Usually. Why not today, when she needed them most?

Jojo loosened her fingers on Rosa's lips. "So let's talk. What are you so upset about, anyway?"

Rosa batted her hand away. "Isn't it obvious?"

"No. When it's obvious, I don't have to ask a question."

"Tony. After all these years together, he chose that little blond bitch over me."

Jojo looked at Lee. "Together? Did you ever notice Rosa was together with Tony?"

"Oh, shut up," Rosa said. "You know what I mean. We've been close."

Jojo had been resting her head on her left hand, fingertips to her temple. She raised her eyebrows and flicked her fingers out. "Close how? You guys been fooling around when we weren't looking? Maybe you mean you've been comforting him when he had troubles, celebrating when he had joys?"

Rosa stared from one to the other. "Why are you doing this to me? Tony and I are close friends."

Lee answered. "Why are we doing this? Because we're your close friends. This close friendship you have with Tony, how did that get started?"

"Who knows how friendships start? They just do."

"Congratulations," Jojo said. "You know how unusual it is to have friendships like yours? Straight men and lesbians, like Tony and us, that's pretty common. Some gay guys have a whole circle of straight women friends. But a straight man and a straight woman? There was a famous movie about how rare that is, that one with the fake orgasm in the restaurant. The movie said either the guy or the woman wants something more, so the friendships don't last. But yours has. For years."

"This conversation left coffee territory long ago." Lee cleared off the mugs and poured three glasses of Refrigerator Red from the box in their almost-empty refrigerator, where they kept it because some wine went down better if it was too cold to taste. "I always thought Tony wanted something more, like that time he proposed."

"That wasn't serious. He just said that because Mama and the family proclaimed him my fiancé. He was just joking." Rosa took a gulp of wine.

"Just joking. But you didn't say yes, did you? As a joke I mean. Why not go along with the fun?"

"Because Mama was right there and she wouldn't have taken it as a joke, I guarantee you."

"C'mon." Jojo topped of Rosa's glass. "We're all his friends. We know he's not stupid, I mean, not more than the average guy. You don't think he knew Mama was there and knew exactly what he was asking? Why would he do that?"

"I know what you want me to say." Rosa took the last cookie and dipped it in her wine. "He's loved me all along. He's always loved me. Are you happy now?"

"And here we thought he was in her blind spot." Jojo tapped Lee's shoulder with a knuckle. "She knew all along he was back there loving her. She just wasn't interested."

Lee tapped back. "In the old days, leading somebody on was looked down upon, but these days with people hooking up and everything so fluid, I don't think that's true anymore. What I admire, she didn't hop into bed with him, even though straight women around here think he's God's gift. That really would have been using him."

Lee looked at Rosa. "Oh, my God. You haven't been fucking him, have you?" She answered her own question, "Nah. We would have known." Pause. "Why not?"

"Because he loves me. If I did that, I'd never be able to leave and hurt him so bad. I'd be with him the rest of my life."

Jojo smiled. "Well it's a good thing that writer came along and took him off your hands. No more worries about 'the rest of your life' and all that crap. You just find a new guy and start with a clean slate. He probably won't be as good in bed, but everything in life has its trade-offs. That gloomy face you wore when you came in here—that was just a practical joke on us. Right?"

"No. I don't want some other woman to take him away."

Lee poured herself and Jojo another glass. "We're okay. We can get plastered. We told her what she needed to hear. We've listened until she got too hard to understand. We've done what friends are supposed to do."

Jojo held her glass up to Rosa. "When Tony came moping around here because he said he'd lost you to Lou Bates, we said, 'No you haven't. Just go fight for her and get her back.' That's what we said."

Lee clicked her glass to Jojo's. "Same to you, girl, same to you. If you want him, which I'm still not clear on."

The next morning, Rosa walked home through the sprinkle of snow on the ground. Old reliable Refrigerator Red. She had a sledge-hammer headache, a stomach trying to digest itself, and an acid breath that could cut through steel.

She couldn't remember much about the evening. He's not gone unless Rosa let her take him. She remembered that. Oh, crap. It was

Friday. She was supposed to be in the Bronx giving touch therapy to the women in the shelter. An hour ago. She'd have to talk to Mary.

Chapter 41

Tatya sat on him, going for yet another one, when she fell forward, face into his chest hair. She looked up at his neck, mumbled "never mind," and purred herself to sleep.

He set her to his side, curled himself around her, and fell asleep himself. He had a weird dream. A dog licked the dried sweat salt off his stubbled face. Waking, he remembered where he was, in Momma's bed, and the licking tongue was Tatya's.

"Please." She tried to tug him on top of her, pulling on one shoulder and his penis.

He climbed over her, arms in push-up position. Rested as they were, they finished together in about two minutes. He rolled off and they lay side-by-side, looking up at Mama's old-fashioned light fixture.

"Sooner or later, we'll have to return to the school, so I can go to work and you can get your car."

She stretched and bridged upwards, her breasts resting on her collar bones and her clenched cheeks pushing her bit of blonde hair toward the ceiling. "No hurry, here."

Pawing around on the nightstand, Tony found his watch. "Jesus Christ. The first class is in ten minutes."

He leaped from the bed, yanking on his pants. Looking around on the floor for where she'd thrown his shirt, he bumped into her just as she'd found her bra. "No time. No time. You can come get it later. Pants and shirt. Please, Tatya, hurry."

He found his shirt, lying next to hers. He picked hers up. Mesmerized again by her breasts, he paused for a second, shook his head, and threw her shirt at them. In his 4Runner, his seat belt over his half-buttoned shirt, he jerked the shifter into gear and raced to the school.

He strode toward the shop door, sockless, his shoelaces flapping against the asphalt, and his long Elvis hair in layers crushed against his scalp.

Tatya slid out her door and hurried toward her car, her shirt wrinkled and not buttoned high enough, her hair as much a mess as Tony's. The boys stared. The girls stared icicles.

Tony shooed the students inside. "Get to work. We started a few minutes late, but we'll catch up if you guys stop staring and start working." As they picked up their tools, he bent his head forward to tame his hair with his fingers. Wafting up from inside his shirt came the smell of his own sweat mixed with Tatya's intimate scent, the unmistakable stink of sex.

Knowing his face probably smelled even more like Tatya, he stepped over to the sink, yanked a paper towel off the roll, and bent toward the tiny mirror while he wet the towel under the faucet. He saw a few fine blond hairs stuck in his dark stubble. Too few and too fine to notice, he was sure. Nevertheless, after he'd scrubbed his face, he checked to make sure they were gone. He scratched his hair into better position with his fingernails, but he could do nothing about the good-time scent clinging to the rest of him. He'd have to brazen it out.

As the day went on, he was surprised to learn, if he showed up for school stinking of sex and managed to avoid the other faculty, he had no problems. His shop students never mentioned it. They whispered in the shop's corners. The boys gave him admiring glances. That blonde was a stunner and he was even more of a stud than they'd heard. The crush girls—that was how he thought of them—stepped up their amateur flirting a notch, now they'd seen the competition. All of the students were on their respectful best behavior, if he didn't count the flirting, which he ignored just like he always did. No discipline problems whatsoever.

Ah-oo-ga, ah-oo-ga. He pulled the phone from his work-shirt pocket.

"Hi. Let's meet at your house. My underwear is lying on your mother's floor."

"Okay. Bring a couple of subs. I haven't eaten since yesterday lunch. Just get two regular Italians." No sense getting her involved in the nuances of Italian subs—what to leave out, what to put in. She was Russian. He gave her directions to the best sub shop, Lucia's old favorite.

Ah-oo-ga, ah-oo-ga. Mama, her voice so low he could hardly hear. "Your sister. She.... Well, better I tell you in person. Meet me at the house."

He appointed one boy to be teacher for the few minutes left in the school day and raced home, to pick up the underwear and make the bed before Mama got there.

He was too late.

As he entered, he saw Mama stepping down the stairs, one of the winter coats from her closet draped over her arm. She wore a fake little grin, until she saw him, when the grin disappeared and her shoulders started to shake.

She stumbled towards him. They met in the middle of the living room and she fell into his chest. "Nikki...Nicki...."

He held her close. Faced buried against him, she stopped crying long enough to ask, "You went to school smelling like this?"

"We were late."

"Yes. I saw the underwear. Rosa at last?"

"No, Mama. Better. She's on her way. She'll be here soon. You can meet her then."

"I hope she takes her time." She backed out of his embrace.

Tony held both her hands. "Is Nicki alright?"

"No. Well, maybe better off than she has been.... I got a call.... She passed." Mama shook her head and talked fast, as if afraid she couldn't get through what she needed to say. "A couple weeks ago—her friends had a service in her homeless shelter. The shelter woman pieced the information together, that she had a mother.... That she had me." Mama ran out of words and ducked her head.

Tony put his arm around her. "A homeless shelter?"

"Oh, Tony. She drank, like her father."

"Hasn't she worked for that airline? For so many years?"

"She lost that job at least ten years ago, Tony. You're oblivious, always have been. That's what we wanted. She and I both wanted. You were a kid. Your father knocked you around—not too bad, not like us. We protected you, and it worked. Now she's dead. No reason to keep up the facade."

"What did she do for a living, then? Protected me from what? What facade?"

"I was afraid to know what she did for a living. She never said. Protected you? From knowing you grew up in hell. You don't know anything about that part, or you couldn't bring your girlfriend here."

"Hell? You mean Papa? I knew about him."

"No you didn't. He had sex by hitting me until I pretended to be unconscious. He started on Nikki when she was thirteen. He banged your head against the wall. You were so little. I finally killed the son of a bitch." She grabbed at his shirt front and buried her face.

Tony hugged her, for a long time. Twenty-four years she'd been living with her secret. God knows how many awful years before that. How could he not know? Maybe he could have done something. If his sister was thirteen, he was nine. What could he have done? His father hit him? He didn't remember. Why didn't he remember?

After a time, cheeks wet, Mama patted him on the back. He let her go and she dug into her purse for a tissue.

Tony went into the kitchen and came back with a paper towel. "How could you have killed him? He was drunk and fell over the edge on his construction job. Did you just wish you'd done it?"

"No. I killed him. I filled his so-called water thermos with grain alcohol instead of his normal vodka. Twice the proof. It took a couple days. Finally, he fell in the right direction."

"Jesus. You killed Papa? I can't believe it. Why was Nikki mad at you, then? You killed him."

"I couldn't tell her that. She blamed me for not protecting her. And I didn't, I couldn't, until it was too late."

"You killed him. You really did."

"Yeah, I did. I was proud—still am." She picked up her winter coat. "Bye." She headed for the door. "I don't want to meet your girlfriend right now."

"Mama. Please stay and meet Tatya. She'll be here any minute."

Mama kissed his cheek goodbye. "Some other time. I just cleaned up after her. Impressive bra. But that other scrap. I don't know why girls like that even pretend to wear panties."

Tony blushed. Mama hadn't even met Tatya. All she knew about her was her bra and panties.

"Don't worry about the mass arrangements. I'll take care of them. You probably have something more important to do." At the doorway, she half turned. "But please don't do it on that bed." Turning back to leave, she bumped into Tatya and her bag of subs.

Tony made Mama stay and share their drippy supper, leaning over the sub wrappers on the kitchen table.

Mama learned Tatya was the Russian writer who'd been snooping around the neighborhood. She stared at Tony, who pretended not to notice. She got up from the table. "I was already about to leave. I've got to go. Nice to meet you, young lady."

As Tatya went upstairs to get her underwear, Tony cleaned the kitchen. Alone, he thought of Nicki, of his big sister. His vision blurred and he sat down, seeing not the kitchen sink, but a gawky teen, head bent forward, long dark hair covering half her face.

Tatya came into the room, holding a little pile, his boxers folded neatly on the bottom, her underwear on top. "Your mother...."

Her voice ran down. She dropped the underwear on the kitchen table and stood next to him, hugging his head with one arm, wiping the moisture off his cheeks with the thumb of her other hand.

After a minute, she pulled him into the living room and sat them on the sofa. She pulled Tony's head down onto her braless breasts and smoothed his hair. Tony wet her blouse with his tears. They sat like that for a long time. Until Tony shifted slightly and wet her blouse some more, with his tongue on her nipple. They rearranged themselves on the sofa.

Chapter 42

"We're about four blocks from Yankee Stadium. Grand Concourse. Probably all day. Four women with disability hearings at the Social Security. Then two appeals. The lawyer's coming for those. I'm in the van. You've been in it before. If you think of it, stop in the McDonalds. You got to pass it on the way from the subway. Bring me an apple pie. Nothing else—just the pie. See you soon."

What luck. A chance to talk to Mary alone. Rosa decided to bring two pies, because of her news.

Rosa handed Mary the MickeyD's bag and settled into the passenger seat, cracked blue vinyl with spongy tufts of foam escaping through the cracks.

Mary peeked into the bag. "Two! Some kind of bribe?"

"Yes. I'm afraid it is."

Mary checked Rosa's eyes. "Spit. You're leaving, aren't you?"

"Paola, Tessa and all the Staten Island Rosa's Angels are trying to get a shelter going, the first on the Island, and they need my help."

"Wow. I'll miss you. We all will. But God decides where She needs you. Not me."

Rosa explained about the women staying in different volunteer's houses, but no central building.

"How are you going to get one of those? Big bucks. No grants anymore. Some Rosa's Angel is rich?"

"No. But we'll have plenty of construction volunteers. Half the men in the neighborhood work in the trades, and some of the women. I just need some wreck for them to renovate."

"Even with the labor. Materials cost money. Plumbing, electric, heat—nothing's cheap."

"I know. I've got one idea. I think it's kind of iffy, but maybe."

Rosa's phone played the chorus of "Volare."

"Hello. This is Jenny Barret."

Rosa ran through her mental phone book. Jenny Barret, Jenny Barret.

Mary leaned over and yelled into Rosa's phone. "Jenny! Is this you?"

"Mary? Did I call the wrong number?"

"Maybe. You still gonna show up for the hearings? First one starts in an hour."

"I'm coming. I'll be there. I'm getting ready to leave right now, but I had to make a couple calls. I'm sorry. I didn't mean to call you." Rosa's phone made the little ending ding.

"*Volare, oh, oh. Cantare, oh, oh, oh, oh.*"

Rosa answered again.

"Hello. This is Jenny Barret."

"Hi. She's calling me, Mary. Hands off. Who are you?"

"I'm your attorney. You're with Mary?"

"Yeah. In her van."

"You poor thing. Convenient though, so stay there. The paperwork is ready. I'll bring it with me and you can look it over and sign if you approve. Okay? See you soon. I've got to make another call." Ding.

Forty minutes later, she pulled up in a chauffeured car. The chauffer, a well-fed older gentleman, stepped out and opened the back door. Gliding on broken-down loafers, he slid around the van to help Mary out of her seat. She evaded his extended hand, said "Thank you," and slipped down from her seat to the ground.

Once settled, three across in the back seat of her big car, Jenny handed Rosa a pile of papers, attached with a black spring clip. "You were brilliant. Best public relations I've ever seen. All the publicity, YouTube, the Rosa's Angels pressure group—perfect. They kept raising their offer without me pushing. Each time, I'd say 'Really?' They'd scurry back to headquarters and come up with another couple hundred thou. Then the *New Yorker* article this morning—I don't know how you swung that. They called and capitulated. Total surrender. Three eight. I'd advise you accept."

Bewildered and repulsed by the whole idea she'd given the speech to get more money, Rosa had trouble following what Jenny said. "Three eight? The *New Yorker* article is out?" She bet that bitch writer made Tony the hero and Rosa the poor-thing victim. Believable, but still.

"Yes, it's out. We made copies. Here's one." She handed Rosa a thick group of stapled pages.

Rosa leafed through it. After the first page, the article continued one column per page, the rest taken up with ads. Titled, "Rosa's Angels," the subhead said, "Staten Island Italians Fight Domestic Violence." As if Rosa's Angels was an Italian-only group, or domestic violence an Italian-only problem. "By Tatyana Kosova." She put the article aside to read later, if ever.

"To answer your other question, three eight is $3,800,000. Your share is $2,532,000, minus expenses. A little over two five total."

Mary had been eyeing her. Did she want some of this for St. Rita's? Fine, but….

Stiff-necked, Mary nodded at the stack of papers. "Was this your iffy idea?"

"Yes. Not so iffy anymore."

Mary relaxed and shook her hand. She yanked on her rope of big wood beads until a carved wooden cross came out of her pants pocket. Kneeling up on the seat to reach, she kissed the cross and touched Rosa with it, on her forehead and her chest, one shoulder then the next. She stuffed the cross back into her pocket before she sat down.

The lawyer handed Rosa another pile of papers. "There are tax implications. We have to do the gift right. Set up a charitable organization. Since this is a charity, we'll work pro bono. Congratulations. You deserve this money. And the women you help? They'll deserve it, too."

The lawyer told her driver to take Rosa home in her car. "Be back here by four," she told him. "You might have to wait."

She went into the office building, Mary waited in her van, and Rosa rode home, remembering when Rex-Aid used to drive her around in a car like this.

On the way home, she looked through the article. The Russian writer portrayed Rosa's neighborhood as some quaint, un-American remnant of a foreign culture, which took some nerve for a Russian to write. The Russians in Brighton Beach just got there since the 1990s. And they had a real mob over there, not some old mafiosos nodding off after their midday meal. But even if everybody in the neighborhood hated it, and they would, the notorious article might help Rosa's cause, and that mattered most.

Remembering Lee and Jojo's advice about going after him, Rosa had the driver drop her off several blocks from her house. She'd walk by Tony's. School was over for the day. Maybe he'd be outside somewhere, walking back from the store. He used to shop at Rex-Aid sometimes.

Nearing his townhouse, she passed a woman sitting on a bus-stop bench, face pressed into a winter coat hung over her knees, hands clamped onto the front edge of the bench, rocking back and forth.

Rosa sat down on the bench.

The woman stopped rocking. "I'm all right. Don't bother about me." She lifted her face out of the coat. "Rosa?"

"Mrs. Prezzi?"

Tony's mother sat up, wiped her eyes with her coat. "I must look awful."

Yes, she did. "Maybe we should go to my house, to Mama's house. She can help. At the least, some cookies, some coffee, some Anisette."

"Okay."

Rosa helped her to her feet. They walked off. Rosa, slowed to match the lady's pace, held her hand. Did something terrible happen to Tony? Horrible scenes raced through her mind.

"Tony never talks about it, but didn't I hear you two were engaged?"

"Is…. Is he okay?"

"Oh. You thought…. No, he's fine. Well, he's with that Russian, but other than that…."

"I know."

"His sister died. My Nikki. She never had a chance. Like her baby sister never had a chance. But we knew the baby was going to…." She stopped walking and moaned for a minute into her coat. "I knew Nikki was…too. But she was out in Alaska, so I pretended I didn't know how bad off she…."

"We're almost there."

Mama put Rosa in charge of readying the coffee and cookies. She took Mrs. Prezzi upstairs to help fix her face. Before they got to the stairs, Mama half turned to Rosa. She pointed to a coffee cup, to the woman in front of her, and then to the Anisette bottle. She held up two fingers, hesitated, than held up a third.

Rosa got the message. Help Mrs. Prezzi drown her sorrows.

The two women came back down. "She looks much better now. Doesn't she, Rosa?"

Her sad face masked behind a thick layer of powder-covered foundation, the lady looked like a botched effort to imitate the news people on TV. Any resemblance to Tony had been erased. Rosa didn't answer Mama's question, bustling to serve the coffees instead.

After her loaded cup of coffee, Tony's mama asked again about Rosa and Tony's engagement.

Rosa stood at the sink, her back to the two mamas, washing plates that were already clean.

Mama explained, "Rosa screwed up twice and she needs her parents to arrange the next one. I chose Tony but it hasn't worked because Rosa is such a stubborn hard-head."

"My Mama and Papa were arranged, and it worked out fine, but that was back in the day. With his father dead, I would never dare tell Tony who…. Hey. Wait a minute. If you're arranging a marriage, aren't you supposed to arrange it with the boy's parents? With me?"

"Yes, technically, I guess. Don't you think Rosa would be good for your son?"

"She'd be great. He's been mooning after her half his life. Especially after Lucia, he needed somebody. What's the matter, Rosa? You didn't want Tony?"

Rosa turned to her mother. "Are you nuts? You gave me such grief and you didn't even arrange anything with Tony's mama? It was just a wild idea out of your own head?"

Mama waved a hand to say, "Eh."

"No, Mrs. Prezzi. I didn't want him. I'd been too hurt by men, it was too soon, and I wouldn't have wanted Leonardo DiCaprio. Now, I think I do want Tony, and it's too late."

"You mean because of that Russian girl? Imagine, I lost my two daughters. My only chance for grandchildren is Tony, and his kids will be speaking Russian. You know the wife's family is the closest. Tony's kids will probably live over in Russkie Beach and I'll never see them."

"Are they engaged already? Because if they're not, Lee and Jojo said I should not give up. I should go after him."

"Good." Mrs. Prezzi patted the back of Rosa's hand while she looked across the table into Mama's eyes.

Mama nodded.

Mrs. Prezzi turned to face Rosa. "Okay. It's arranged. You and my son are engaged. Now go after him."

Chapter 43

A memorial mass was like a normal funeral mass except there was no body. The priest never said anything about Nikki but her name, Nicola Nunciata Prezzi, and her baptism, and something about God's mercy and grace were beyond human understanding. In other words, even though the church taught she should be headed for hell, maybe they were wrong.

Tatya had never been to a Roman Catholic mass before. She said the Russian Orthodox ones were more beautiful and more elaborate, but took a lot longer. A trade-off.

After mass, the family processed out of the church with the priest, than stood ready to accept the condolences of everybody who followed them out. Mama and her boyfriend were now officially engaged. Consoling her grief had led him to propose. According to Mama, he'd said, "My kids? Fuck 'em. Will you marry me?" He stood next to Mama at the start of the line.

Next stood Tony, with Tatya after him, even though she'd objected that she wasn't Roman Catholic and she wasn't family. Sure enough, the mourners didn't know what to make of her. Should they murmur condolences? Most settled for shaking her hand.

Among the first families to emerge into the sunlight were the DeAngelos. His Mama and Mrs. DeAngelo embraced a long time, whispering. After that, Mama's fiancé handed her a tissue and she wiped her eyes. Next, Rosa got her turn to give his Mama a hug.

Mama introduced her fiancé to Rosa, then firmly placed Rosa into the receiving line between the boyfriend and Tony.

Rosa tried to leave.

His Mama held her shoulder. "Please stay with us."

Looking bewildered, Rosa stayed in place.

Everybody leaving the church hugged her as if she had lost a sister, as if she were a member of his family. With her there, people coming out of mass were even more confused about who Tatya was and why she stood at the end of the line.

Mama and Tony held a small reception at their house. Lee and Jojo had skipped the mass to arrange the donated food and the drinks. They'd volunteered for the duty. "The church and we have an agreement. They prefer we stay away, and we do too."

Tony kept an eye on Mama. The first second she wasn't surrounded by well-wishers, he took her hand and led her out the back door.

They crowded together on the tiny back stoop. "What was that thing with Rosa about?"

"What thing?"

"Don't play innocent. After the mass."

"Oh. Because you and Rosa are engaged."

"That was just Mama DeAngelo's nutso notion."

"Yes, it used to be. But two days ago we made it formal. She and I agreed."

"C'mon, Mama. That's crazy. I'm with Tatyana now."

"That's right. Like you say, 'for now.'"

"I didn't say 'for'—."

But Mama had already turned to go back inside.

Tony finished painting the second-story trim. He climbed down the ladder, laid it flat on the sidewalk, and went into the house for one last check. Upstairs, the chipped toilet and the yellowed sink had been replaced; downstairs, the antique refrigerator and stove were gone, replaced by gleaming white Whirlpools. Everything was freshly painted, inside and out.

He'd had put all his painting gear in the back of the 4Runner when the real estate ladies stopped by. They toured the house, admiring his work. He refrained from narrating the tour. Here's where Papa slept drunk in front of the TV. The big room upstairs, that's where he raped Mama. He did my sister in the little room in back. That's why we call it Hell House. Good luck selling it.

Instead, he accepted their compliments, signed some papers to set the asking price, and watched one of them put a sign in the front window.

Tony headed to his furnished rental, a third unit in the basement under what originally had been a two-family house. The place was cheap, because it was in the basement and because it was next door to an ugly boarded-up warehouse. Cheap was good. The house he'd lived in was Mama's, not his, and she'd asked his permission to donate the money from the sale to Rosa's shelter project. He said, "Sure." He could save a down payment and pay a mortgage the same as everybody else, so Tatya and he would eventually have a house. Meanwhile, all he needed was a bath and kitchen and a bed for Tatya's visits. He lived fine in the cheap apartment. Especially when Tatya visited, like today. She should arrive any minute.

She walked in and they sat side-by-side on his bed. "Remember that scene at your sister's mass?"

"What scene?"

"Don't play dumb. Your mama and Rosa, and me treated like a nobody."

"Yes. I'm sorry. They were all rude."

"They were all Italian, and I'm not."

With one hand, he gently rubbed her shoulder. With the other, he ran his fingers through her blonde curls. "No, you're not. What you are is beautiful."

"Thank you. What I am is Russian. Do you remember back at the beginning when I asked you to pretend we were in love? And you said, 'Maybe we already are?'"

"How could I forget?"

"Are we?"

Shit. A woman question. No man would ask this. There was only one possible answer. "I am. Aren't you?"

"Of course. When I'm with you, I feel so content, so safe."

Tony kicked off his boots and unbuttoned his shirt. "So why the question?" He reached up under her loose top, wishing for the umpteenth time she didn't have to wear that iron bra.

She pushed down on his arms and his hands emerged from under her shirt. "Because I've met your mother, and even attended your sister's funeral, but I've never taken you to Brighton Beach to meet my family. Well, mostly not to meet my Otets, my Father. When I'm not with you, my love makes me afraid."

"Afraid of your father?"

"Yes. He wanted to kill my professor. And he's not happy I'm with another foreigner, another non-Russian."

"You'll bring me home when you're ready—and he'll get used to me. Since we're in love, can we make love now?"

She pushed him back on the bed and unbuckled his belt. After pulling off his pants, she quickly undressed and sat on him. This position never worked too well for him, but let her have her first one this way. They didn't have to start with his French kisses every time.

He watched her breasts bobble, mesmerized by the sway. Oh shit. The position of Lucia's Rosa accusation. Then Lucia's revelation. Lucia as Rosa. Rosa.

Shaking his head to clear his mind, he grabbed Tatya's cheeks, pulled her tighter down onto him, arched his back to push deeper, and ground them both to a fast finish. He rolled out from under her and stretched himself on his back.

She leaned over to look into his face.

Crap. He wanted to cover his eyes with the back of his forearm. But that would look defensive, so he didn't.

"What was that about? What happened to giving me a head start, helping me cross the finish line first?"

"I don't know. I had this feeling I needed to hold onto you tight, to love you with everything I had."

Tatya kissed his forehead. "How sweet. Fast thinking, too."

"What do you mean?"

"I'd call what we just had 'hungry sex.' Wouldn't you?"

He sat up. Where was she taking this? "I guess so. After all our times together, it's good we still—"

"That's what I thought at first." She sat up, too, feeling around the floor till she found her underpants. "But why would you be hungry for me? I give myself to you whenever you want, I mean whenever we want. I'd give myself to you for a week at a time, if we could."

Tony sat, head hung and shoulders tense, waiting for the inevitable.

She fastened her bra and her stunning breasts disappeared, gone forever. "We both know who you were hungry for, don't we?" She finished getting dressed. "Don't bother getting up. I'll let myself out."

He heard the sound of her car door shutting, her car starting up, its little engine purring with the perfected timing he'd given it. The sound grew softer until he could hear it no more.

He flopped back on the bed. Freed again, his fantasies went where they wanted to go. Where they'd always wanted to go.

Chapter 44

The five-woman planning team for Rosa's Angels gathered in Lee and Jojo's apartment—the host couple, Rosa, Paola and Tess. It had snowed two days ago. They'd skidded down sidewalks between shoveled ridges of New York City's blackened snow, and stomped their boots in the hallway outside the apartment.

Jojo set out the coffee mugs. "…hard to tell. I think we'll make it to the playoffs again this year. Beyond that…. Tony doesn't fire them up like he did the last two years. Too preoccupied with the writer. That's my guess."

The anise cookies arranged on a plate and set in the center of the kitchen table, Lee sat down in her chair opposite Jojo. "That's not fair. He had to paint the whole house and move. He hasn't had as much time for basketball as he did last year."

"What? He moved? Where? Did he move in with the Russian?" He moved and Mama hadn't told her?

"No. Not yet, anyway," Jojo said. "You still fighting for him?"

"It's hard. He's never around anymore. His Mama agreed with my Mama on that arranged marriage thing. So now he's probably as rebellious as I was."

"What do you mean he's not around? I see him at b'ball practice every day. He's at school all day just like he always was."

"I can't go there. He's at work. Where did he move to?"

"Rosa, what the hell happened to you? When we are on the team together, you were always push, push, push, go, go, go. Sure you can go to school, if you want him enough. The blonde's not with him when he's at work."

"You get beaten up twice by your men—by your partners. Then we'll see how, 'go, go, go,' you are when you want another one. Just tell me where he moved to."

Paola put down her coffee mug. "Beaten up…. Now we're back on topic. He lives in a run-down house next door to that abandoned warehouse—okay, that's done? What's the agenda for today? After all this time, Rosa, why'd you call a meeting today?"

"Oh. Great news. I got the money."

Paola bowed her head to look at Rosa over the top of her glasses. "What money?"

"You know, from Rex-Aid. Mary's lawyer sued them for me, remember?"

"Mrs. Prezzi told Mom she's donating the money when her house sells, too." Tessa slapped her fist into the palm of her other hand, just like her coach Tony always did. Maybe we'll have enough to get something started."

"Two and a half million. I got two and a half million. That's great about Mrs. Prezzi. But I think we've already got enough to get a shelter finished, never mind started."

After the hubbub died down, Tess asked where.

Lee looked at Jojo. "We know a real estate agent. A pair of them, actually."

"Tell them to start with that warehouse next to Tony." Rosa gave Lee a high five.

The person who'd put herself in charge of the remodeling job was Jojo's Aunt Mike. Recently retired as a construction foreman, she was the one who'd told Jojo to go ahead and come out, back when Jojo was still in high school. That was almost twenty years ago. Impossible, Jojo had thought. Now in 2008, high school kids had their own LGBT club.

Early on, after she'd made her first walk-through, Mike called Rosa to meet over beer at the tavern.

"I'm buying, Rosa. I called the meeting." She went to the bar and came back with two drafts. "When you bought the warehouse, did you know it was an old mob operation?"

"The mob? You think?"

"Yeah. Built in the twenties. Two floors of apartments upstairs.

Normal. Storefronts on the ground floor. Normal. A big warehouse hidden behind extra-shallow stores. Not normal. Three apartments set up as a secret suite of offices. Even more not normal."

"I see what you mean. Wow."

"Yeah. Interesting. They probably used it to warehouse booze, back in the day. What do you want us to do with the office suite? Divide it into one-room studios, like we're doing everywhere else upstairs?"

"No. Make an apartment for the shelter manager."

"Okay. Who's that?"

"Me, I think."

"Good. Hard job, though. But when I'm done you'll have a new apartment. Not much new construction around here, not like you'll have—a nice place for downtime, if a shelter manager ever has any downtime."

"Thanks. Do you want another beer? My turn."

"Nope. Gotta go."

"Me, too. Bye."

The warehouse was a mess, unused since the mid-nineties. Squatters had torn out all the saleable scrap, the plumbing and the wiring, and replaced it with piles of garbage—disintegrating mattresses, torn blankets, moldy clothes, cans and bottles, feces and rats.

The first stage, before the pros came in, was to clean out the garbage. Women from the neighborhood and Tony's shop students did most of that work. The work day started whenever people got out of school or work, and it ended at nine. Since it was basketball season, Jojo and Tony didn't arrive till late, Tony with Tatya always alongside.

Rosa asked Jojo. "How am I supposed to go get him? She's never more than three feet away."

"I don't know. But that pout on your face won't help."

"Thanks. Fuck you. And her."

"That won't help either."

Rosa turned away to pick up a damp clump of clothing. Insects buzzed out of it, so she held the bundle at arm's length as she headed for the dumpster.

Tony appointed two of his shop boys to trap and kill the rats that swarmed away from the warehouse clean-up.

"I hope the kids can stop them before they get to my apartment," he told Tatya and Rosa. "In any random group of high school boys, a few will like to kill rats. Most of them, actually."

Once the construction pros took over the volunteer work, Jojo became her aunt's assistant, driving Mike's truck to the store if something was needed at the last minute, coordinating guys who often worked two stories away from each other. Lee was the bookkeeper, keeping track of expenses and budgets. Paola and Tessa ran the Staten Island branch of Rosa's Angels, boarding women in this house or that apartment, duct-taping the organization together until the shelter could open.

Rosa called Karl. "Do you guys want a salon and a studio apartment? Free rent?"

He put his phone on speaker, so Birgit could hear. "What's the catch?"

"You'll be in the women's shelter building. One storefront for the salon, another for your apartment. I hope you will give the women your therapy. They will all have trauma, the worst kind, what you called "love trauma."

"I want to take you up on the offer. But each woman will need more than one session. We want to help them, but we have to serve our paying clients, too. I don't know if we'd have the time. Damn."

"Finish my training. Before the shelter opens, while I've still got the time. Then I can help do our women, too."

Birgit took over their end of the conversation. "How soon can you start?"

"Tomorrow?"

"See you then, we open at nine."

The next morning, Rosa worked alongside Karl. It took ten sessions over two months, but at last she could sense the traumatized areas almost as well as Karl.

Rosa and Mike met regularly, to straighten out small problems. The most common small problem was a construction volunteer ready to quit. They worked for free—under Mike, who was not good at bossing nicely. Sometimes Rosa had to smooth things over, to keep the volunteer on the job, along with the guy's buddies, who might have walked out in solidarity. Like the old wildcat strikes.

The work was a little behind schedule. Mike wasn't worried. "We'll be done by the opening. I've charged up the women pros, and the men won't let themselves be shown up."

"Okay. We'll stick with our date. May 17th, the Saturday before Memorial Day weekend."

"We'll be done. Don't worry about it."

Chapter 45

The day before Mary Center's dedication, Mike gave a tour to some VIPs. She walked backwards around the corners and through the major spaces, explaining every feature, like a tour guide in a museum. Mary followed with her usual impatient scurry, leading the little group that straggled behind—Mama, Rosa, Jojo and Lee, Paola and Tessa, Tony and his mama, Birgit and Karl.

Rosa noted, with heart-pounding hope, the absence of Tony's Russian shadow. Was she gone?

Lost in hopes, she fell to the rear of the group. She didn't need to hear Mike. She'd been here yesterday, and every day before that. Half the group had.

The tour was mainly for Mary, who had first learned the name of the shelter when she arrived for the tour. "This is named after the real Mary, right?" Rosa assured her it was. Marys didn't get any more real than the 87-year-old nun.

When they got to her new apartment, Rosa lingered to look it over once again. All new. Better than the Residence Inn in Connecticut.

Tony stepped into the apartment's bathroom. The usual sink, toilet and shower-tub, but all brand new. He called to Rosa, "This is a shelter? I've never lived in luxury like this my whole life."

Up in front of the group, Mama told Mike, in a voice loud enough for everyone to hear, "We've been going too fast for Rosa. She obviously wants to show Tony all the details. We'll keep going, and they can come along at their own pace."

Tony's mama swept the group through the apartment door. "When you're right, Mrs. D, you're right. Let's get a move on."

Mary was left behind, standing in the doorway. "Nah. It's only this apartment Rosa wants to—oh." She stepped over the threshold and shut the door behind her.

Rosa looked at the closed door, slowly absorbing what Mama had done to her, had done for her. She heard the quiet sound of his boots sliding across the wall-to-wall carpeting, but he didn't say anything. From behind, he stroked her unscarred cheek with his fingertips. His other hand slid its fingers across her forehead.

He'd gotten down to her lips and the tip of her chin when she slowly turned around. Checking his big dark eyes, she pressed her lips against his, cautious touches slowly giving away to pressure until the backs of their lips pressed firm against their teeth. She was about to open her mouth to admit his tongue, when he moved on. His lips caressed her scar at its top on the cheek, in front of her ear, and moved slowly down as far as the top of her dress allowed.

Good. He was sensitized. He liked the one scar on her cheek. One scar. Would he like the ugly tangle that covered her back and her left side, from her shoulders to the soles of her feet? In theory, she thought he would, but her life wasn't in theory. She was afraid his first tentative start would shrivel away at the sight of her body.

She hung on his shoulders and he sunk down onto the carpeting. She pushed him flat and knelt beside him, trying to unbutton his shirt, green with "Tony" embroidered on his pocket. Her fingers trembled.

He took over the job.

She moved down to his belt. She couldn't make it budge.

He unfastened it.

She yanked at his green mechanics pants. But his boots were in the way. Her trembling fingers were no use on their knots and laces.

He removed his boots.

She tugged at his pants. He was too heavy for her to slide them out from under his butt.

He sat up and removed his own pants.

His socks, she could manage. She went for his boxers.

He took hold of her hand. "Your turn."

She went through the removal ritual that the design of her dresses demanded. Gathering her skirt up over her waist, she bent double and let the mass of material slide over her head into a pile on the floor in front of her.

Tony had propped himself up on his elbows to watch. "I can't believe that. Five seconds and all that clothing, from ankles to wrists to neck – it's all gone." He stared at her chemise. "You took off your dress, and there's another one. Like a Russian doll.... Oh, crap. I didn't say that! You didn't hear that!"

His distress was so genuine, Rosa kneeled on the floor and leaned over to kiss the top of his head. The shiny Elvis hair was held in place by some thick mousse. His hair scratched her nose. She preferred the feel of the hair on his chest. Probably his other hair, too, if she ever got his boxers off so she could touch it.

"Holy... There are no more layers, are there? I can see right through this one." He reached up and gave her bodice an experimental pinch. He truly could see right through, he pinched what he was aiming for, and the place he pinched stood up in gratitude. "Please leave that layer on, at least for a while. It's so sexy." He lay back down.

Rosa had a temporary reprieve. Relieved—and anxious.

Tony embraced her, learning how sheer the chemise was, that he could feel through it as well as see through it. Her breasts. The dark triangle between her legs. She had to move his hand away from there, or she'd come before she even got undressed. He moved to her rear. Hugging her to him, he felt the mass of scars and explored up her back, down the back of her thighs.

"You can stop trying to feel where they end. They're everywhere." Rosa's fear welled up, making her lower lip tremble and her eyes water.

Tony darted for her lip, enfolding it in his. When her trembling ceased, his lips moved into a full-on kiss, drawing her lips into his, and touching tongues as he slowly let her go. He pulled up the hem of her chemise and used it to dab the water from her eyes.

While he tended her face, her brain got urgent messages from down below. "I'm exposed down here. Naked. Surrounded by nothing but air conditioning. Cover me or make him pay attention." Unfortunately, like shadows, her scars also sent unwilled messages— "That's right, cover me up."

Finished with her eyes, Tony dropped her chemise back on her thighs, maybe unaware of the chaos he'd caused. He kissed the scar on her cheek.

Touch

"These scars saved your life. If they hadn't healed your bleeding wounds, you'd be dead. I saw you covered in blood. That was ugly. The signs of healing you have now? They're beautiful. I love the way they feel, I'll love the way they look, and, most of all, I love that they exist, that they brought you here to me. Let's get past this. Show me."

Rosa rose to her knees and repeated the undressing maneuver. Her chemise fell at her feet. He wanted her naked—so he could see her scars. Touch therapy worked, but it made its clients weird.

She stood and pirouetted in fake bravery, showing off her tangle of wounds. He rose to his knees. The second time her breasts came into sight, he held them and stopped her twirl. He kissed them, slow and long. He nuzzled his face in her hair. He kissed her there, long and slow again. She rippled under his lips. Her knees shook and she feared she couldn't stand.

He leaped up, put his hands under her rear and lifted her in the air, pulling her hard against his boxers.

She put her arms around his neck, threw back her hair, and pressed her breasts against his chest.

When she had slumped to pudding, he set her feet down on the floor and held her in his arms.

She'd taken care of her need and she hadn't even let him in! She slipped out of his embrace and yanked down his boxers to take a look. He was ready, not spent. "I'm sorry. Guys are supposed to be the ones with the prematurity problem."

"Don't worry. You'll have more. I loved to see you. Next time, we'll join together and really have fun." He noticed how unsteadily she stood and sat down on the floor, pulling her down next to him.

She lay on the floor. "Watch me make Angels." Like a little girl in new-fallen snow, she waved her arms up and down to make wings, narrowed and widened her legs to make a gown. She ended her Angel-making pantomime with her arms up and her legs wide. The defensive position, only horizontal.

As she'd hoped, Tony pounced.

At one point, Tony rubbed his rough fingers all over her, what she called her normal and her abnormal skin. She shied away from his fingers on her scars.

He stopped caressing her skin. "Are your scars ever going away?"
"No. I don't think so."
"So they are a part of you now. If your lover—that's me—truly loves

you, he will love all of you. Your clear skin and your scars. Never mind this 'normal' and 'abnormal' talk. If I love your scars, it doesn't mean I have a touch therapy fetish. Well, maybe a little. It means I love every part of you. I am not going to touch some parts of you and avoid others."

Rosa stirred uncomfortably.

"Let's try an experiment." He began to rub only her scarred thighs, her back, the side of her breast and especially her butt. Softly at first, then harder. He squeezed her and spanked her lightly.

The heat within her built up yet again, and she shuddered. Each time he made her come, she flew higher and glided longer.

"So much for 'abnormal,'" he said. Your scars are a part of you. Love you, love your scars. Get over your fear. They're badges of courage, not of shame. A part of you to love, not to shun."

Rosa sighed. "I'll try. They're ugly, though, no matter what you say."

"No. Your future husband thinks they're great. Who else will you show them to?"

"Nobody."

"See. The whole world loves them."

"Maybe."

Still later, she'd fallen exhausted into a drowsy state. Something down there woke her up. She felt downwards. The back of his head. Of course, his famous move. She opened her legs and came. And again. She rippled continuously, unable to catch her breath. "Please…. Please…. Please…stop."

He kept her going another thirty seconds and let her shudder to a halt.

In the late May evening, the earliest colors of dusk shone through their windows. It seemed like they'd been making love for days, but only a couple of hours had passed. They dressed, combed their hair with their fingers, and headed downstairs.

"Let's get a pizza," Tony said.

Rosa was hungry, but what she really wanted was a beer.

As they hurried down the stairs, Rosa heard the quiet murmur of voices. The sound abruptly stopped, just as she caught sight of the other members of the tour, sitting on folding chairs in a circle, looking like residents in a group therapy session.

She stopped, a few steps from the bottom.

Tony, behind her, piled into her back. He had to hold her waist to keep her from toppling down.

Nothing to do but finish their descent and face them.

Mama looked in Rosa's eyes and smiled. "Well?"

Rosa looked back. "Well, what?"

Tony's Mama held out the back of her left hand towards them. "Well, we arranged your engagement. After all that time up there, do you agree?

Tony looked at Rosa. Did she agree?

Her eyes swept the group, settled back on him. "I think so."

Rosa kneeled on the floor in front of him.

"Tony, I love you. Will you marry me?"

He kneeled facing her. "I'm supposed to ask."

"Well, go ahead."

"Rosa, I love you. Will you marry me?"

Focused on each other's eyes, they knee-walked closer for a kiss.

Mary stood up, only a little taller than when she'd sat. "Oh, for God's sake. Somebody answer the question."

They both said, almost in a whisper since their faces were so close, "I will."

They embraced, still on their knees. They kissed—softly, in front of their mothers and a nun.

From their audience, a collective sigh.

Chapter 46

The whole block in front of The DeAngelo house was decorated for the festivities and closed to traffic, filled with tents to shade the rental chairs and the tables soon to be piled with food. DeAngelo women scurried from the front door to the nearest table, carrying carafes of wine, glasses, big pitchers of water and plates of antipast'. Under Mama's direction, those Mary Center women who could safely leave the shelter distributed the food and drink among the tables. A young woman in torn jeans tested the sound system, fiddling with knobs and slides until she was happy. Earlier in the morning, squads of nephews had swept litter from the streets between the reception block and the church.

When Mama was satisfied everything was ready, she and Rosa and the women in the wedding party squeezed into the family's fanciest cars to ride the four blocks up the hill to St. Anthony's church. Tony and his tuxedo troop already waited at the church.

An hour later, a strong melodic line grew louder as its source proceeded from the church. A folk accordion, Sicilian bagpipes, the tamburello drum—basically a huge tambourine—and a big guitar came nearer, their sounds sometimes overridden by the voices of the tenor and the bass who strolled along in front of the band. Falling farther and farther behind the music, holding hands and showered by bits of shredded paper, Rosa and Tony moved slowly down the street, stopping frequently to receive congratulations and kisses from neighborhood friends. The ushers and bridesmaids stayed behind the bride and groom, standing patiently or chatting with their own friends.

Touch

Rosa wore a new creation from Mrs. Billetsky, a shiny white angel-sleeve gown half covered by a robe of sparkling silver net. Her hair fell over the net in waves of black, accented by one white rose. Tony, his gleaming hair slicked back on the sides and the little curl bouncing lightly on his forehead, wore a rented tux. So did Rosa's papa, Tony's Best Woman Jojo, and all of Rosa's brothers.

Rosa's Matron of Honor, her sister Aggie, walked alongside Jojo. Behind them followed the Angel's Paola, Rosa's baby sister, and Jojo's Lee. They and Mama all wore whatever long dress they wanted, topped by the same sparkling silver net that Rosa wore.

Rosa and Tony sat at the head table surrounded by the wedding party. The guests and the rest of the group ate the home-made food. Rosa and Tony had to socialize and pose for everyone who had a phone. She had no time to eat, which was okay because she felt a little nauseous again.

Just before the cake-cutting ceremony, Rosa whispered, "Remember, hubby, you go first. If anything but the most delicate piece of cake is placed lovingly into my mouth, I get the last word."

"The wife gets the last word. I remember that. I think it was in the vows. Your throat will have never known such loving nourishment." Tony kept his promise. Rosa feinted left and right—she had the last word, after all—but in the end she placed the bite of cake neatly on his tongue.

She threw her bouquet bullet-straight at her little sister, who'd asked for help to get her guy to make the move.

Sis caught it and handed it to him. "Here. Hold this for me."

When Jojo gave them the big silver tray, the tray being her main job besides not losing the rings, Rosa and Tony went around collecting envelopes, smiling thank-yous like ushers collecting money to fix the church roof. Lee and Jojo retreated into Mama's house to open the envelopes, keep track of who gave what for the thank-you notes, and count the take. While Tony danced in the street with Mama and all the women, Rosa danced with Papa, Jojo, her brothers, and almost every man present, shy young teens and not-shy-enough old men.

Every few songs, the tenor and the bass led the guests in an old song that everyone knew, then moved into a tarantella, inspiring everyone to get up and dance around the dinner tables.

Every woman told Rosa this was her big day. Their weddings had been the high points of their lives. Rosa was exhausted and hardly able to stand. She had already given a speech and become famous—come to think of it, exhausted and hardly able to stand then, either. She'd already spent that unbelievable time with Tony in her new apartment, with the mamas and the nun waiting and noticing how low long they took. She was exhausted and unable to stand then, too.

Tony had strong fishies, because his sperm needed only one afternoon to do their job. Excited, she'd told Aggie her news. Mama told everybody, so all the women spent the ceremony in church trying to see the signs. Aggie swore she didn't tell Mama. Mama claimed she'd seen the glow. Maybe.

Besides, the "big day" was for the family, not for her. After one little dance with Tony, she saw him only for official events, the cake feeding, the envelope collecting. He charmed the aunts, just as she charmed the uncles, but charming each other would have to wait till later. Even then, she'd probably put on her special first-night lingerie and fall asleep.

Right after the church ceremony, before the reception, Tony had led her to their rented black classic, a 1959 Cadillac convertible with the tallest tailfins Rosa had ever seen. From the dual headlights in front to the bullet-shaped tail lights emerging from the fins, the car was huge, too long to fit in a garage.

"The kids are around here, I can hear them giggling. They're mostly your nephews. Just stand there and look stern." He called each nephew by name. "You can't hide. Get your skinny butts out here!" A straggling collection of young teens appeared, looking uncomfortable in their outgrown confirmation suits. "Things would be different if this was my car. But it's a valuable rental. Every scrawl and sign and whatever mess you have planned has to come off without leaving a mark. You'll clean the car and pay the rental agency for damages. If I were you, I'd make sure no other group of kids gets at the car, because you'll have to pay for their work, too."

They protested. "That's not fair. Aunt Rosa—even if we didn't do it?"

"Yep. Not fair."

Tony pointed at the back of the trunk. The convertible's windows were down, nothing to write on there. "You want to use painter's tape to put on a 'Just Married' sign, fine. Don't let your buddies do worse than that, capiche?"

Tony led Rosa away. "I think I just saved us a lot of hassle."

"Tony. They're kids. Causing hassles is what kids do. Ours has already started. I'm throwing up every morning."

"Yes, but you hang over the toilet with such beauty and grace."

She elbowed him in the ribs.

He held her chin. "We should try again. I don't think we got it quite right in the church." He gave her one of his specialty kisses. So gentle it would have told her body to grow a baby, if her body hadn't already gotten the message.

Five hours later, after the reception had gone on so long the older uncles slumped asleep on their folding chairs, so long the aunts reviewed the wedding as if it were already over, so long the wedding party had changed out of their gowns and tuxedos, so long the Mary Center women chatted among themselves while they waited to clear the last of the dinnerware, so long Tony and Rosa stood impatiently waiting for Jojo to show up with the Cadillac, Tessa brought everything to a halt.

Still in her wedding clothes, she and two other Rosa's Angels slipped among the wedding tables, gently pulling two reluctant girls toward Rosa. The girls looked like baby whores. They had the uniforms—boots, skirts barely long enough to cover their butts, bikini tops—but they were far too young for the job. The aunties, their wedding reviews run out of steam, stared at their next two discussion topics.

The party arrived at the head table. "I'm sorry, Aunt Rosa. I know it's your wedding, but Mama said it was okay to ask. Nina and Alma need a safe place. Now."

Mary Center was full. Rosa hesitated for a moment. "Put them in our apartment. Maybe space will open up by the time we get back."

Tessa backed away because Jojo pulled up in the Caddy. A pink "Just Married" placard was taped to its trunk. "Oggi Sposi" signs were taped to each door, similar to the English and just as traditional.

Jojo got out and slipped the roll of envelope cash into Tony's pocket. Tony held the door for Rosa. She got in and slid along the bench seat just far enough for him to fit behind the wheel. Everybody waved and cheered, throwing the last of their confetti. Tony glided away. Rosa raised her hand and waved one last time, then slumped her head on her husband's shoulder. At the first corner, Tony slowly swept the big Caddy to the right, and they were gone.

The Author. Casey Costra comes from the New York City area, married an Italian-American not long after graduating high school, and spent Sunday afternoons with all the cousins at Nona's house. The Costras both earned undergraduate and graduate degrees while raising their three children. Casey eventually became a professor. The family has returned multiple times to Italy and Sicily, has lived in Mexico, Guatemala, and Peru, and currently lives in Delaware. Casey has written nonfiction before, but this is the first novel. Rosa and Tony will return at least two more times in the Rosa DeAngelo series. Watch for the next installment, *Traffic*.

The Neighborhood. Yes, Casey knows that Staten Island is the only New York City borough that has no neighborhood called "Little Italy." The whole island is "Sort-of Italy," since Italian Americans are almost half the population. The neighborhood in this book is made up of pieces of different New York neighborhoods, plunked down somewhere west of the Staten Island Railroad and some distance from the Ferry Terminal. There is no St. Anthony's or Rex-Aid on the Island, and the novel's high school has no name.

Getting Help. If you are the victim of domestic physical or sexual abuse, the *National Domestic Abuse Hotline*, 1-800-799-7233, will be answered by trained counselors 24/7. The website is www.thehotline.org, but the organization warns that contacting the site may leave a dangerous trail on your computer. Better to call. In New York City, the organization is *Safe Horizon.* Its hotline is 1-800-621-HOPE (4673). The Staten Island branch office is located at 51 Stuyvesant Place, (718) 442-4613. If you are in immediate danger anywhere, call 911.

The Numbers. The national Center for Disease Control (the CDC), Division of Violence Prevention, has put together the results of national surveys to conclude: 27-40% of women will experience violent abuse or rape by an intimate partner in their lifetime. The range reflects different technical definitions of what constitutes domestic abuse. Half of those women will experience violence or rape in the youngest years of adulthood, between the ages of 18 and 24. Since the start of the Afghan and Iraq wars, husbands and boyfriends have killed twice as many American women as battlefield enemies have killed American soldiers.

Acknowlegements. Thanks to my many valued editors of an earlier version on Critique Circle. Thanks to Nadja Van der Stroom, Lisa Suda, Jim White, and Toni Morgan for their further editing help. Elena Kusterer and Charles Gouraud provided valuable technical support. Thanks to my beta readers, including Carol Lucia-Passo, Joyce Blakeslee, LaVerne McIntyre, Melissa McClean, Judith Cianci, and others whose names I never knew. Faith and Todd Kusterer provided advice, support, and many discussions of the technical aspects of writing fiction. Linda Minkowski and JD&J Design created the visuals and the design for the book. I am grateful to all.